Praise for Frank Anthony Polito and *Renovated to Death*

"Not since Sarah Graves's Jake Tiptree mysteries has home remodeling been so deadly entertaining." —*Library Journal*

"The fabulous and fun Domestic Partners in Crime in this wildly entertaining new home makeover murder mystery don't cut corners on the laughs or suspense with suspects coming out of the woodwork! You'll want to both love it and list it as your favorite new cozy series!" —Lee Hollis, author of *Death of a Clam Digger*

"[A] sprightly cozy . . . Some crackerjack renovation tips, including the proper procedure for refinishing woodwork, will appeal to DIY enthusiasts." —*Publishers Weekly*

"The real estate market is hot and so is Frank Anthony Polito's debut mystery, *Renovated to Death*. If you're addicted to HGTV, if you've dreamed of flipping a house, or if your DIY skills are limited to changing a lightbulb, you'll enjoy this trip to Pleasant Woods—where no one's ever been murdered, until now!" —Leslie Meier, author of *Mother of the Bride Murder*

"*Renovated to Death* is fast-paced, modern, and sparkling with irreverent humor. It's easy to envision *Domestic Partners* as a real-life HGTV series. Let us inside Peter and JP's Craftsman Colonial, show us the menu of their favorite brunch spot, and save us a spot at the gay karaoke bar. The first Domestic Partners mystery is a winner—bring on more adventures in murder and home design." —*Criminal Element*

Please turn the page f

T0188718

Haunted to Death

Books by Frank Anthony Polito

BAND FAGS!

DRAMA QUEERS!

REMEMBERING CHRISTMAS

Domestic Partners in Crime Mysteries

RENOVATED TO DEATH

REHEARSED TO DEATH

HAUNTED TO DEATH

Published by Kensington Publishing Corp.

Haunted to Death

FRANK ANTHONY POLITO

Kensington Publishing Corp.
www.kensingtonbooks.com

KENSINGTON BOOKS are published by
Kensington Publishing Corp.
900 Third Avenue
New York, NY 10022

ISBN: 978-1-4967-5006-8 (ebook)

ISBN: 978-1-4967-5005-1

First Kensington Trade Paperback Printing: September 2024

10 9 8 7 6 5 4 3 2 1

Printed in the United States of America

To Charlene,
my psychic cousin,

And to Aunt Toni,
who told us scary stories,

Come back and haunt me anytime, you two!

Halloween 1997

Emma stood on the third-floor balcony in the white wedding gown.

Tears streamed from her piercing blue eyes as she listened to the melancholy tinkling of her favorite music box. The automated instrument rested atop the nightstand in the room behind her, next to the canopy-covered bed she shared with her husband. The melody gave her comfort as she struggled to come to terms with the realization she'd known for far too long . . .

Bill Woods *never* loved her.

She gazed out at the garden party below, her costumed guests dancing in the dark. She felt a surge of anger and betrayal, amplified by the effects of alcohol on her physical and mental state. How could he do this to her—his own wife? And if her suspicions were correct, he'd also been keeping a secret since the day they were married, three years before.

Her thoughts were interrupted by his voice calling out her name from the hallway.

She spun around, clutching tightly the key to their bedroom door, and shouted across the master suite for him to leave her alone.

Her other hand found its way up to the diamond necklace hanging about her neck, a birthday present from her husband, earlier that evening. The lavish piece of jewelry probably cost a small fortune. He had the audacity to surprise her with it, in front of all their friends, when all along he knew the gift had no meaning. It was purely a gesture of *show*—nothing more.

Bill ordered her to open the door. His command was muffled through the heavy wood, but she could hear the fear in his voice.

When she confronted him about the affair, moments ago, his face went white with shock. He stammered and stuttered, struggling to find the words to explain his infidelity. His eyes darted around the room as he looked for an escape. He tried denying her accusations. His shoulders slumped, and his head hung low, as he realized there was no way out.

Emma decided she'd had enough. She was tired of Bill's lies more than anything. She knew in her heart that he didn't care for her . . . and she didn't care for him. Their marriage was one of convenience, arranged by their fathers, to join their two dynasties into a single powerful union.

Still, Emma couldn't bear the thought of Bill leaving her. Not for their *housekeeper* and the son he fathered with the older woman, over nine years ago. She couldn't let him win. She needed to find a way to take control of her own life, to break free from the deceit surrounding her world for far too long.

Bill called out to her again, this time with great conviction.

She twisted a lock of her honey-blond hair and took a deep breath. She thought of her precious daughter, asleep in the nursery one floor below. Emma didn't want their child growing up in a home filled with dishonesty. She thought of the shame and embarrassment she'd feel, pretending everything was all right when everyone else knew otherwise. She knew staying with Bill would only perpetuate the cycle of deception, and she refused to subject her daughter to that. The shame of remaining in a loveless marriage was far too much to bear. She had to be strong for her daughter's sake. She needed to make a difficult choice that would ultimately be in their mutual best interest.

Turning back to the balcony rail, she came to a decision. She gripped the cold wrought iron, her knuckles turning white . . . and she leaned forward.

Someone appeared in the bedroom behind Emma. Hearing the footfall, swiftly she spun around. Then, she screamed out.

The fall happened in slow motion, as if time had stalled to watch Emma plummet three floors to the flagstone patio below. The white wedding gown billowed around her as she descended, her body twisting and turning in the pale moonlight.

As she hit the ground, the sound of live music was stifled by the shock and silence filling the crisp autumn air. Her startled guests rushed to her side, calling out for help, for an ambulance, for *someone* to do something! But it was too late.

Emma Woods was *dead.*

TWENTY-FIVE YEARS LATER

Chapter 1

No one really knew if the old house was haunted.

According to local legend, the stately Arts and Crafts–inspired manor was cursed from day one. Built in 1913 by lumber baron William Royce Woods, the home's original owner had made a deal with a powerful Native American shaman. The shaman warned that if Woods disturbed the spirits of the land, a curse would be placed upon his family for generations to come. William, a man of science and reason, dismissed the shaman's warnings as mere superstition. The lumber baron laughed off the hex, believing it to be nothing more than the tales of some old Indian. Woods proceeded clearing the 1.3-acre plot of land on the outskirts of town and constructing his grand mansion, Woods Hall, ignoring the consequences of his actions.

But as the years passed, the curse seemed to only intensify. Visitors to the manor reported an overwhelming sense of unease, and many refused to spend the night when invited.

All around, strange things started happening. Woods's once loyal employees deserted him, and the market crash of 1929 decimated much of the fortune amassed by his company, Woods Lumber. The unfortunate events of Black Tuesday, some believed, led to poor William's untimely demise. Or was the hex of the Native American shaman responsible for the lumber baron's downfall?

Convinced of his failure—and fearing he'd let down his family—the elder Woods believed he no longer had reason to live. In the early hours of a cold winter morning, the once wealthy and powerful man hung himself. He was just shy of forty-two.

This was only the beginning of the effects felt by the shaman's inescapable curse.

Fortunately, for the Woods family, the lumber business bounced back after the Great Depression. Nearly thirty years passed without incident. William's wife, Fern Elizabeth Woods, née Ridge, had long ago been made aware of the wicked spell cast upon her husband. Having already reached her seventieth birthday, Fern was certain that her privileged world would forever remain untarnished. However, in the fall of '58, the woman's relatively long life was cut short by a deadly virus. The pandemic caused by the H2N2 strain of influenza had already killed thousands across the globe, and soon it found its way to the tiny historic town of Pleasant Woods, Michigan.

A series of unfortunate deaths followed.

First, there was William and Fern's son, William Royce II, and his wife, Dorothy, who died on the same February evening after their luxury car became stranded in four feet of snow during the Great Blizzard of 1978. The couple, both in their middle fifties, preferred wintering in a warmer climate. That season, however, they chose a ski trip to Boyne Mountain instead of their usual Caribbean Island vacation.

Less than two decades later, Barbara Woods, the spouse of William III, lost her battle with liver cancer. She'd never drunk a drop of alcohol.

Shortly thereafter, William Royce III himself perished, claimed by a massive coronary that took him kicking and screaming into the hereafter while enjoying his morning coffee.

William Royce IV, aka Bill, died later the same year, along with his brand-new bride and former housekeeper, a single mother named Kathleen. Tragically, the private plane carrying the newlyweds to their Mackinac Island honeymoon went down over Lake

Huron. They left behind a pair of orphans, a two-year-old girl belonging to Bill, and Kathleen's eleven-year-old son.

But perhaps the most questionable passing occurred a quarter century ago. Bill's first wife, Emma Wheeler, a beauty-queen-turned-model—and the mother of Bill's orphaned daughter—fell from the third-floor balcony of Woods Hall during her own twenty-fifth birthday–Halloween celebration.

Or did she jump . . . ?

Or was she *pushed* . . . ?

No one quite knew for sure.

It was this mystery—and the alleged haunting by Emma Woods of the home she and her family once shared—that we *Domestic Partners in Crime* would soon be tasked to solve.

JP held open the door as we entered the Top Dog brewery in downtown Royal Heights. At close to nine o'clock on Labor Day weekend, the bar was full of patrons ranging in age from Gen X through Z. My partner and I fell smack-dab in the middle, both millennials in our mid-thirties.

Well, at thirty-four I considered myself *early* mid-thirties. JP, however, turned thirty-six this past June 27th, so he was definitely just plain *mid*. Me, I had almost three full months till my next birthday on November 21st, making me a Scorpio to his Cancer.

As per my preferred astrologer, Miss Zelda—I read her horoscopes every night before bed, as soon as they were posted—our coupling made for one of the best in the Zodiac, so long as the couple in question was willing to put in the effort to support each other.

> Both water signs, Cancer and Scorpio share common traits, resulting in a good potential for a harmonious relationship. Both signs are also known for being deeply emotional, intuitive, and empathetic, which help them understand each other on a deep level. Cancer is a nurturing and protective sign, while Scorpio is pas-

sionate and intense. This combination can create a strong bond between the two signs, as Scorpio is drawn to Cancer's gentle nature and Cancer is attracted to Scorpio's intense energy.

That last part, I totally felt in terms of my current stress level.

Growing paranoid, I craned my neck like an anxious ostrich. Or whatever bird or animal might crane their neck to get a better view of his or her surroundings. As a pocket gay, I had a hard time looking past anyone taller than my five-foot-seven inches. Thankfully, at six-two, JP could serve as my personal guide dog.

"You see them anywhere?"

JP surveyed the jam-packed room with its high tin ceilings draped with Edison bulbs and strands of twinkling white lights. "Not sure."

The air practically pulsated, thick with the scent of hops and the sound of lively chatter and upbeat music. People gathered in every corner, soaking in the vibrant atmosphere at one of the hippest spots in Metro Detroit. All were dressed in a mix of vintage and contemporary fashion, their outfits carefully curated to create the perfect Instagram-worthy look.

A visual feast for the eyes, giant murals and framed artwork adorned every inch of available space on the exposed brick walls. At long communal tables groups of friends laughed and chatted excitedly over shared small plates and charcuterie boards. They munched on street tacos of *al pastor* topped with cilantro and pineapple, bacon-wrapped hot dogs, and beer-battered fried pickles.

A sense of FOMO seized me . . . and suddenly I was super hungry. Once we found the other couple, I definitely needed a beer and some fried brussels sprouts.

"I sent you the link to their latest video," I reminded JP, mildly annoyed. "Midnight Musings" off their sophomore album, *Hazy Days and Lazy Afternoons.* Clearly, he didn't know who, exactly, we were looking for. "Did you watch it?"

JP stared down his broad nose, a slight bump across the bridge caused by a sucker punch he got one time leaving a college sports bar back in Pittsburgh, long before we met. His nostrils flared and his jaw clenched.

I knew just what he was going to say: *For Pete's sake, Pete!* Even though most everyone else called me *Peter*, he always dropped the *R*. Especially whenever he got defensive. I couldn't help noticing, in that tension-filled moment, the hotness factor of the man standing with me.

"I did watch it! But how am I supposed to remember what they look like? These Zoomers are all the same. You can't tell them apart."

I heaved a heavy sigh at his indignant attitude. Still, after almost six years, I counted myself lucky to have found him.

John Paul Broadway was by far the most beautiful man I'd ever set eyes on. *Tall, dark, and sexy* didn't begin to describe the star of screens both big and small. Dressed in a pale blue polo that hugged his baseball biceps and made his bright eyes pop, he looked gorgeous as always. His pecs still had the pump from a trip to our local community Wellness Center earlier that afternoon, a free perk paid for by our property taxes. I felt it too. My Tigers T-shirt always clung a little tighter after a good workout.

Pulling my phone from my shorts pocket, I took a quick peek at my texts. The thread we exchanged earlier that day assured me they'd be there.

Hey! We still on for tonight?
Fer sure!
OK. 9PM @TD in RH?
Perfect. C U then! XO
☺

I considered sending another message. But I didn't want to come off as being too eager or annoying. Having access to her personal number was a privilege. It would only make things weird if I overused it. No need to give her a reason to block me on day one.

But what if they were delayed? Or, God forbid, something

went wrong, and they couldn't make it after all? Though in that case, wouldn't she have texted again to tell me? Or took the time to put the phone to her ear and actually call? The one thing I couldn't stand was a lack of communication. If I said I was going to be somewhere, I showed up. And if I was ever running behind schedule, I made it a point to let the person I was supposed to be meeting know I'd be there ASAP.

Still, this was a pair of twenty-five-year-old, semi-famous musicians we were dealing with. Compared to me and JP, they were children. Maybe their mothers never instilled in them a sense of responsibility? I hated to be all *heck, yeah.* But come on, kids. Get it together!

Before I could work myself into a frenzy, ruminating over the rules of proper etiquette and decorum, JP piped up. "Is that them?"

"Where?"

"The cute couple with the entourage."

Sure enough, it was the members of my new favorite band, Low-Fi. The moniker not only indicated the type of music they made, but it also combined the duo's names: *Fi*ona Forrest and Finn *Low*enstein.

Near a high-topped table in the corner, a diverse crowd of a dozen adoring followers congregated, all clamoring to take a selfie or score a signature on a crumpled napkin.

My pulse quickened in expectation of the event about to befall us. Were my palms sweating? Talk about a total cliché! But . . . I'd been looking forward to this appointment for months, ever since Ursula picked Woods Hall as the next project we'd tackle on *Domestic Partners.*

The fact that the house—an historic manor located at 13 Woods Way in our hometown of Pleasant Woods—was rumored to be *haunted* only sealed the deal when it came down to her final decision.

Chapter 2

JP acted all casual.

"Shall we?" He took my hand and led us across the concrete floor, gently clearing a path through the sea of bodies. The sound of chatter and clinking glasses filled the brew pub. But I could hardly hear a thing over my own beating heart.

"Excuse us?" I waited a second before interrupting.

"Yes?" Fiona Forrest looked at me with piercing blue eyes. Her honey-blond hair fell in waves across a pair of delicate shoulders. She wore a vintage crop top the color of sunshine, paired with high-waisted jeans—cut off at the knees and folded, à la 1991—and well-worn leather sandals. She blinked in recognition. "Hey, PJ Penwell!"

The J stood for James, after my father.

I breathed in the scent of patchouli as Fiona pulled me close. She was shorter, I'd guesstimate around five-three, so she rose up on her tiptoes to embrace me.

We exchanged a round of pleasant introductions, then headed to a semi-private booth off the back bar. Before we departed, Fiona took the time to thank her followers for stopping by to say hello. Her fiancé, on the contrary, couldn't be bothered. He didn't even say goodbye.

Finn Lowenstein was a tall guy with a lean and lanky build and perpetual scruff. Not quite JP's height, he stood about six-one, maybe? His dark hair hung into his even darker eyes. His style was a mix of edgy and everyman. He sported a plaid flannel button-down atop corduroy jeans, his feet clad in Carhartt brown work boots. A trail of tattooed musical notes floated up the inside of his right forearm. On his left, a Star of David signaled his Jewish heritage, as did the yarmulke covering the back of his head. When we first arranged our get-together, we had to make sure to wait till sundown, on account of Shabbos.

"Finally! I'm meeting my favorite author," Fiona gushed once we were seated.

My neck growing hot, I blushed with embarrassment. Sure, I enjoyed hearing the praise. What author didn't want to be labeled as someone's most beloved? But, while I enjoyed my own writing style, I found it hard to imagine anyone else would feel the same way.

"I've read all of your novels. More times than I can count. *Death of a Drama Club Diva* is the best."

"You just made Pete's day," said JP, patting me on the shoulder.

Fiona touched my hand across the tabletop. A hand-inked hummingbird flew about in the soft crook between her thumb and first finger. "Please! I'm only telling the truth."

"Well, that's very kind of you," I humbly told Fiona regarding her devotion to my literary endeavors.

Over the finest in Michigan craft beers, we toasted to the success of *Domestic Partners'* third season. Fiona took a group selfie and posted it to Low-Fi's official socials for all the world to see. *#lowfimeetsdomesticpartners #business #topdog*

She tucked away her mobile device. "I love your doggies! I follow TheDailyClydeandJack. The reel you posted of them chasing each other around the tree in your backyard . . . So cute! They're not twins, are they?"

"Not biologically. They just look a lot alike," JP said. "We say they're brothers-from-another-mother. Clyde's a beagle–pit bull mix and Jack's a Parson Russell terrier."

We adopted both of our boys from a dog rescue called Home FurEver. Clyde, I found on the Adopt-a-Pet app early last summer. In the posted photo, a tiny white doggie with brown brindle markings on the right side of his face, and a half-moon-shaped patch over his left almond-shaped eye, peered sadly at the camera. His head tilted to one side, ever so slightly. He had the stubbiest little legs and the tiniest pink toenails. At first sight, JP and I both fell madly in puppy love with Mr. Clyde Barker, as we christened him on his official adoption papers.

Clydie Boy was the sweetest pup. Thirty-two pounds of pure muscle! Sure, he had his moments. Like when another dog passed by our house, walking with its owner up the alley right off our driveway. Clyde would leap onto the window seat cushion and pound the pillow with his big front paws, barking ferociously. We couldn't fault him for protecting his domain, could we?

Lord Jack Strohein, as per the name on his pedigree, joined the Broadway-Penwell family this past spring. We called him *Jack* or sometimes *Jackson*. Fortune smiled on us while having Sunday dinner with my parents, Jim and Patsy, at their home in nearby Madison Park. Over cake and coffee, Mom shared the story of how the poor little dog's dog-daddy up and died, leaving him an orphan. The resemblance to our Clydie was uncanny: same brown-and-white color; about the same size. He even had the same half-moon patch over his left eye. That night, I reached out to Home FurEver, informing them of our desire to bring Jack into our family . . . and then we did.

Jackson, aka Mr. Fuzzy Face, was a total charmer. While he weighed a good ten pounds less than his big brother, his long limbs gave him a slight advantage in the height department. He did this thing where he'd lie down, flat on his belly, with his two front legs crossed one over the other in a jaunty fashion. We called it *fancy paws*.

"Thought pits are illegal around here," Finn scoffed.

I hated how pit bulls got such a bad rap. "Not in PW. And he's only *part* pit."

Pleasant Woods was an accepting and tolerant town, a part of the reason JP and I chose to make it our home. According to the most recent census, the neighborhood boasted the seventh-highest rate of same-sex couples in the nation and received top marks, annually, from the Human Rights Campaign.

Situated between upscale Royal Heights to the north and modest Fernridge to the south, a mere fifteen hundred residents counted the Detroit suburb as their home. On the west side of Woodward Avenue, the main thoroughfare bisecting the community, spacious dwellings rested on oversized lots belonging to the upper middle class. The east side—affectionately dubbed *Peasant* Woods—gave way to smaller properties whose owners, while still well-off, earned far smaller incomes.

It was here that JP and I made our lives, after roughly five years together in Brooklyn. Back then, we never dreamed we'd ever own our own house. As an actor and a playwright, respectively, we resigned ourselves to being life-long renters.

Then, one day, our luck changed.

JP booked a supporting role on the highly rated TV cop show *Brooklyn Beat* as openly queer detective Sam Hardy. Meanwhile, my young adult mystery series *Murder High*, featuring queer teen detective TJ Inkster, hit the *New York Times* bestseller list. Soon, we stopped eating canned tuna and ramen for dinner. We saved up some money and moved to my native Michigan. Thanks to my best friend, Campbell Sellers, Realtor Extraordinaire (his descriptor, not mine), we purchased a 1924 Craftsman Colonial with a mortgage payment equaling two hundred dollars *less* than what we paid in Williamsburg . . . and with *double* the space.

For the better part of the first year, we fixed up the sixteen-hundred square foot, four-bedroom home, located at 1 Fairway Lane, for all the world to see. As cohosts of a hit home renovation show called *Domestic Partners*, we became household names—at least in the world of Home Design Television, aka HDTV.

"What do they got good here?" Finn scanned the QR code with his smartphone and pulled up the Top Dog menu.

"Everything's good. They've got a great arugula salad. Comes with toasted walnuts, goat cheese, and sliced apples," JP answered.

I chimed in. "The burger's huge! I always end up taking half of it home for the boys."

Finn's nostrils flared as he glanced up. "Meat is murder, bro! We can't eat either of those. We're *vegan*."

"I knew that," I said, in reference to our dining companions' dietary restrictions.

Because I did.

I knew all about the band, which *Analog Ear* called (quote) a refreshing departure from the polished and overproduced sound that dominates much of the mainstream music scene today (unquote).

An Aquarius born in mid-February, Fiona Forrest grew up on a small farm in a small Northern Michigan town, outside of Traverse City. After being home-schooled, she attended the Motown Music Academy, where she met Finn Lowenstein, born on the Ides of March, making him a Pisces.

"The salad sounds yummy! We can always get it sans the goat cheese," said Fiona sweetly.

At nineteen, F and F formed the aptly named, Low-Fi. Finn played keyboards, upright bass, and harmonica. Fiona sang, played acoustic guitar and ukulele, accompanied by her beau. They began their ascent to fame by posting songs and videos online. Before the crazy kids knew it, indie label Blank Canvas signed them to an exclusive recording deal, launching the lovebirds' music careers.

But it was Fiona's twenty-fifth birthday, this past February 14th, that would forever change both their worlds.

After celebrating back in Brooklyn, where she and Finn also lived for a time, they returned home to Greenpoint for some post-dinner dessert. Her parents shipped the birthday girl a frozen Sanders Bumpy cake, a delicacy rarely found outside Michigan, along with a case of Vernors pop. Fiona called to thank her folks. The generous gifts reminded her of home, a place she hadn't visited since Low-Fi's debut album *Static Dreams* scored them a Grammy nod as Best New Artist.

On speaker, her mother and father told Fiona she should probably sit. The news they needed to share would surely come as a shock. Soon, the young woman learned the truth of a long-held family secret.

As a twist of fate would have it, she was *not* Fiona Forrest, daughter of Gregg and Gina, a humble farmer and his wife. Her given name at birth was Fiona *Woods*, as in William Royce Woods, the cursed lumber baron who died by his own hand after losing much of his fortune. Fiona's birth parents were none other than William Woods IV, aka Bill, and first wife Emma, the former Miss Great Lakes and Wheeler Automotive heiress, who on Halloween night 1997 fell from a third-floor balcony during her own birthday celebration.

After her biological father's death two years later, while on honeymoon with his new bride and former housekeeper, custody of two-year-old Fiona was granted to the girl's nanny and her groundskeeper husband.

In his will, Bill Woods left the married couple enough money to comfortably raise his only child, far away from the tiny historic town of Pleasant Woods and the curse that had befallen his people for generations. A clause in their contract specified that neither Gregg nor Gina would utter a word pertaining to Fiona's true identity. The girl was to be raised—and to live—as a Forrest, until she reached her twenty-fifth year. On that St. Valentine's Day, all would be revealed.

As the sole remaining heir to the Woods Lumber dynasty, Fiona Forrest inherited the Woods family's fortune, along with the stately Arts and Crafts–inspired manor known as Woods Hall.

Her life would never be the same again.

Chapter 3

A man and woman approached our semi-private booth.

"Hey, sorry to interrupt . . ."

Tall and rugged looking, the guy appeared around my and JP's age. A thick beard covered his face, and he was blessed with an even thicker head of sandy hair. He wore a tight DETROIT HUSTLES HARDER T-shirt, while a pair of well-ripped jeans hugged his meaty thighs.

The woman, smaller in stature, was slightly younger in years, most likely mid-twenties. Her curly red hair she wore in an up-do. A vintage floral dress showed off a curvy figure. Her bright green eyes sparkled under the bar lights. Judging by the way she clung to the man's big arm, she seemed to be his girlfriend. "Told you it was them!"

She didn't sound like the brightest bulb in the box, as my mother would say. But I made it a point to give people the benefit of the doubt before passing judgment.

"We're a couple of Low-Fi superfans," the guy confessed.

Fiona gently touched his arm with her hummingbird-tattoo-hand. "Awww! Thank you so much!"

"What brings you to the Motor City?" asked the woman. "I'm Ashley, by the way. This is my boyfriend Corey."

So, I was right. They *were* BF and GF.

Fiona greeted the couple kindly, as if they'd been besties forever. "Hey, Ashley and Corey! Finn and I live here now. Well, we're moving here. Soon as our new house is ready."

Corey did a double take, gaping at me and JP. "You're the *Domestic Partners* dudes! Man, we watch your show all the time."

"Thanks," we both said, pretty much in unison.

"Nice meeting you." JP addressed the man and woman, as I sat back and kept silent. Even after two full seasons of beaming into the homes of 1.1 million HDTV viewers on a weekly basis, I couldn't get used to being recognized in public.

"These bro-hams are fixing up our place next," said Finn, cutting into the conversation.

Corey ran a big hand through his thick hair. "Cool! Whereabouts?"

He wasn't being nosy, I could tell. It was simply a Midwest kind of question. In Pleasant Woods whenever you met a fellow neighbor, the first thing they wanted to know was the street you lived on. Nine times out of ten, people would just rattle off their address. *We live at 1 Fairway Lane, right off the alley.* As if to say: *Feel free to come and stalk and/or rob us!* When JP and I resided in New York City, we barely talked to the people in our building let alone asked for such personal information.

Before Fiona could reveal the exact location she and Finn would soon call home, Finn cut her off. "Bro, you and your lady want a pic with us, or what?"

Ashley squealed. "That would be awesome!"

Fiona flagged down the nearest server, a cute blond boy I recognized as a regular from Drag Queen Queeraoke at the not-so-gay-anymore gay bar, Shout! He happily snapped a photo of the six of us, then gave back Fiona's phone.

Ashley gave her boyfriend a firm nudge. "Go on, boo . . . Ask them."

Corey brushed his girlfriend off, slightly embarrassed by her blatant instigation. "You guys don't happen to need any extra help, do you? Right now, I'm outta work. Pretty handy with a hammer . . . if I do say so myself. I can paint, build stuff, whatever you might want done."

JP explained how it wasn't up to us. Our executive producer did all the crew hiring. A disappointed Corey asked if we could at least pass his info along. I said we would, no problem, knowing it'd be a long shot. Ursula was the type of woman who liked doing things *her* way. If you wanted something, you pretty much had to convince her it was *her* idea. My mom did the same sort of thing when it came to my dad.

Was it manipulative? Probably. Did it work? 99.9 percent of the time.

Pulling out my mobile device, I added Corey's number to my contacts. As he spouted off his digits, I took note of the area code: 818. "That's LA, no?"

"Yeah, we used to live there. I never changed it when we moved back to The D. I figured, why bother with all the hassle?"

"I get it. Me and Pete kept our Brooklyn numbers when we left New York. These days, what's it matter? So long as my agent can get ahold of me."

Ashley beamed brightly. "I'm an actress! But I *hated* LA. All the girls out there are sooo skinny and sooo plastic. So here we are back in The Mitten." She snorted through her upturned nose, laughing like she'd said the funniest thing calling Michigan by one of its several pseudonyms. Personally, I preferred *Great Lakes State* and *Water Wonderland*.

Finn cleared his throat, deliberately. "Sorry, bro. We're kinda in the middle of something."

Taken by surprise by his bad manners, I said a silent prayer, hoping Finn Lowenstein wouldn't turn out to be a total D-bag. Somebody somewhere once said: *Never meet your idols.* With any luck, the adage wouldn't apply to the current circumstance.

"Right on. PJ, be sure to give my number to your EP, okay? Tell her she can call me anytime."

"Thanks for coming over to say hello," Fiona said to Corey and Ashley before they bid us goodnight.

They walked away from our booth, blending in with the crowd of hipsters.

JP took the reins and launched us into our official meeting. "Okay. We'll meet at Woods Hall tomorrow night and shoot the walk-through. Basically, we go from room to room and talk about what you guys like and don't like, and how you want us to fix it."

"Ursula wants to make sure it's dark out when we shoot . . . To add to the ooky-spooky haunted house factor," I mentioned.

Finn laughed nervously. "She doesn't think Woods Hall is *really* haunted, does she? I mean, there's no such thing . . . right?"

Personally, I didn't believe in ghosts. Though my sister Pamela sure did. When we were kids, after our grandmother died and we'd visit our grandpa, Pam would try and scare the bejesus out of me, saying she spotted Granny lurking around the old house.

"Ursula's all about the ratings. I love her, but she's a shrewd businesswoman," JP said.

Last season, we worked on a 1929 Tudor Revival across the street from us, owned by a pair of twin brothers, Tom and Terry Cash, who grew up in the home. Long story short . . . On a Saturday afternoon in late summer, JP and I stopped by 4 Fairway Lane, only to discover one of the twins lying dead at the bottom of the rickety old staircase. Good old Ursie! She took advantage of the poor man's broken neck by playing up the angle, as our show's executive producer, that JP and I were some sort of crime-solving duo. She even took out a full-page ad in *Variety* when the season aired, dubbing us *Domestic Partners in Crime*.

"Once we film the walk-through, me and Pete will come up with a plan for how the actual renovation will go."

Finn sipped his beer, pausing to lick his foamy upper lip. "Gotcha. You guys really need us?"

"We do. Ursula thinks, since you're both celebrities and the house is yours, it'll look good having you both on-camera," I answered. "It won't be much. Mostly stuff like painting and furniture shopping."

"Fi does like to shop. But if you need help with anything dangerous, count me out." Finn held out his hands. "I can't go damaging these babies."

"We've only got like eight weeks to finish up this project. Originally we were supposed to have three months . . . but you guys were off on tour all of August," said JP, laying on a bit of a guilt trip.

Fiona meekly apologized. "Sorry."

"No worries," JP lied. "It's just . . . Ursula wants everything done by Halloween. She's got this grand plan to get PNN to come in and tape a segment on our season finale."

Finn's face drew a blank. "Bro, what's PNN?"

"Paranormal Network."

They should've called it PN since *paranormal* was one word, but . . . who was I to tell them what to name their channel?

I further elaborated. "They've got this one show, *Ethereal Encounters*. They want us to hold a séance and see if we can contact the spirit of Emma Woods. Try to find out how she died . . . and if the rumors are true and someone *killed* her."

When I said these words, Fiona fell silent. Her already pale complexion grew paler as she contemplated what she'd just been told.

Finn shook his dark head. "I don't know, guys . . . I'm not a fan of the supernatural *or* haunted houses."

JP and I exchanged glances, both realizing how insensitive it was to spring something so serious on Fiona in the middle of a brew pub. Plus, we didn't know the first thing about conducting a séance. Hopefully Ursula and the PNN people would figure all that out.

Finally, Fiona spoke up. "I've been wanting to know more about my birth mother. Ever since my adoptive parents told me about her. I did some online research, of course. But I'm a little nervous to think I might actually *see* her."

JP made a promise. "We understand your concerns. We'll take every precaution. Nothing'll go wrong. And if at any point you're uncomfortable, we'll stop."

I concurred. "Exactly. Ursula won't take any chances. She can't afford to lose her job. And HDTV won't risk getting sued."

Finn still seemed hesitant.

Fiona held his hand. "Baby, if there's a chance I can talk to my birth mother . . . and find out what *really* happened to her, I need to do this." She sighed at the thought of finally meeting the woman who gave her life. Even if it was through an otherworldly encounter.

After a moment of contemplation, Finn caved. "Okay, doll. But if the ghost of your dead mom *does* appear . . . we are def moving outta that house."

"It's like you said, Finn. Haunted houses aren't *real*," JP reminded the musician. "The whole séance thing . . . it's probably just some stunt Ursula's cooking up."

I hoped my partner was right. A lot could go wrong during the taping of a home renovation TV show. But . . .

Being *haunted* by the ghost of a former beauty queen wasn't something I wanted to deal with.

Chapter 4

We left Jack and Clyde with my parents.

"You boys be good for Grandma and Grandpa!" JP called as we attempted to head out the door.

At home, we literally had to bribe them in order to go anywhere. The ritual went something like this: JP took his position in the mudroom, located at the rear of our house. I lured the boys into our living room, past the Tobey dining table we got for a steal from an antique dealer in Pennsylvania, along with a matching buffet and a set of Parkersburg dining chairs, all circa 1910.

Both dogs waited patiently while I broke in half a chicken-flavored edible bone, feeding a piece to each before *quickly* making my way back across the dining room and swiftly shutting the French door behind me, thereby preventing the pups from escaping. Most of the time, the dogs paid me no attention, preoccupied with wolfing down their snack. But every so often, Clyde got wise to the plot and would chase after me. One time he even bit me on the butt, the crazy pooch!

As we pulled onto the property of the grand manor estate, I admired all the opulence.

Woods Hall was a beautiful and timeless example of a traditional American home. After sitting vacant since the late 1990s, the once beautiful stucco façade had aged considerably. The cream-colored paint peeled off in places, exposing the underside to the harsh elements of many a Michigan winter. The large roofline, once a significant feature, revealed several missing slate shingles. Gutters and downspouts were now rusted and damaged. Vines and other various vegetation grew on the walls and around the porch, further adding to the unruly appearance.

The once pristine lawn was overgrown and neglected. Weeds seized control of the yard, and the grass grew tall and unkempt. The edges were no longer well-defined, and the lush area blended into the surrounding foliage. Brittle fallen branches and dead leaves littered the ground, with small scrub trees randomly sprouting up all over the place. The garden beds along the perimeter sat empty, their soil hard and dry.

The limestone steps leading up to the porch, once a welcoming entrance, were cracked and uneven, presenting a climbing hazard. Much of the wood trim framing the lead glass windows had rotted and needed replacing. The windows themselves were covered in a quarter century's worth of dirt and dust. A few of their wood shutters had fallen off over time. The rest hung haphazardly, giving the impression of a house long abandoned.

Despite the deterioration, we could still see some beautiful features as JP and I parked our crystal-black SUV in the drive. The stone fireplace and chimney had both aged gracefully, adding to the home's classic Arts and Crafts character. The mature oaks and surrounding shrubs, unfortunately, had grown wild, obscuring much of the property from view. But, overall, the historic manor home still retained a certain charm, showcasing the natural materials and craftsmanship that went into building it over a century before. With some restoration and care, JP and I possessed full confidence that we could restore Woods Hall to its former glory. No doubt she'd be a beautiful home for Finn and Fiona Forrest-Lowenstein to raise their children.

"Hey, guys!" I greeted our *Domestic Partners* crew, waiting for us on the stone walkway out front.

They were a small but capable trio: Kevin the cameraman, Dave the sound and lighting guy, and Adam, aka Gopher, the production assistant.

Kevin gave us his customary salute. His last name was Canon, coincidently enough, though he shot the show using a Panasonic. Hailing from Cincinnati, the man in his mid-fifties had a stocky build and a friendly face. He stood only a few inches taller than me, with salt-and-pepper hair, a bushy beard, and dark-framed glasses he removed whenever we rolled. A slight gap between his two front teeth added to his charm and approachability. He was the jokester of our TV show family and could always be counted on to entertain us with one humorous tale or another.

Dave Dolby was a fifty-year-old Hoosier from outside of Indianapolis. With a medium build and average height, his soft brown hair was starting to thin on top. No matter the season we were shooting in, or the location, Dave made it a point to dress his professional best. He always wore a collared shirt and what my mother referred to as *slacks*. Though his choice of footwear was more practical. Since he did a lot of standing around all day, he sported sneakers instead of hard-soled shoes.

Adam the PA was a good guy, a junior in the Film Studies program down at the College for Creative Studies in Detroit. This was only his second year with us on set. From the little interaction we had with him, JP and I could tell he was both ambitious and passionate about the entertainment industry and eager to learn as much as he could. I envied him a little, having the opportunity to work on a television production at such a young age. Back when I was a student, there weren't any such programs for playwrights to gain practical experience. I also envied his style. He always looked super cool, dressed in colorful graphic T-shirts. Me, I pretty much lived in a navy hoodie, jeans, and tennis shoes, and a ballcap could be found perched on the top of my head.

Regarding Adam's nickname, I never thought it my position to

ask where he'd gotten it from. I assumed everyone called him Gopher because, as a PA, he was always running errands or fetching
equipment for the crew. JP thought maybe it was his tendency to
be a little clumsy. One time at the Tudor Revival during the taping
of season two, he accidentally knocked over the scaffolding we set
up to use for painting the coffered ceiling. He sort of did resemble a
rodent burrowing through the ground as he fumbled about making
a big mess. But being twenty-one and a cutie to boot, he totally got
away with it.

"So get this . . ." Kevin launched into his spiel as JP and I approached. "I'm on my way to the hotel, and I stop for gas before I
get there. I'm standing outside the car, filling up, when I look over
to see an older fella next to a beater car with two or three other
guys in it. He's shirtless and barefoot, leaning over the guardrail
rimming the parking lot . . ."

"Oh no!" I said, playing my part as a member of Kevin's captive
audience.

"Throwing up."

"Sounds like somebody had a rough night," JP teased, laughing
along with Kevin's account.

"Oh, it gets better," Dave the sound and lighting guy said. Obviously, he'd already heard the whole story from Kevin before our
arrival.

"After one particularly violent transaction, the guy yells: *My
dang teeth!* I assume he stopped heaving enough to bend down and
retrieve his dentures. But I didn't stick around long enough to find
out."

The five of us chuckled at Kevin's little ditty, before getting
down to business.

"Anybody hear from Ursula?" JP checked his phone for a message, text, or voicemail.

As per usual, she was late. Why any of us was surprised was the
actual surprise. For as long as he'd known her—since their days

working together on *Brooklyn Beat*—JP teased Ursula about one day
being late to her own funeral. I couldn't talk. I had my own problem with punctuality. *Better late than never* was a personal motto.

A few minutes passed when we heard the roar of an engine. A
classic car pulled up in the gravel driveway behind my and JP's
more modern-day vehicle. The glossy Acapulco Blue body was
both sleek and aerodynamic, with a long hood, a short rear deck,
and a sloping fastback. The mag wheels, large and shiny, had a five-
spoke design that complemented the overall muscular appearance.

Right off, I recognized the 1967 Ford Mustang. Not because I
considered myself a car buff. Far from it. But my dad owned one
just like it when he was in high school. Constantly, he showed it off
in pictures, lamenting the day he ever listened to my mom and sold
it to buy a more family-friendly station wagon.

"Nice ride!" Kevin the cameraman called out.

Finn climbed out of the car, full of masculine pride.
"Thanks, bro."

Taking it upon myself, I presented the homeowners to our
trusty crew.

"Always been a big fan of a classic muscle car. Where'd you
ever score such a beautiful baby?" said Kevin, continuing with his
compliments.

"Fi got it for me as a gift when she found out she's the long-lost
daughter of the great-great-grandson of a lumber baron and auto
heiress."

"That'll do it," said Dave the sound and lighting guy.

"I need to find me a girlfriend like yours," added Gopher.

Finn took a deep breath, trying to put his emotions into words.
"I grew up pretty poor. When I got my driver's license, my folks
couldn't afford to get me a car. I thought about buying one after
our first album went gold. But you guys know how it is . . ." He
addressed his statement to me and JP. "Living in New York City,
even if you can afford a vehicle, it's a pain in the butt to park it."

Finn looked over at the Mustang, full of gratitude. "Owning a car like this now, it's like a dream come true." He slipped his arm around Fiona and pulled her close. "Thanks, doll."

She kissed him tenderly on the cheek. "You're welcome, baby."

One look and anyone could tell this was a young couple totally in love.

For their sake, I hoped this upcoming home renovation project wouldn't put *too* much of a strain on their seemingly perfect relationship.

Chapter 5

Ursula showed up a full thirty minutes *after* our scheduled call time.

She rushed across the overgrown front lawn, looking like a cat burglar dressed head-to-toe in black, and nearly tripped on a tree root. "I know, I know . . . My flight from LaGuardia got in late. When I checked into the hotel, my room wasn't ready. To top it off, I had to walk the last quarter of a mile just to get here. All because my idiot Uber driver refused to drop me at a *haunted* house."

Ursula Boss was a thirty-six-year-old cisgender female (she/her/hers) with red-brown hair, expressive brown eyes, and a curvy build. She was what my mother would call *buxom*. Like Kevin our cameraman, she also hailed from Ohio—Dayton, to be exact—and her strong Midwestern accent often came through in her speech, particularly whenever she was giving orders, which was more often than not.

Could a surname be more fitting? Ursula was *the* boss, capital B . . . and she never let a soul forget it.

"What happened to your rental?" JP wondered. HDTV always supplied a car for Ursula to drive whenever she came to Detroit to shoot *Domestic Partners*.

"It wasn't ready either. This whole day is turning into a total nightmare. Gopher . . ." She handed off her overstuffed Louis Vuitton handbag to Adam the PA.

As the executive producer for a hit TV show, Ursula was a natural leader, skilled at keeping the production team on track and ensuring everyone worked toward the same goal. So what if she had a problem, herself, with being on time? (She was the boss!) If nothing else, she was highly organized and detail-oriented, with a keen eye for spotting potential issues before they could become problems.

She was also in love with my soon-to-be husband.

It was a tale as old as time, and oh-so typical: the single straight woman, pining away for her gay best friend. Of course, she'd totally deny it if ever confronted. And it didn't bother me one bit. Well, only when things came up like wanting to take a vacation, and having Ursula inform JP how she'd have to make sure she could get time off before we booked the trip. Oh, and could JP go with her to the Galapagos Islands—just the two of them, for old times' sake—to celebrate her fortieth, three years from now? Nothing like planning in advance, Ursie!

Not that I didn't love her, don't get me wrong.

Without Ursula, there'd be no *Domestic Partners* on Home Design TV. She's the one who first pitched the idea, after we told her about our plan to leave Brooklyn. The premise for season one involved a handy gay couple who purchase an old house and complete the renovations over the course of a ten-episode arc, all the while bickering back and forth—albeit affectionately—and providing some requisite eye candy for the network's target audience of mostly women and gay men. The show was a breakout hit and promptly renewed for a second season, following a rave review in *Variety* . . .

If you're looking for a home renovation show that's both instructive and entertaining, look no further than Domestic Partners, now airing on HDTV! Hosted by a fabulous queer

millennial couple, actor JP Broadway and author PJ Pen-
well, this show is a must-watch for anyone who loves home
improvement projects, interior design, and all things DIY.

   What sets Domestic Partners apart is the delight-
ful chemistry between JP and PJ. These two are not only
incredibly talented and knowledgeable when it comes to
home renovation, but they're also hilarious, charming, and
downright adorable. Watching them work together as they
renovate their very own historic house is like watching a
master class in teamwork. They bounce ideas off each other,
problem-solve together, and always manage to keep things
light and fun.

   Overall, Domestic Partners is a top-notch production
that's as fun to watch as it is informative. If you're a fan of
home improvement projects, interior design, or just good tele-
vision, do yourself a favor and tune in. JP and PJ are the
hosts you never knew you needed . . . and once you start
watching, you'll be hooked!

"Just breathe . . ." JP firmly massaged Ursula's tense shoulders.
Anyone with two eyes (who wasn't blind!) could see the look of ecstasy on her face as she melted under his firm but gentle touch.

   Once Ursula finally relaxed enough to move forward, she
spoke. "You must be Fiona and Finn. We appreciate this opportunity to help you guys out with your home. Let's get started, okay?"

   JP and I assumed our marks in front of Kevin's camera, while
Fiona and Finn observed from off. Dave double-checked both his
lighting and sound instruments. Adam, aka Gopher, held up the
clicker, aka the slate.

   Ursula stood behind Kevin's right shoulder and shouted: "Picture's up! Roll sound, roll camera!"

   After a second, Dave declared: "Sound is speeding!"

   Whatever that meant. I still hadn't figured it out after two full seasons. But I wasn't about to be annoying and ask someone to explain it.

Kevin called back: "Rolling! Camera's set."

Gopher read off the words written in marker on the white board with the black lines and the stick across the top. "*Domestic Partners*, episode three-point-one, opening, take one."

The clicker snapped in front of my face, making me jump, the way it did every single time the PA clicked it. One of these days I'd get used to it, I kept telling myself. For now, I tried not to flinch too noticeably. I had a fear someone was putting together a reel of outtakes, featuring all my skittish moments, to be shown at some future end-of-season wrap party.

"Action!"

Taking a beat, JP and I mentally prepared ourselves. It'd been a good ten months since either one of us stepped in front of a camera. Once we got back into the swing of things, I knew we'd both be fine. For now, I was a bit of a nervous wreck, to coin yet another phrase of my mom's.

"I'm JP Broadway. This is my partner in crime, PJ Penwell."

He never called me *PJ* in real life, hardly anybody did. Mostly, I used it as a pen name, at the insistence of my editor, Sabrina James at Huntington Publishing. Apparently, placing an author's initials on a book cover sold more copies. But since the pseudonym gained me the most notoriety, HDTV insisted I also use it as my on-camera persona.

"Hey, guys! We're super excited to be back for another season of *Domestic Partners*," I said, reciting from memory the opening speech I also helped write.

JP continued with his copy. "And let me tell you . . . This time, we've got a truly intriguing project on our hands."

"We're renovating a 1913 manor home that's rumored to be *haunted* . . ." I resisted the urge to turn and gesture behind me, knowing Kevin would take a shot of the house, to be inserted later during what they called *post*. My guess was they'd also be adding some sound effects for emphasis.

"Yep, you heard PJ right. Twenty-five years ago, this Halloween, the former beauty queen and model who lived here *died* under mysterious circumstances."

"Some say she still haunts the halls, looking for answers about her untimely demise. And we're here to give this old house a new life and uncover the truth, along with the deceased woman's daughter and her fiancé."

Here, I figured we'd cut to a shot of Fiona and Finn, smiling and nodding as they were introduced.

"This house definitely has a history. And we're not just talking peeling wallpaper and creaky floorboards. But don't worry, we're not scared. Are we, PJ?"

"JP, speak for yourself. Guys, I'm totally freaking out."

He slung a big arm around my shoulder and squeezed me jovially. "It's okay, I'll protect you."

"So come along for the ride, as we take on this haunted renovation and discover the secrets this old house has been harboring for decades."

"We promise it'll be a season of *Domestic Partners* like you've never seen before."

Ursula kept stressing the importance of making the show's opening snappy and quick, so we could move on to the good stuff. We only had forty-five seconds for the entire spiel. During our initial season, I had the toughest time getting used to appearing on-camera. *But come on!* I was a writer. I didn't know the first thing about stage presence and projecting. Apart from the Intro to Acting class I was forced to take as a Theatre major, I'd never performed a day in my life when this TV stint began. It wasn't *my* idea to cast a playwright-turned-Young Adult mystery author as the cohost of a home renovation show.

Thankfully, the lessons I learned over the past two seasons eventually paid off. This past spring, my play *Blue Tuesday* received its world premiere at the Royal Heights Playhouse, starring none other than JP Broadway in the leading male role. After losing one of the other actors last minute, due to unforeseen circumstances, I agreed to shirk my writerly duties and step into the spotlight as a member of the ensemble. With only *four* days of rehearsal, I made my Theatrical debut, opposite my real-life domestic partner as his onstage lover. Fortunately for everyone involved, I'd already memorized most of my character's dialogue due to hearing it spoken by the original actor every night during rehearsal. Oh, and I also wrote the lines, so I could pretty much say whatever I wanted if I forgot any.

"And cut!" Ursula gave the cue for Kevin to turn off his camera and for Dave to stop doing whatever he did as the sound engineer.

"That's a cut! Moving on to interior shots of the property now. Finn and Fiona, stand by!" cried Gopher.

They weren't the least bit nervous. On their last tour, Low-Fi played to sold-out crowds across the country. Sure, our TV audience numbered around a million, but we didn't have all those adoring eyes trained directly on us. The Royal Heights Playhouse only sat a few hundred. Getting up on that stage six different times over a two-week run was bad enough. I couldn't imagine what it was like for Finn and Fiona, doing what they did, singing and making music all the time.

"Okay, guys . . . Ready for the walk-through?" Ursula enlightened F and F on what, exactly, this next step would entail. Pretty much the same thing JP told them last night when we met up at the brewery.

If Ursula were there—and hadn't insisted on flying out from New York this afternoon, instead of yesterday morning—she would've known what the four of us already discussed.

Finn responded, a little condescendingly if you asked me. "Yeah, yeah . . . Just turn on the camera. We're professionals. We know what to do."

Ursula held her tongue.

Chapter 6

The house was in good shape, for the most part.

Considering the property had been shut up like a proverbial clam since the turn of Y2K—when Bill Woods and his second wife, Kathleen, perished en route to their honeymoon destination, and their children were shipped off to new homes—the interior of Woods Hall fared rather well over two decades time. Except for a few structural improvements, much of the work JP and I needed to do, renovation-wise, was merely decorative.

As my real estate agent bestie, Campbell Sellers, liked to say: *The house had good bones.* A few coats of fresh paint, rip out some old carpet and refinish the hardwoods underneath, bring in some period-appropriate furniture and . . . voilà! The historic manor home would easily be restored to its former glory.

Kevin started up his camera. "Rolling!"

We entered the wide front door leading into the marble-tiled foyer. JP allowed Finn and Fiona to go first, as it was their house after all. I followed close behind, attempting to walk backward and talk without falling.

"Welcome to Woods Hall! We're here tonight with the home-owners, who *some* of you might recognize . . ." JP said.

He and I separated to reveal our *Domestic Partners* very special guest stars.

"The members of the hit indie band Low-Fi . . . Fiona Forrest and Finn Lowenstein!" I said, all smiles, thrilled to be sharing the same space with my new BFFs.

"Hey, everybody out there in HDTV Land!" said Fiona, waving delightedly at the camera.

Finn gave a cool nod. "Wha's up?"

The young couple looked as hip as ever. She wore a loose-fitting, pale pink baby-doll dress with a high waistline and flared skirt. A pair of dark leggings (or were they *jeggings?*) clung to her shapely legs, and on her feet she sported chunky Doc Martens in that reddish-purple color I could never remember the name of . . . *cordovan*, maybe? Finn's look tonight was along the same lines as last: plaid flannel button-down over white undershirt. But instead of cords, he wore basic blue jeans and Chuck Taylors, along with a suede yarmulke. I'd never seen him without the head covering on, not in any of the pics posted on any of Low-Fi's socials. Maybe he was Orthodox? I didn't know much about Judaism, other than the little I learned working a part-time job as a desk clerk at a luxury hotel on Manhattan's Upper West Side called the Promenade, home to many Jewish retirees.

"Finn and Fiona have offered to join us this season," JP explained to our loyal viewers, who were used to watching us as a duo.

"Can't promise I'll be of much help," said Finn, chuckling warmly.

"You guys'll do a great job, I'm sure," I said, downplaying the negative attitude.

We hadn't even lifted a finger yet, and the guy was already trying to get out of doing any sort of actual work. Talk about a slacker! If he had his way, Finn Lowenstein would probably spend his day in front of a ginormous flat-screen, playing video games with his friends, online.

We continued the tour of Woods Hall, shooting what we in showbiz like to call a *walk-and-talk* shot. JP and I had intentionally

avoided seeing the interior of the house until that very evening, so
as to catch our spontaneous reaction to what we discovered waiting
for us. Finn and Fiona, of course, paid a visit to the property a while
ago, when they first returned to Michigan from New York. They
needed to see what they were getting themselves into by agreeing
to pack up and move their lives to Pleasant Woods, after being on
their own back in Brooklyn.

A French door comprised of twenty lead glass windows led into
a grand entrance hall, paneled with a rich mahogany. After two
decades of neglect, the once stunning chandelier that hung from the
high ceiling looked tired and worn. The brass had lost its shine, and
the crystals no longer sparkled with the light. Corrosion accumu-
lated on the surface, obscuring its ornate details. The chain supporting the fixture had rusted, while some of the accent pieces were
missing and broken, leaving gaps in its pattern.

On our right we discovered an amazing flight of steps leading
up to the home's second floor. They were "worst of the '90s," covered by a narrow polyester runner that reminded me of my childhood, with its pattern of triangles and half circles in navy, pink, *and*
yellow. Oh, and little black squiggles that looked like confetti floating about Times Square on *New Year's Rockin' Eve*. I think we had
a similar rug in my kindergarten class, not even kidding. Along both
sides, we could see exposed hardwood, so I knew all we needed to
do was rip up that hideous rug and replace it with a nice Turkish
wool number.

"The runner needs to go," said JP, totally reading my mind.

Fiona agreed. "Def perf obv! I'm thinking something more traditional and stylish."

"*Moi aussi,*" I said, speaking *en français* (my college minor) for
no apparent reason.

Finn took a step closer to inspect the tacky carpet. "I don't
know. I kinda like it."

Fiona looked at her significant other like he'd lost his mind.
"Then you can put it in your man cave . . . which we are *not* mak-

ing one for you in this house, so don't even think about it." She turned to me and JP, hands on her hips. "I've already told him: no man caves and no giant flat screens to play video games on with his friends."

What did I just say? I said to myself. At least Fiona was on the same wavelength as me and JP. Something told me we and this guy Finn were going to butt heads on more than one occasion. And I was *not* looking forward to it, not one little bit.

In general, I tended to avoid conflict at all costs. I realized it made things difficult being a dramatic writer when you didn't like putting your characters in tense situations. My personal philosophy just so happened to be: I wanted to show an audience a world where people *don't* do things, so the people viewing my characters *not* doing wouldn't make the same mistake and *not* do themselves. I think it made pretty good sense, no?

After the camera cut, Ursula gave us our next set of directions. "Hey, you guys . . . Let's head up to the second floor now, okay?"

She was The Boss, so what were we going to say? *Um, I don't think so. Let's go down to the basement and see if there's any ghosts lurking around in the cellar.*

This was when we made our first startling discovery on that very first night . . .

At the top of the stunning staircase, hanging high on the wood-paneled wall, we came upon a hand-painted portrait. Framed in rich, ornate gold that perfectly complemented the opulence of the painting, the carved wood frame itself was decorated with swirls, flowers, and other intricate designs, adding to the overall grandeur of the piece. The painting depicted a young woman in a regal and elegant pose, seated on a plush red velvet chair, her back straight and her head held high. Waves of honey-blond hair cascaded over her delicate shoulders, framing her pretty face. Her bright blue eyes sparkled with a hint of mischief.

The breathtakingly beautiful gown, a shimmering shade of cerulean, complemented the young woman's sparkling eyes, while the delicate lace detailing and intricate beading hugged her curves in all the right places, emphasizing her natural beauty and grace.

In the painting, her expression was one of serene confidence and self-assurance. Her posture exuded elegance and poise, and it was evident to all who gazed upon her image that she was a woman who knew exactly who she was and what she wanted.

"Fi, when did you pose for this?" asked Finn slyly, gazing up at the life-sized portrait of what appeared to be his girlfriend.

He was kidding, we all knew for a fact. The painting's subject couldn't have been Fiona Forrest, née Woods, born just five years *after* the portrait was commissioned by the young woman's automotive industry CEO father. Her identity would become evident upon reading the engraved nameplate affixed to the bottom of the gold frame: EMMA ROSE WHEELER—MISS GREAT LAKES 1992.

"She looks just like you," Ursula said.

Fiona stared in awe at the hand-painted image of Woods Hall's former First Lady, whose resemblance to her long-lost daughter was uncanny. "She *does* look like me. Except for the pageant gown and spiral perm."

Finn shuddered. "Well, she's creeping me out. Looks like her eyes are following us." He moved side to side, keeping his own eyes fixed on Emma's. "I say we get rid of her, A-sap."

Ursula pointed at the painting. "Kev, get a shot of this."

Fiona held up her phone and snapped her own photo. Her thumbs began tapping on the screen. Ursula caught her mid-action.

"Do me a favor . . . Don't post any pictures till after the open house on Saturday, okay?" She phrased her sentence as a question, but really it was a command. "We can't give away too much, otherwise people won't come. And we're counting on the money we'll raise for JP and PJ's dog rescue."

It wasn't *our* dog rescue, per se. It was Home FurEver, the organization we adopted both Clyde and Jack from. The woman who ran it, Margot, grew up in Pleasant Woods and went to school with Tom and Terry Cash, the twin brothers whose family owned the

Tudor Revival we renovated on *Domestic Partners* season two. She also personally knew the previous owner of our house, Whit Voisin, an older man who died of a heart attack in his sixties, poor guy! If anything, our new hometown was a tight-knit community. Everybody knew everybody . . . or so it seemed.

"Sorry. Wouldn't wanna take away from charity." Fiona returned the mobile device to from whence it had come.

Glancing up at the hand-painted portrait of Emma Woods, I swear I saw her eyes move.

Chapter 7

We headed down a narrow corridor.

On both sides of the long hallway, we faced a series of closed doors, stained a dark walnut color. Most likely, these were the bedrooms where the Woods family once slept. The third, smaller than the first two we inspected, seemed to belong to a child, based on the twin bed we found inside.

A large wooden wardrobe leaned against one of the drably painted walls, calling to mind one of my favorite childhood novels, C. S. Lewis's *The Lion, the Witch, and the* . . . Framed posters of popular horror movies decorated the others. *Scream 2, The Haunting,* and Tim Burton's *Sleepy Hollow* were a few I recognized from my own youth. On the nightstand next to a twin bed, a stack of Goosebumps books by R. L. Stine lay collecting dust, their pages yellowed with the passing years. Based on these objects alone, the child who owned them had to be around my same age, now.

"I did some research when I first found out Bill Woods was my birth father," said Fiona, stepping through the doorway. "His second wife, Kathleen Anger, was his former housekeeper."

The atmosphere in the bedroom felt eerie, giving me an anxious feeling. The air was thick with dust particles, dancing in the moonlight shining through a single dirty window. Kevin captured our actions while Dave recorded the conversation.

"What kinda name is *Anger*?" Finn asked no one in particular. "Wouldn't wanna meet up with her in a dark alley, late at night."

Fiona ignored her fiancé's attempt at humor. "When Emma, my birth mother, died, Bill married Kathleen. She had a nine-year-old son, Royce."

I found this bit of info rather interesting. Call me inquisitive, but . . . "Isn't *Royce* the middle name of all the Woods family men, dating back to William Royce Woods, the lumber baron?"

"It is. My assumption is Kathleen did it as a gesture," Fiona stated. "She wasn't married to the baby's father, so she picked a name that meant something to her. Maybe she chose *Royce* after William's middle name since he gave her and her son a home when they needed one?"

Thinking it over, Fiona's premise sounded plausible enough. So, I let go of my misgivings. Sometimes a name was just a name.

"This must've been Royce's room. Truthfully, I have no memory of him," said Fiona sadly. "I was like *two* the last time we saw each other."

Out of nowhere, JP let out a wail. "Aw, man!"

I pivoted to see what my partner-slash-cohost was so upset about. "Well, shoot," I said, noticing a baseball-sized hole in the wall. The edges were jagged and rough, revealing the wood lath behind. Loose bits of plaster and white powder dusted the floor below.

"Looks like somebody took a hammer to it. Probably that Royce Anger kid," Finn, the detective, deduced.

"Don't worry. We'll get Chippy to fix it up," I told JP.

Chip Carpenter was our jack-of-all-trades contractor, but everyone called him Chippy. He handled construction, plastering, painting; pretty much any projects JP and I couldn't manage on our own.

"Can't you just cover it up with this?" Finn reached down and retrieved a framed *Blair Witch Project* movie poster resting against the wall.

"No! We can't just—" JP started to say when Ursula stopped him, causing our conversation to crash to a halt.

"Cut! While this topic is indeed fascinating . . . let's see what we've got behind door number four."

Ursula slipped out of the child's bedroom and strolled across the hallway. She turned the cut crystal doorknob, but the door wouldn't budge.

"What do you think is in there?" asked Fiona.

"It's probably where the ghosts hang out," joked Finn.

We toured the master suite next. As was common in many large homes constructed in the early 1900s, the room consisted of a spacious sleeping chamber, a personal dressing area, and a private bath.

"This was my birth parents' bedroom," said Fiona, marveling at the massive third-floor space.

The centerpiece was a grand canopy bed made of dark, polished mahogany and draped with heavy curtains, still set up in the spot where Bill Woods and his second wife, Kathleen, last slept upon it during the last century.

"Now these are nice . . ." JP stepped across the tan carpeting over to a pair of fancy double doors, their leaded panes cracked and stained from years of neglect.

The portals opened onto a large balcony overlooking the parterre garden, with its symmetrical pattern of hedges separated by walking paths. The once sturdy railing was now rusted and worn out in places. A layer of dust and debris covered every surface, including the few remaining pieces of rattan furniture, the cushions torn and soiled. In the corners, cobwebs stretched from the beadboard ceiling down to the warped, wood planks of the floor.

I joined JP outside, followed by Finn and Fiona. As the four of us stood together, we could feel the weight of history . . . and the tragedy that took place on that balcony, nearly twenty-five years before. The waxing gibbous moon cast a glow over the yard, illuminating the twisted branches of the old-growth oak trees and throwing long shadows across the uneven ground.

"This project is gonna be a *ton* of work," said JP, sounding defeated.

Finn placed his hands on the wrought-iron rail. "What about that dude from the brewery? The one we talked to about getting him a job. Can't you guys just hire some more help?"

"I already gave Corey's number to Ursula, like I said I would. She didn't seem the least bit interested in having another crew member join us," I said bitterly.

Had it been *her* idea, maybe I would've gotten a different response?

"Careful of those pots," JP warned Finn as he leaned over the balcony and looked down at the patio below.

A trio of moss-covered terra-cotta planters had been left behind, each one placed atop a stand and situated against the railing's edge. Their once vibrant flowers had long ago withered, the leftover dirt now dry like the desert.

Finn took a step backward. "I see 'em! Wouldn't want one of them falling off here and landing on your head, would you?"

Fiona stood in silence, taking in the view. She gazed down at the flagstone patio spanning the back of the house. Her voice was tinged with sadness as she spoke. "So . . . this is where Emma Woods died. I still wonder how it really happened . . . and *why*."

It made me uncomfortable discussing such a personal event with the daughter of a dead woman. Especially since Kevin and David—at Ursula's coaxing, no doubt—had snuck onto the balcony with their equipment . . . and now our every word was being recorded.

"Well, the story I've heard is she fell. Right in the middle of her twenty-fifth birthday party. Twenty-five years ago, this Halloween."

"I know that much, PJ. I read all about Emma online. For her costume, she wore a white wedding gown; a replica she had made of the one Princess Di wore when she married Prince Charles. Diana was killed in a car crash two months before. Emma thought it would be a nice tribute to her memory."

Vividly, I recalled the night of August 31, 1997. I was nine-going-on-ten. It was a Sunday, but it was still summer vacation, so I got to stay up till eleven o'clock. Me and my dad were playing Super Mario 64 in our family room. When we turned off the console, a CNN breaking news report flashed across the TV . . .

Princess Diana Dead.

Images of the mangled car she rode in with her companion, film producer Dodi Fayed, accompanied the story, along with a detailed description.

It appears to be official . . . Princess Diana, at the age of thirty-six, has died of massive internal injuries she suffered in a car accident.

At the time, I remember thinking how sad it was, but at least she lived a wonderful and *long* life. To think now, she was the same age JP just turned a few months ago—the same age I would be in a little over a year. It wasn't fair someone so *young* could be gone so soon.

"Campbell Sellers told us all about the night Emma died," JP said to Fiona. "He told us how she fought with her husband in front of the guests. Then she ran upstairs and locked herself in their bedroom. The next thing everyone knew, she screamed and fell to her death from the balcony."

Fiona's eyes pooled with tears as she envisioned the final moments of her birth mother's life. "Or did somebody *push* her?"

This was another theory floated by Cam that didn't quite track for me. "If Emma locked herself in the bedroom, how would someone get inside to push her off the balcony?"

"I found an old news item. It mentioned the door was broken in," Fiona said. "Bill Woods told the police he broke the door down *after* he heard Emma scream. But what if he broke the door down so he could get inside to kill her?"

Finn shrugged. "Too bad your real dad died in that plane crash with his housekeeper wife. Guess we'll never really know what went down, babe."

Fiona turned to me and JP, pleading. "Maybe you guys could help me?"

I had an idea what she was asking, but I needed some clarification, just to be sure. "Help you . . . ?"

"Find out what happened to my birth mother on the night she died. And I'm not talking about staging some silly séance as part of a TV show. I need real answers."

The look on JP's handsome face betrayed his hesitancy. "What can *we* do? If you think Emma Woods died under suspicious circumstances, talk to Detective Paczki of the PWPD. Pete can introduce you, he's a close personal friend."

Fiona sighed, frustrated. "I did talk to him! He dug up the police file from Halloween night 1997. According to the report, there was no sign of foul play. The coroner ruled Emma's death an accident, the result of a traumatic fall from this very spot."

The four of us observed a moment of silence, our eyes cast down on the ground below, where the former beauty queen once lay dying.

"No disrespect, Fiona," I said, my mouth suddenly dry. "It was a party. Emma probably had a few drinks to celebrate. She could've lost her balance. If the police report said—"

"I don't care about some stupid police report! Emma didn't just trip and fall off a balcony in the middle of her own twenty-fifth birthday–Halloween party. Somebody *killed* her."

"*Why* do you think she was murdered?" JP asked, the more pragmatic of our pairing.

"I don't know. It's just a feeling I've got. Something isn't right. But she was my *mom* . . . and I need to know the truth."

If my own mother died under mysterious conditions, I know *I'd* want to get to the bottom of things. I couldn't just keep living my life knowing she'd lost hers, potentially at the hands of a cold-blooded killer. Thinking it over, seriously, I put myself in Fiona's place.

As the self-proclaimed *Domestic Partners in Crime*, how could we possibly refuse her request?

Chapter 8

On Saturday, we held the official Woods Hall open house.

This community-wide event was something we'd done at the start of each *Domestic Partners* season, so far. We literally opened the front doors to the house we were working on and invited all the neighbors to enter. Giving them a chance to tour the property, early on, allowed the locals to take in the *before* version. Once we finally finished the project, we'd hold a second showing so they could admire the *after*.

As per Home Design Television, we charged a suggested donation of five dollars. All proceeds were then donated to a favorite nonprofit organization. Margot from Home FurEver was on hand this morning to help me, JP, Fiona, and Finn greet the line of Pleasant Woodsians that stretched down the stone walkway and around the corner.

Each one of us took a turn at saying hello to the hoard of visitors. "Welcome to Woods Hall!"

The weather that morning had, thankfully, held out. Early September in Metro Detroit often saw milder temperatures than those of the preceding month. Typical sunny skies gave way to partly cloudy conditions. It felt quite pleasant to be standing outside for hours on end, smiling at strangers and friends alike, while posing for pictures and taking selfies.

Margot beamed with appreciation. She gazed up at the impressive stucco and wood structure behind us. "I can't thank you guys enough for doing this."

Fiona grinned. "Of course, anything for the pups!"

"We're just happy to help. You let us adopt Clyde and Jack. It's our way of returning the favor," said JP.

Margot blushed, before addressing Fiona and Finn. "If you're ever looking to bring a new fur baby into your beautiful home, be sure to get in touch with me, okay?"

"We will for sure!" Fiona promised.

"You bet we'll be getting a dog. Or *three*. If this place turns out to be haunted like everybody says, we're gonna need protecting," Finn said.

Margot chuckled nervously. "I've heard about Woods Hall being haunted. I don't mean to scare you guys, but I don't think *I* could ever live here."

"That's what I told Fi. When she first brought up moving to Michigan and living in a haunted house . . ."

"I never said Woods Hall is haunted. I said there are *rumors*. And even if it's true, I'm Emma Woods's daughter. I seriously don't think she'd hurt me."

Finn playfully folded his hands and pretended to pray. "I hope not!"

For a full two hours JP and I stood side by side at the front entrance of Woods Hall, pleased as punch at the turnout. Dr. Naveen Vaidya and his lawyer wife, Rana Vakeel—whom we hadn't seen since she portrayed the female lead in *Blue Tuesday* that spring— stopped by to show their support. Our friends Miguel Canto and his husband Ricardo Abogado showed up with their German shepherd Angus. Miguel taught music at Fernridge High School and Ricardo worked with Rana Vakeel at the same law firm. We referred to Angus as the Sheriff, since he made sure to keep the other dogs in check whenever things got a bit chaotic at the local community dog park. Clydie loved Angus so much, he allowed the bigger dog to place his entire mouth over his head (in a show of affection, of course!) after they formally bowed to each other.

One by one, our neighbors from Fairway Lane made an appearance, starting with Hank and Hennie Richards. The octogenarian couple resided in the very first home built on our block: a 1920 canary-yellow Cape Cod located at number 6, right next door to the Tudor Revival we renovated last season on *Domestic Partners*.

Mr. Hank, as everyone called him, wore polyester plaid pants that morning. He came to the open house fresh from playing a round at Detroit Golf. Mrs. Hennie sported a heather-gray sweatshirt stenciled with an Old English *D* across the front. The woman was a diehard Tigers fan—much more than me or my mother—and never missed a ball game down at Comerica Park, come rain or shine.

Mr. Hank gazed up at the old manor from the porch. "We haven't been to Woods Hall in twenty years."

"Twenty-*five*. You were still in office, darling, the last time we were here." Mrs. Hennie smiled sweetly at me and JP. "Mr. Hank was mayor of Pleasant Woods during the 1990s. Did you boys know that?"

We did.

She told us the story right after we met her and Mr. Hank when we first moved to Fairway Lane, almost two years ago. And she told us *again* at the first block party we attended that fall. And *again* in December at the holiday party held at Chianti, the wine pub directly across the street from our house. And *again* over Sweet Treats ice cream at the summer ice cream social in Gainsford Park.

"That's right. We were here on the night of the *accident*," said Mr. Hank, his memory jogged.

Mrs. Hennie took a deep breath. "Oh, yes. I remember it like yesterday. Poor Emma Woods! She fell off that balcony up on the third floor . . . landed not ten feet from where we were standing, outside on the patio."

"Such a shame," said Mr. Hank, hanging his balding head.

JP and I looked at each other, surprised. "You were both at Emma's twenty-fifth birthday–Halloween party?" I asked our elder neighbors.

Hennie nodded, a far-off look in her eyes. "We were. We had a wonderful time too. Everyone was dressed in costumes. I came as Jessica Fletcher . . ."

"And I was Amos Tupper," said Mr. Hank, sounding just like Tom Bosley, aka Belle's dad from the *Beauty and the Beast* original Broadway cast recording.

"How fun!" I could just picture the Richards in their *Murder, She Wrote* cosplay gear.

Mrs. Hennie beamed. "There was all this delicious food! June from June's Diner—this was back before she retired, and The Depot took over—she baked the most wickedly fun birthday cake. A live band played music, and everybody danced."

"And how about that drag queen? You boys know Stephen from the block? Gave his very first performance, if I'm not mistaken, right here in this house."

The neighbor in question was none other than Stephen Savage-Singer, who lived two doors down from us at 5 Fairway in a mid-century modern ranch, the newest house on the lane. Stephen's burly bear husband, Evan, was a Gulf War vet and father to a tween trans girl named Gracie. As his drag persona, Harmony House, Stephen hosted Drag Queen Queeraoke every Friday and Saturday night at Shout! A trained musical theatre professional with an amazing alto belt, he opened each set *entertainting* (his verbiage, not mine) the mixed, standing-room-only crowds that gathered in the cabaret room.

"Emma was such a gracious hostess . . . but then something went terribly wrong. The next thing we knew, the poor girl was dead," Mrs. Hennie informed us.

Mr. Hank gazed up at the house once more, looking solemn as he spoke. "Hard to believe it's been twenty-five years. You boys were probably in diapers back then, huh?"

Flattered, both JP and I chuckled. "Not quite," he confessed. "But close."

Quickly, I ran through the Halloween costumes of my youth. I distinctly remembered dressing up like the blue Power Ranger in 1997, mostly because blue is my favorite color. But also, I thought Billy Cranston was super cute. Especially when he wore his glasses! In all honesty, that year I wanted to go trick-or-treating as Scary Spice. Not because I liked Mel B the best. I was team Emma Bunton all the way. But the name *Scary* seemed more apropos to the holiday.

Realizing they might know more about that awful night, I decided to risk it and ask the Richards a point-blank question. "But it *was* an accident, wasn't it? Emma *fell* from the balcony. She didn't jump . . . and she wasn't *pushed* . . . was she?"

"According to the official police report, it was nothing but an unfortunate incident," Hank Richards assured us.

"That's what we heard too. But Fiona is convinced otherwise," JP told the one-time mayor. "She thinks maybe her mother's death *wasn't* so accidental."

"Well, she has no reason to think that. You can tell her I said so!" While his tone seemed a tad gruff, we came to learn as neighbors, that's just how Hank Richards sounded. "When Emma Woods died, I made sure the police conducted a thorough investigation. As town mayor, if anything suspicious turned up, I would've known all about it."

"Are Fiona and her fiancé here? We'd love to meet them!" Mrs. Hennie said.

JP searched the yard in a show of looking for the couple. "They are . . . Not sure where."

In all actuality, less than ninety minutes into our stint as open house hosts, Finn started complaining about his blood sugar levels being low. He stated emphatically how he needed to find food— *fast!*—before he passed out from hunger. Tired of listening to his whining, Ursula gave Finn and Fiona permission to break early. But

I didn't mention any of this to Mr. and Mrs. Richards, lest it should make dear Fiona look foolish for being engaged to such a big baby.

"I can't imagine what that poor girl must be going through. I read all about her in the *Detroit Times*," said Mrs. Hennie, shaking her head softly with sympathy.

The story, written by Arts reporter and a fellow Pleasant Woodser, LaRena Judge, detailed how Fiona had recently come to discover her real identity as the sole remaining member of Pleasant Woods's namesake family.

"She's having a tough time. But she'll get through it. What other choice does she have?" I said.

We all fell silent, each one lost in their own thoughts.

The old manor home creaked and groaned around us, as if it too was holding its breath in anticipation of the truth finally being revealed.

Chapter 9

Campbell Sellers was a master manipulator.

The guy *always* got what he wanted, since our meeting freshman year at Madison Park High. I'll never forget the first day I saw Cam, sitting on the bleachers while everyone else ran laps around the gym. Somehow, he convinced our hunky phys ed teacher, Mr. Goodbody, to excuse him from any sort of physical activity. But the second the bell rang, I swear I saw Cam sprinting out the double doors and down the hallway.

Later that afternoon in honors choir, a miracle occurred. When it came time for us to stand up and sing, Campbell's injury suddenly healed itself as he rested his full weight on his sprained ankle. Turns out, the guy faked his doctor's note! After class, I couldn't resist calling him out. Unapologetically, Cam confessed to the forgery and forced me to keep his secret by producing another fake note the very next day . . . this one with *my* name on it. According to the convoluted backstory he created, I hurt myself falling off the choir room risers and would need to join Cam on the bleachers for a full two weeks while we both recovered.

This was only one of many hijinks concocted by Campbell Sellers over the course of four years. When we were sophomores, he conned me into breaking into our band teacher's office to borrow something. That something ended up being the Polaroid proudly displayed on Mr. Musick's bulletin board, a photo he posed for with the ladies of Destiny's Child, whom he unexpectedly bumped into while waiting for a flight at Metro Airport.

Junior year, Cam talked our drama teacher, Miss Stratford, into letting us put on a stage version of *The Breakfast Club* under one condition: If he and I watched the movie and wrote down all the dialogue, she'd grant us permission to produce it. Forget about this scheme being totally ridiculous . . . it was totally illegal! As a produced playwright, I now knew better.

Sadly, after graduation Cam and I went along on our own ways. I stayed at my folks' house and went to Wayne State. Cam moved up to Mount Pleasant to attend Central Michigan. Sure, we saw each other every so often, mostly on Christmas break and summer vacation. Then, another four years later, Cam announced he'd be moving back to the Detroit area, which was right about the time I decided to pack up and head to New York City.

We were two ships passing each other by. But here we were, once again, residing in the same little town on the very same street. Cam lived in a boxy-shaped Prairie-style Four Square that loomed like a bastion on the opposite corner of Fairway Lane at number 11. He'd been there for over a decade, moving into the 1915 home soon after college graduation. He also rescued his dog—a fawn-colored American Staffordshire terrier called Snoop—from Home FurEver, which was part of the reason Cam made it a point to stop by and say hello that Saturday afternoon, during the Woods Hall open house.

"Well, hellooo!" Cam stepped out of the Jeep he drove and scurried up the stone walkway, greeting me with a peck on the cheek.

"You look nice," I said, commenting on the navy pants and khaki blazer he wore, fresh from his own open house for a home he was selling up in Royal Heights. Cam never seemed to have a weekend free, so it pleased me to see his smiling face at my and JP's event.

His eyes lit up at the sight of Margot, standing with me and Fiona on the porch, decked out in her purple HOME FUREVER T-shirt. "OMG! How *are* you? It's been *sooo* long!" He enveloped the fifty-something woman in a warm hug.

Margot tucked a lock of her dyed red hair behind an ear. "I'm good, thanks. Busy as ever. I'm sure you are too."

Cam groaned dramatically. "Ugh. We got a ton of looky-loos today, but no real buyers. I don't know why. It's a great property in a fantastic location. This market is *kiiilling* me . . . and my profits!"

As the top Realtor around town, Cam sold more houses in a month than others did in a single year. On more than one occasion, he slapped a SOLD sign out front of a house that never even made its way onto the MLS, along with the eye-catching caption on the on-line profile: *Listed, Pending, Same day!*

"You know what they say. It can only get better," I said.

"Who says that? Tell them they can pay my mortgage!" Cam spat sarcastically.

Always one to crack a joke in the face of adversity, my best friend had me, Margot, and Fiona in stitches in no time. The longer the day wore on, the more slaphappy (and sleep deprived) I began to feel. Desperately needing a jolt of caffeine, I sent JP on a mission to The Depot Diner across Woodward Avenue to bring me back an extra-large coffee.

No sooner had I relayed my partner's whereabouts, I remembered my manners. "I'm sorry, Fiona. You know Campbell Sellers?"

She offered her hand. "We haven't officially met. But we've spoken on the phone a few times."

"*Riiight!* You and your boyfriend sing in that band, Hi-Low."

Fiona laughed at the quip. "*Low-Fi.* Yes, Finn. He's around here somewhere."

After they returned from an early lunch, Finn Lowenstein decided to make himself scarce. The last time I saw him, he was wandering around the backyard garden. From the looks of his behavior, he was either up to no good . . . or he was searching for a place to sneak in a nap.

Margot prepared to take her leave of us. "If you'll excuse me . . . I see a very big donor. I should probably go and chat her up. It was wonderful seeing you, Cam. Oh, real quick! How's Snoop doing?"

"Snoop is good. Other than when I took him to get neutered, no complaints."

"Good! Give him a belly rub from Momma Margot," she said before stepping off the porch and heading across the long grass.

Cam returned to his chat with Fiona. "So, I see you decided to keep the house. I lost out on a *huuuge* commission when you guys wouldn't let me sell it. But good for you!" he teased, albeit seriously.

"I know, I know . . . I just couldn't allow some corporation to swoop in and turn my family's home into a Disneyland ride."

Okay, now I was confused. "Sorry, what's this about Disney World?"

"Disney*land*, she said," said Cam, always one to correct me when I got something wrong. "Didn't I tell you? I'm sure I did. You're my best friend, you know everything." He took a quick beat. "Well, you *don't* know about the guy I met on Lads4Dads the other night, but . . . a girl's gotta have some secrets. Fiona, why don't you do the honors?"

Now Fiona looked confused. "Sorry . . . What's Lads4Dads? I assume it's a hookup app for young guys who want to meet older men. Or vice versa."

"It is! But sexual proclivities are *not* what we're discussing. At least not right now. I'm referring to the call I received a while back. Go on, tell Peter about the nerve of that man."

"Yes! So, shortly after I learned about Bill and Emma Woods being my birth parents, I got a call from Cam, asking if I'd be interested in selling Woods Hall. Apparently, some guy from some company here in Michigan heard it was *haunted* . . . and he wanted to buy this place and turn it into an actual haunted house."

"Like at an amusement park?" I asked, perishing the thought. I couldn't stomach the concept of walking through a series of creepy hallways with a bunch of total *strangers*, surrounded by piped-in screams and strobe lights, just waiting for lord-knows-who to jump out and scare me to death.

Among other things, I wasn't a fan of forced frivolity.

"*Maaaybe* . . . I'm really not sure. I just knew I wasn't interested, no matter how much money the guy offered. And it was a *ton*."

"Well, Nancy Drew. Smell you," said Cam, cocking his head in Fiona's direction. *"I'm kidding!"*

"I'm sorry, I am. But I don't need any more money. I've got this house, and everything that comes with being the long-lost great-great-granddaughter of a lumber baron. Now if Finn had his way, I'd sell this place to the highest bidder and we'd move back to Brooklyn, lickety-split!"

"Your scruples are much to be admired, Fiona Forrest," said Cam sincerely. "Or should I call you Fiona *Woods*?"

"No need. I'm sticking with Forrest. It's the least I can do out of respect for the people who raised me."

Hearing this made me smile. *"Your scruples are much to be admired, Fiona Forrest,"* I said, stealing my BFF's phrase.

For a twenty-five-year-old, the girl had a good head on her shoulders.

Cam crinkled up his nose like he smelled something foul. "Is *scruples* the right word? Eh, what do I know? I sell real estate. It's certainly not brain surgery!"

Regardless of the outcome, I found it interesting that someone had contacted Campbell Sellers about reaching out to Fiona about parting ways with Woods Hall, so the supposedly haunted property could be retrofitted for a legit haunted attraction. With the topic on the table, I could remember something along the same lines being stated, back when Cam first took me and JP on a tour of run-down houses to consider for our next renovation project. We couldn't gain access to the home, since Fiona and Finn were off on tour, so I told Cam to use his handy-dandy Realtor's passkey to let us in and show us around.

"What key?" he asked on that April morning. *"Woods Hall was never listed for sale, so I never had one . . . Fiona Forrest inherited this house. It never hit the market. A potential buyer saw one of my billboards and reached out to inquire about the status of the property."*

It struck me odd someone was willing to pay a (quote-unquote) ton of money to buy an old house they (quote-unquote) heard was (quote-unquote) haunted. What if they'd gone to all the trouble—and spent all those dollars—only to discover the ghost of Emma Woods and her haunting of Woods Hall was a complete hoax?

Something told me there was more to this mystery than any of us were aware of.

Chapter 10

The sun set over 13 Woods Way.

The bright blue sky turned a soft shade of pink, then deepened to a rich orange-red as the sun sank lower toward the horizon. The clouds were painted in shades of purple and orange, creating a stunning contrast against the suburban backdrop. As the light shifted, the warm glow of the old manor home's exterior became even more pronounced. The cream-colored stucco glowed a deep, warm gold in the fading light, while the chocolate-brown shutters and olive-green trim gleamed in shades of bronze. Shadows grew longer and the light that bathed the oak trees along the property became more intense.

My sister was the next familiar face to find me doing my open-house hosting duty. "Hey there, stranger!"

"Hey!" I said, embracing her as she bounded up the limestone porch steps.

We weren't a touchy-feely family, but Pamela and I hadn't seen each other since our parents' Fourth of July barbecue, so we both made sure to go the extra mile in our show of affection.

"I like this *ensemble*," I said, employing a French accent.

Pam's outfit that evening consisted of formfitting, stretch cotton yoga pants and a matching lightweight jacket with hood. I knew she didn't work out, so I had no suspicion she just came from the gym.

"Thanks! A little treat for myself . . . just because. Where's JP at?" Pam searched the crowd that, hours later, showed no signs of thinning.

By that point in the day, I counted a total of six-hundred-plus visitors to Woods Hall, meaning we raised well over three *thousand* dollars for the rescue dogs of Home FurEver.

"Pa-*mel-a*, Pa-*mel-a*, Pa-*mel-a*!" JP sang out. He snuck up behind my big sister and threw his big arms around her, giving her a big hug.

They had this inside joke that involved them both going to Cancun on separate high school class trips, years apart, and frequenting the same dance club, La Boom. As the story goes, the DJ took a liking to my sister who—due to his Latin accent—he called Pa-*mel-a*, em-*pha*-sis on the second syl-*la*-ble. Evidently JP remembered the DJ—due to his Latin good looks—and when he and Pam first made the discovery, they found the coincidence hi-*larious*.

"Hey, brother-in-law!" Pam said cheerfully, squeezing JP in return.

She always preferred my other half to me.

Pamela Penwell-Parker was a woman who exuded a confident and mature aura, befitting her thirty-nine years. She favored our father when it came to her physical attributes. Her warm smile could light up a room, and her dark hair framed her face in a flattering way. Never having had children, her figure remained slim yet curvaceous. This fact was a bone of contention with our mother, and she gave Pam and her hubby Mason a hard time over their elopement to Las Vegas, years before.

"So . . . who's taking me on a tour? I'm dying to see this place!" my sister said, her sparkling brown eyes full of curiosity.

I opened my mouth to offer.

Pam grabbed hold of JP's arm. "Okay, let's go!"

"I'll stay here and greet any newcomers," I said, trying not to harbor hurt feelings at being thrown over by my only sibling.

JP cupped his hands together and shouted across the yard. "Yo, Finn! Could you cover the door? Me and Pete are showing his sister the house."

Before Finn could come up with *another* excuse as to why he couldn't help, JP led us through the wide front door of Woods Hall.

Stepping across the foyer, Pamela's jaw just about fell open. "Wow. This is amazing!"

"Ignore the musty smell," I begged. "We tried airing it out. That's what happens when a house sits shut up for almost twenty-five years."

We made our way into the living room, with its neutral-colored wall-to-wall carpet and oversized burgundy leather sofa, matching recliner, and ottoman. An entertainment center cluttered up much of one corner, on which sat a so-called big-screen TV. At a whopping twenty-six inches, the thing looked like it weighed close to a hundred pounds.

Pam covered her mouth as she took everything in. "Oh god! Is that a VCR?"

It was.

"A JVC four-head with hi-fi stereo sound," I said, cracking up my sister.

"Remember the time Dad got on his kick?"

"Which one?"

"Peter! Remember all the VCRs?" Pam turned to JP. "Around, I don't know . . . 2002, maybe . . . our dad somehow got it in his head we needed a VHS player in *every* room of our house."

"Except the bathroom. But only because there was no place to mount a TV next to the toilet."

"He bought Peter and me, both, our own TV/VCR combos.

We rushed home every day from school, fixed a plate in the kitchen, then locked ourselves in our bedrooms for the rest of the night. What kind of parents let their kids do that?"

Looking back this probably explained my mom's insistence that JP and I come for dinner on most Sundays, and why she made us all eat together around the dining table while partaking in actual conversation.

"It worked out good for me. Got to see *Will & Grace* when it first aired, no questions asked. And whenever Cam spent the night, we snuck and watched the original BBC *Queer as Folk* on VHS," I said, reveling in the memory.

"Good times," said JP, shaking his head at the silliness.

Pamela took a few steps further into the room and then, suddenly . . . she stopped.

"What's wrong?" I asked, noticing a fearful look on her face.

"I detect a *presence*," she said, her voice trembling. "Petey, you know I'm psychic."

Pam always made this claim . . . and I was always skeptical whenever she did.

"Are you sure?" asked JP, his brow furrowed.

My sister nodded slowly. "I am."

The three of us stood still for a moment, the silence broken only by the sound of our breathing. My pulse quickened as I tried to rationalize what Pamela was saying. Maybe it was the musty smell or the creaking of the old hardwood floors under our feet. But as I glanced over at the staircase leading up to the hand-painted portrait of Emma Woods as Miss Great Lakes 1992, I got a definite chill.

JP was having none of the Penwell siblings' supernatural nonsense. "Let's show your sister the rest of the house. Pammy, wanna see the kitchen?"

Off the back of the home, the room was a mix of old-world charm and late twentieth century functionality. The real wood cabinets, installed when the house was first built, remained. I envied the butler's pantry and the additional shelving and counter space. The granite, I could do without. I wasn't a big fan of the dark veining and gold speckles that were on trend back when Emma and Bill Woods were married and redecorated Woods Hall. In our current house, we had quartz, which was a pain to keep clean, but . . . the slate-gray sure did beat the brown and beige of the 1990s!

As we strolled down the hallway, the row of wall sconces lighting our path began to flicker. Pamela's eyes opened in alarm, and she lowered her voice to a whisper. "You feel that? There's someone else here with us."

JP and I looked nervously at each other, trying our best to remain calm. Maybe it was just me, but the air suddenly felt thick and heavy. There was a strange energy in the house that neither one of us could quite put a finger on.

"It's probably just some faulty wiring. We can have Sparky take a look on Monday," JP said, making a snap judgment.

Sparky was our on-set electrician. His real name was Sam.

"I'm telling you guys—" Pam started to say. But she stopped short as a loud *thud* rang out from behind us, followed by the sound of shattering glass.

We scurried into the kitchen, only to find one of the cabinet doors flung open. Several pieces of expensive china lay on the ceramic tile, shattered to pieces.

Pamela gasped in horror and took a step back, her voice shaking when she spoke. "Okay, I think I've seen enough . . . Get me outta here!"

Hurrying back to the front foyer, the wall sconces flickered again as we passed by. But this time, a booming *bang* erupted from behind one of the wood-paneled walls.

"It's just the plumbing!" JP called out, quickening his pace.

Bolting through the wide front door, the three of us stumbled onto the porch, finally safe and sound in the twilight.

"You sure you guys wanna renovate *this* house? It's like something out of a horror movie in there," Pam said, her tone serious.

I couldn't blame my sister for feeling this way. The old manor did seem eerie and unsettling . . . and I didn't believe in evil spirits! Yet somehow, it felt like we were being watched.

Was the ghost of Emma Woods haunting Woods Hall for real?

Chapter 11

My heart leapt right out of my chest.

"Did I scare you?" Ursula asked, after doing just that.

She had snuck up behind me, JP, and Pamela standing on the porch of Woods Hall—totally freaking out—and literally shouted in our ears: *BOO!*

JP audibly exhaled. "Um . . . yes. Don't ever do that again."

Ursula tilted her head as she scrutinized us. Our closed-off body language was enough to convey the lingering fear of our recent mutual experience. "What's up? You guys look like you saw a ghost. OMG! Did you?"

My sister shrieked. "We did! Well, we didn't *see* it . . . but we felt it. At least I know *I* did."

"No, I felt it too," I said, reluctant to acknowledge my stance on the existence of spirits was being reconsidered.

We shared with Ursula the details of our ghostly encounter, to which she replied without sympathy. "Why didn't you guys take the crew with you? Man! Kevin could've totally got some footage."

"Pete and I were just showing his sister around. Some wall sconces flickered, and a pipe rattled in the wall. It's an old house. Stuff happens all the time."

"Okay, whatever. I'll make Gopher clean up the mess in the

kitchen. We need to get out back. Everything's all set up for the concert."

She was referring to the performance Fiona and Finn agreed to give that night, to close out the open house. When she first approached them, Fiona said she was all-in. Finn, on the other hand, acted hesitant. He wanted to know if Low-Fi would be paid for their time and talent. Not surprising. With a little coaxing and coddling, Ursie managed to convince Mr. Lowenstein that giving a *free* show for their followers would make for a good first episode of *Domestic Partners'* new season. And, if he wanted, they could set up a merch table on the grounds. Ursula would make Gopher the PA man it, selling CDs, T-shirts, and beer cozies or whatever. They could also live stream the event on their social media channels.

Fortunately, for the sake of everyone involved, Finn agreed.

On the flagstone patio, Chippy, our contractor, built a makeshift stage. It wasn't anything fancy, just a small platform put together with some two-by-fours and planking. He made sure to elevate it high enough off the ground so folks standing in the back could see.

Before the concert officially started, JP and I stepped up to make an announcement as Finn and Fiona took their positions. She tuned her guitar while he tickled the keys of his keyboard, quietly warming up his fingers.

Being a trained actor, JP was always the one to speak when it came to public appearances. Me, I just stood idly by, trying not to look like a deer caught in the headlights. "Hey, guys! First off, we wanna thank everyone for coming out to Woods Hall today. Isn't this a beautiful home?"

The crowd clapped and cheered, showing off their enthusiasm for the amazing piece of property most had never seen up close and personal before.

JP smiled at the audience. "We're thrilled to be here and to kick off season three of *Domestic Partners* . . . with this incredible performance by Low-Fi. PJ and I are super excited to be helping

Finn and Fiona with the renovations on their new house. We can't wait to have everyone back when we're finished to see how everything turns out."

The crowd cheered again as Finn and Fiona smiled appreciatively, behind us.

"Okay, I'll shut up now," JP joked. "On with the show!"

Accompanied by thunderous applause, Fiona gazed at the audience. "Good evening! We're Low-Fi. And we're beyond thrilled to open our home to you all. Thank you so much for your warm welcome. Finn and I are looking forward to living here in Pleasant Woods for a long, long time. Most of you know the history of my family. It hasn't always been the brightest. But I'm back where I belong, and I know things can only get better now."

"Who wants to hear some music?!" Finn shouted, interrupting Fiona's heartfelt moment.

They say *actions speak louder than words*. The more I got to see of this guy's behavior, the more I was beginning to wonder: *What did Fiona Forrest ever see in Finn Lowenstein?*

The audience didn't seem to mind. They showed their unconditional love for Low-Fi, cheering and stomping their feet in a deafening roar. From where I stood with JP, his strong arms around my waist, I searched the sky for the full moon. Earlier, I could see it clearly. Suddenly, it was gone, hidden behind a dark cloud that seemed to come out of nowhere. If it started raining in the middle of a *free* Low-Fi concert, a very happy camper I was *not* going to be!

Finn and Fiona launched into their first tune, a sorrowful ballad showcasing their unique sound. But I didn't recognize the melody from either of their two albums.

Fiona gently strummed her guitar. "This is a new song. It's called 'Haunted by Your Ghost' and it's dedicated to my birth mother, Emma Wheeler-Woods."

> *Shadows on the wall*
> *Remind me of your face*

> *Whispers in the hall*
> *Echo memories of your grace*
> *I'm haunted by your ghost*
> *In this empty space.*

The lyrics, written by Fiona, depicted the profound impact of losing her mom at a young age, even though she couldn't remember the woman. The reference to *shadows on the wall* and *whispers in the hall* implied she was haunted by a presence she couldn't fully comprehend. The line *echo memories of your grace* spoke to the idea that her mother's absence left a void in Fiona's life, despite not having any concrete memories of her. It suggested her mom was a source of comfort and love, and she was left to grapple with the absence of that presence.

Overall, the lyrics captured the complex emotions that can come with losing a mother as a child. The use of sensory cues, such as shadows and whispers, created a vivid and emotional image. Fiona's feelings of longing and loss were palpable, making the song a poignant tribute to those who experienced the absence of a parent from their lives.

> *Haunted by your ghost*
> *I can't escape your hold*
> *My heart is your host*
> *And I'm left out in the cold*
> *Haunted by your ghost*
> *I'm lost and all alone.*

In the chorus, Fiona repeated the idea of how she's haunted by her birth mother's memory, unable to escape Emma Woods's hold on her heart. The use of *host* in the line *my heart is your host* evoked a sense of possession and control over the emotions she continued to feel. As an author, I envied the songwriter's ability to pen such deep and meaningful poetry.

The memories of your touch
Etched into my skin
The echoes of your voice
Haunt me from within
I'm haunted by your ghost
And I can't begin again.

I try to run, I try to hide
You're always by my side
I can't shake this feeling deep inside
I'm haunted by your ghost, every night.

So, those dark clouds I noticed . . . the ones that came out of nowhere, obscuring the full moon from our view? Well, along with them, a not-so-gentle breeze began blowing across the backyard, rustling the leaves of the old oak trees.

JP tightened his grip around my middle. "Looks like it's gonna storm."

I reached for the phone in my pocket. "My weather app doesn't show any rain."

One thing I hated was an inaccurate weather forecast. As far as I was concerned, the weather people got paid the big bucks to get it right. They should be held accountable! People like me planned their daily activities based on their predictions. There was nothing worse than being out on a dog walk with Clyde and Jack and getting drenched because I had no idea there was a hint of rain coming.

JP took a quick look around as the wind whipped up and a dense fog rolled in over the garden. "Should we make a break for it?"

Glancing over to where Kevin stood with his camera, I knew our every move was being recorded. Again, I remembered the reel of outtakes we'd watch at the end-of-season wrap party, worried how foolish we'd look if we went running for shelter.

"Let's just wait it out. I don't wanna be rude to Finn and Fiona."

Apparently, F and F weren't taking any chances. The second Fiona's mic stand blew over, they both stopped singing and playing, mid-song.

Fiona bent down and snatched up her microphone, her voice barely audible over the fierce wind. "Hey, guys! I'm sorry we're gonna have to cut the show short."

There were groans and disappointed murmurs from the crowd.

"We really appreciate you being here tonight. We're so sorry we can't finish the set."

"Yeah. We don't want anybody getting hurt on our property, okay? We can't afford to get—"

Before Finn could utter the word *sued* . . . a huge gust knocked one of the moss-covered terra-cotta planters off the third-floor balcony, above. The enormous clay flowerpot came plunging down, heading right for the makeshift stage where Fiona stood frozen in terror, directly below. The planter seemed to be moving in slow motion as it tumbled through the air, turning end over end, its rough texture and earthy tone illuminated in the dim light of the stormy sky.

As it fell, Fiona could feel the rush of air as the heavy object hurtled past her, missing her by mere inches.

The planter hit the ground with a loud *crash*, sending shards and soil flying in every direction. The once beautiful container was now a jumbled mess of broken pottery.

And just like that, the wind died down and the fog rolled out.

Fiona kept still, visibly shaken, staring up at the balcony.

JP and I jumped onto the stage beside her. "Are you okay?" I asked, panicked but relieved to discover the Low-Fi singer unscathed.

"I think I just saw my birth mother," she answered, her eyes still fixated on the spot high above.

At Ursula's insistence, the remaining open-house attendees were all sent home. Kevin pulled up the footage he shot on his camera of the entire incident. As the terra-cotta planter fell from the balcony, a flash of white materialized on-screen, near the railing's edge.

Kevin rewound and played back the tape. "You guys hear that? Sounds like some sorta music . . . all tinkly. Maybe one of them music boxes? My daughter's got a bunch of 'em."

It was hard to hear over the whipping of the wind, but Dave's sound equipment had definitely picked up *something* on the recording. He covered his ears with noise-canceling headphones, to get a better listen. "Play that again, Kev . . . Think I'm hearing a woman . . . *crying?*"

Finn screamed and pointed at the monitor. "Emma Woods!"

"As much as I want this house to be haunted, we can't be sure *what* that white flash is," said Ursula.

Finn threw a hissy fit. "It's a ghost wearing a wedding dress . . . and she just tried killing her own kid!"

To quell everyone's anxieties, JP headed inside Woods Hall with Kevin, Dave, and Gopher the PA. I stayed behind with Fiona, making sure she didn't need anything. Moments later, the men stepped onto the third-floor balcony.

JP called down to us. "All clear! No crying spirits, no music boxes, no nothing!"

"You sure?" I shouted back. Desperately I wanted to believe what happened was nothing more than an honest accident . . .

Not the evildoings of a dead woman.

Chapter 12

JP stood at the stove cooking breakfast. With a plastic spatula he flipped over four thick slices of brioche bread. They turned a golden brown, sizzling in the nonstick frying pan, coated with a not-too-generous amount of salted Irish butter.

"Starving!" I sang out, observing my partner in culinary action.

A quiet noise erupted from my middle.

"Is that your belly?" JP laughed lightly.

"I said I'm starving!"

"Almost ready . . . Is the syrup on the table?"

Glancing behind me to make sure, I caught a glimpse of Jack and Clyde, both sitting on their bums in their usual spots beside the dining table. They were smart boys, and they both had their daddies wrapped around their little paws. Well, Clydie's paws were *big*, but . . . These pups knew right where they needed to be, come mealtime. Scrambled eggs with Parmesan Reggiano was one of their faves.

In the kitchen, JP transferred the warm bread to a pair of scarlet Fiestaware plates, sprinkled cinnamon on top, then dusted each one with powdered confectioners' sugar. The presentation looked like something straight out of *Martha Stewart Living*.

"May we please eat now?" I begged in my best little-boy voice.

JP picked up his phone off the countertop. He snapped a pic—in portrait orientation, after being taught by Fiona to do it that way—and posted the shot to our official *Domestic Partners* socials. "*Ooone* sec."

#sundaybrunchgoals #frenchtoastlove
#domesticpartnersincrime

After we ate, we finished our coffee in front of the living room television. Mr. Clyde curled up next to Daddy JP on the Stickley spindle sofa. Daddy PJ sat with Jackson Boy tucked against his hip, all snug beneath his special dog blanket from Grandma Patsy. Mom purchased the super-soft sherpa from a sale to benefit Canine Companions, yet another Michigan-based dog rescue. She gifted both our boys one, when they first joined the Broadway-Penwell family. The blankets were black, white, and red and decorated with tiny hearts (*to show Grandma's love*, she said) and big paw prints.

"Turn this up, would you?" JP asked me as a shot of Woods Hall popped up on the TV.

To our surprise, *Good Day, Detroit—Weekend Edition*, aired a story on the recent scare we faced at 13 Woods Way, when a freak windstorm blew a terra-cotta planter off the third-floor balcony . . . missing Fiona Forrest of Low-Fi fame by *that* much.

"How'd they hear about what happened?" I said, sipping my Starbucks home brew from my favorite cherry-red Le Creuset coffee mug. It held a full fourteen ounces, so I only had to get up off the couch once for a refill.

JP dipped a cookie into his cup and took a bite—forget we'd already had something sweet with our morning meal—talking as he chewed. "One guess."

Miss Ursula strikes again!

If anything, it was good publicity for our show. The news item also mentioned how *Domestic Partners* helped raise close to $5K for

Home FurEver. In a brief on-camera interview, Margot said she was super pleased with the support, which made both JP and I super pleased to know we, once again, did some good for the dogs of Metro Detroit.

Reaching beneath the sherpa blanket, I gave little Jack's fuzzy hindquarters a gentle squeeze. Clyde let out a nervous yawn as JP attempted to pet him under the chin. We sure did love our boys!

On Sundays, we made it a point to spend quality time with Jackson and Clydie. We had one more day free before work at Woods Hall officially began. As production ramped up and our deadline loomed tight, there would surely be some panic on Ursula's part (there always was!), causing The Boss to start cracking the old whip.

But for now, we could enjoy just being together.

En route to the local neighborhood dog park, we bumped into our friends, The Marshalls, out strolling with their trio of dachshunds, Moto, Rex, and Phippie, aka Mr. Phipps.

"Yoo-hoo! Domestic Partners!" called Vicky, her high-pitched Michigan accent projecting down Sylvania Street. She and her husband Quinn were Pleasant Woods's current First Couple.

In spite of it being September on the calendar, Vicky sported one of her infamous floral print caftans, while a pair of Bermuda shorts showed off her mayor husband's hairless legs. I wondered what they did with their days now that our community swimming pool was closed for the season.

Married way back in the mid-1980s, Vic was in her late sixties, and Quinn recently celebrated his Big 7-0. Vicky spent well over thirty years teaching English and drama at Fernridge High. They were both officially retired, with Quinn being a former executive at a prominent Detroit ad agency.

On the corner of Mayfair Drive and Wisconsin, while the dogs sniffed each other inappropriately, we adults chatted. Vicky's gray eyes crinkled at the corners as she regaled us.

"How was the open house yesterday? We're so sorry we couldn't make it. Rex had a tummy ache. We didn't feel good about leaving him home with just his brothers. Moto and Phipp tend to gang up on him whenever Quinn and I aren't around."

"No worries! The open house went well. We got a nice turnout and raised a good chunk of change," I told the silver-haired woman.

"Wonderful!"

Vicky, we hadn't seen much of since *Blue Tuesday* closed. I got to know her rather well during the six-week rehearsal period, serving as her assistant once she took over the reins from the original director, Xander Sherwood Deva. He was a man befitting of the alternate pronunciation of his surname—*Diva*—that was for certain! A total nightmare to work with, Xander had a bad habit of cutting down my play, and dissing my dialogue, whenever he spoke to the actors . . . and he did it with me sitting right there in the room.

I say he *had* a bad habit because, two weeks into the rehearsal process, Xander was unexpectedly strangled by his own extra-long cashmere scarf. As *Domestic Partners in Crime*, JP and I donned our Encyclopedia Brown caps and helped Pleasant Woods's resident police detective, Nick Paczki, figure out how the director with the posh British accent died on that fateful April Fool's Day night.

"We caught the story on the news this morning . . ." Mayor Marshall's grin appeared extra bright, set off by his late summer suntan. "Crazy about the windstorm at Woods Hall, huh? We didn't get anything like that over on this side of town."

"Oh, no?" JP replied, raising an eyebrow in my direction.

This was his silent signal, as if to say: *Don't mention what happened when we took your sister for a tour of the old house, Pete.*

We never even told Fiona or Finn about our little run-in with whatever caused those hallway sconces to flicker and made that mess of broken glass in the kitchen. They'd already dealt with enough after Fiona's near miss with the falling planter.

Before I could button my lip, Vicky piped up. "Any ghost sightings?"

"Nope. No ghost sightings," JP answered easily.

He wasn't fibbing when he said this. We really didn't *see* anything. Well, there was the flash of white caught by Kevin's camera in the footage of Low-Fi's performance. But we had no real way of knowing just what that was.

Could it have been the spirit of Emma Woods, back from the dead, dressed in the Princess Di costume she wore at her Halloween birthday party in 1997? Sure, it could. Was it most likely? Probably not.

Vicky lowered her voice slightly. Not that anyone else was around to overhear us. "You know, we were at the party on the night she died?"

The streets of Pleasant Woods were calm and quiet on this Sunday morning. Most folks we knew were still spending weekends Up North at their cottages or lakefront beach houses, as was customary in Michigan. JP and I dreamed of one day owning a second piece of property. But the thought of driving two-plus hours to get to it, then having to cut the grass when we got there and clean it before we came home . . . Well, it didn't seem worth the hassle or expense.

"I don't know if we knew you guys knew the Woodses," JP said, carrying on the conversation. He attempted to untangle Clyde's leash as he and Moto got caught up giving each other puppy kisses.

"Sure! Emma did some modeling for the ad agency. She and Bill were quite a bit younger than us, by like twenty years or so," Quinn said. "But they were both good kids."

Vicky visibly blanched. "Personally, I didn't care for either one of them. Not to speak ill of the dead, but . . . that girl was *always* flirting with my husband. And her own husband could never be trusted!"

Mr. Marshall blushed at his wife's unabashed transparency. "Emma

Woods was a nice girl. She was maybe a little overly friendly, but she never crossed a line that I can remember."

"Because you were too blinded by her flattery! That twenty-fifth birthday–Halloween party she threw for herself back in . . . Sweetheart, what year was that? Gosh, they all just blend together, don't they?"

The mayor nibbled on his thumbnail, doing the mental math. "In 1996, I think it was. No, wait. It was '97. Because *Ally McBeal* just started that same year. Remember, honey?"

Vicky nodded with recognition. "I never cared for that Calista Flockhart either! How she ever landed Harrison Ford . . ."

Quinn brushed off his wife's negative critique of Mrs. Han Solo and turned his attention toward me and JP. "We used to tape the show on Wednesdays and watch it on Fridays. But that week, we waited till Saturday morning instead."

"What made you wait?" JP asked out of curiosity.

"By the time we got home from the party, Vic and I were both too distracted by what happened to Emma . . . and what we over-heard before she fell off the balcony."

If the Marshalls knew something that might shed a light on how Emma Woods really died—*and by whose hand*—it was up to us, as *Domestic Partners in Crime*, to start asking questions.

"What did you overhear?" I asked, hoping I wasn't prying by being so personal.

The mayor's wife placed a hand on her husband's shoulder. "Do *you* wanna tell them?"

Quinn Marshall hesitated. "How about we take these pups and head back to our place? We can sit out on the deck and have a nice chat."

Our trip to the dog park could wait.

Halloween 1997

The Marshalls arrived at Woods Hall shortly before nine o'clock.

As they stepped through the marble-tiled foyer, the middle-aged married couple was barely recognizable as the forty-second U.S. President and First Lady, William Jefferson and Hillary Rodham Clinton.

In the dark of the grand entrance hall, the lights of the brass and crystal chandelier flickered dimly. Streamers in orange and black wove their way between the spindles of the staircase. A wispy spider web stretched across the wide archway. In the corner of the web a large black arachnid, with its three pairs of furry limbs, waited for the arrival of its prey.

The dining room that evening was a masterpiece, with an opulent feast of miniature quiches, tarts, and finger sandwiches—cut and shaped to resemble actual severed fingers! At the carving station, a chef outfitted as the grim reaper wielded his scythe as a carving knife.

Quinn took a step toward the dessert table. Positioned dead center was a thirteen-tiered layer cake in black and orange, complete with twenty-five ghost-shaped candles. Vicky shuddered as she quietly read the cake's inscription: *Happy Deathday, Emma.*

In the spirit of Halloween, the baker frosted a slash through the word *birth* that preceded the word *day* and added an edible tombstone to the cake's top tier.

A young woman's voice rang out over the roar of live music coming from outside on the flagstone patio. The Marshalls twirled round to discover their hostess, Emma Woods, stunningly beautiful in her birthday-slash-Halloween party outfit.

The gown was ivory silk taffeta, a replica of the original worn by Lady Diana Spencer at her wedding to the Prince of Wales. The dress—heavily embellished with lace, hand embroidery, and pearls—had a fitted bodice with a sweetheart neckline, covered with delicate lace appliqué. The long, puffed sleeves made of billowing silk tapered at the wrist and ended in a ruffle around the cuffs. The full skirt was fabricated from layers of tulle and silk organza that cascaded down to the floor.

Around Emma's neck dangled a magnificent diamond necklace, a lavish birthday gift from her husband, Bill. She greeted the ad man and his school teacher wife, complimenting their costumes.

Quinn returned the kind words, proclaiming the automotive heiress a natural princess.

Coyly, she adjusted the diamond tiara perched atop her head, affecting a soft British accent as she commanded him to bow in her presence.

Mr. Marshall played along, bending deep from the waist. His wife was having none of it. Emma's breath reeked of alcohol . . . and the party only began an hour ago! But Vicky realized she needed to be affable for the sake of her husband's business. Woods Lumber and Wheeler Automotive were two of the biggest accounts represented by Renaissance Advertising, the agency where Quinn held his position as deputy director.

Vicky Marshall curtsied demurely in Emma Woods's honor.

Quinn surveyed the crowded room for any sign of the prince of the house, William Woods IV, aka Bill.

Emma suggested they go in search of the housekeeper, who knew her husband longer—*and perhaps better?*—than she did.

Mr. Marshall laughed lightly, picking up on the not-so-hidden innuendo in Mrs. Woods's tone. Much like the royal affair reported in the tabloids between Prince Charles and Camilla Parker-Bowles, he'd heard the rumors of the apparent one taking place at Woods Hall.

A cater-waiter passed by, dressed as a royal footman. He nodded his powdered wig and held out a tray of crystal flutes.

Vicky Marshall detested champagne. But she happily accepted, raising her glass in a celebratory toast to Emma on her twenty-fifth birthday, and wishing the young woman a long and happy life.

Emma knocked back the expensive bubbly. She hiccupped slightly, before her focus was diverted to the opposite side of the manor. At which point, she excused herself and rushed off to speak with someone she deemed important.

This was the last time the Marshalls ever saw Emma Woods alive.

Chapter 13

J P and I listened with rapt attention to Quinn and Vicky's story.

The four of us lounged on the back deck of the tan vinyl-sided two-story with a side dormer and attached flat-roofed single car garage. Located at 82 Sylvania, perhaps the most fun feature of the property (apart from the purple front door) was the decorative half-dozen colorful bowling balls half-buried in the front garden bed.

While our puppies roughhoused down below in the yard, we enjoyed freshly brewed iced tea as the afternoon sun bathed us in a warm glow. Personally, I preferred iced *coffee*. But I wasn't going to be rude and refuse when Vicky offered it.

Beyond the eight-foot cedar privacy fence, Gainsford Park bustled with Sunday activities. Screaming children played on the playground while their helicopter parents kept a close watch. The sound of a bat hitting a ball echoed through the air, followed by the sight of an older boy (or was he a *she*?) sprinting around the baseball diamond, seen from our elevated position. The leaves of the trees were already beginning to turn, a sign of the fast-approaching fall.

"And then Emma walked away," said Quinn, picking up his story where he'd left off, "and we went to look for Bill Woods. I wanted to make sure he saw us there. You know, showing our faces at his wife's birthday and all that? I hated being such a suck-up to a twenty-five-year-old kid, but . . . his dad's company brought in big money for us at the agency."

"Did you ever end up finding him?" I asked, shifting into sleuthing mode.

"That's the thing. We did find Bill Woods," said Vicky. "He was right where Emma said he'd be . . . with the housekeeper . . . looking very suspicious."

"How so?" asked JP.

"At first they didn't see us. They were huddled in a corner of the kitchen near the butler's pantry," said Quinn.

Vicky lowered her voice like she had before, standing on the street corner. "When we got closer . . . we distinctly heard Kathleen whisper something to Bill."

JP and I both leaned forward in our Adirondack chairs. "What did she say?" I asked, the suspense building as Vicky's gray eyes narrowed.

"*You promised you'd do it tonight,*" she said, quoting the words spoken by the late Kathleen Anger.

"And what did Bill promise he'd do?" JP asked curiously.

Quinn shrugged. "No idea. We didn't want them thinking we were eavesdropping, so we pretended we didn't hear a thing. Remember, Vic?"

"I always assumed Bill planned to tell Emma he was leaving her. Maybe he changed his mind and Kathleen was upset about it? Everyone in Pleasant Woods thought they were having an affair."

"And why is that?" I asked.

Campbell Sellers told me and JP the same thing on the day he took us for our home tour of Woods Hall that didn't happen, back in April. Cam's exact words were something along the lines of: *Soon after Emma's suicide-slash-accident-slash-murder, vicious rumors started circulating. It seems Bill Woods and the live-in housekeeper, Kathleen Anger, were having a scandalous love affair.*

"Well . . ." As Vicky prepared to reveal more about the rumored liaison between Bill Woods and his live-in housekeeper, a look of hesitation crossed her face. Her gray eyes flickered back and forth, searching for the right words. Her body language was guarded, with her arms slightly crossed in front of her and her shoulders drawn up toward her ears. It was evident that Mrs. Marshall was torn between her desire to share the full story and not wanting to come off as a gossip.

"Vicky and some of her friends, they've always believed Bill Woods is . . . *was* the father of Kathleen Anger's little boy."

"She named the baby *Royce William* . . . That doesn't sound like a dead giveaway to you?" Vicky rolled her gray eyes at me and JP. "Gentlemen, my husband . . . Mr. Naïve."

"Well, it's not like she named him *William Royce the fifth*. To me, that would've made it obvious," said Quinn, coming to his own defense.

Vicky waved a resigned hand at her husband in a gesture of defeat. "Kathleen Anger wasn't fooling anybody by reversing the two names, okay? I give up!"

"Pete actually brought up the same point," said JP, referring to my earlier qualms. "Fiona told us about Kathleen's son being named after the middle name of Bill Woods's father."

Vicky scowled. "Royce was Bill Woods's middle name too! Maybe she didn't name her son after Bill's dad, but after the boy's own father . . . Bill Woods!"

She continued to enlighten us.

"The story I've always heard was this: When Bill Woods was sixteen and Kathleen was nineteen, they became romantically involved. Bill's father caught on and put a stop to the affair. But soon after, Kathleen announced she was pregnant. William Royce Woods the third wasn't about to allow his son to marry a common housekeeper. So, in exchange for her silence, he permitted Kathleen to remain at Woods Hall with the baby. She wasn't allowed to list Bill's name as the boy's father on the birth certificate, out of fear of the truth getting out. And if the girl ever told anyone, William would see to it she was prosecuted for corrupting a minor."

"Not sure you can corrupt a teenage boy," Quinn teased, "but yes, I heard that same story around the ad agency when I worked on the Woods Lumber account. It wasn't until Bill's dad died, he and Kathleen could finally marry."

"What about the theory saying Bill killed Emma?" asked JP, re-hashing what Cam also told us. "Maybe that's the promise Kathleen was talking about when she said what you overheard her say."

Cam's version of the story went something like so: *Emma got wind of Bill and Kathleen's affair—no one quite knows how—and in the middle of the birthday-slash-Halloween party, she accused her husband of being unfaithful. What did he do? In a fit of rage, Bill Woods followed his jealous wife upstairs to the master suite and onto the balcony. That's when he supposedly shoved her off.*

"Then, with Emma gone and Bill's father eventually out of the picture, Bill and Kathleen could live happily ever after," said JP, wrapping up his hypothesis.

"Except for the Woods family curse!" Vicky cried. "Talk about ironic. Bill and Kathleen never even made it back from their honeymoon. And Bill died before he got the chance to adopt Kathleen's son—*his* son."

The mayor's face contorted into a puzzled expression and his lips pursed tightly. "But here's what I don't get . . . If Bill Woods planned on leaving Emma on the night of her twenty-fifth birthday– Halloween party . . . why did he bother giving her that diamond necklace?"

A wistful expression crossed Vicky's face. "Oh! That necklace was gorgeous! John Paul and Peter, you boys should've seen it. A large pendant in the center, encircled by a bunch of smaller dia-monds in a beautiful halo pattern. I don't even wanna know how much it cost! And to think, we got her a silly old music box."

"That music box wasn't silly. Emma collected music boxes. It was a good gift."

"It was a *cheap* gift."

The Marshalls' bickering reminded me of the tinkling sound we faintly heard on the footage taken during the wind storm at the Woods Hall open house. Maybe the white blur on that tape *was* the ghost of Emma Woods?

Still, I couldn't shake the most obvious question.

"What *I* don't get is . . . If Bill Woods was the prime suspect in Emma's death, why was he never investigated?"

"The Woodses are—*were* a very powerful family, Peter. William could've easily paid off the right people, covered up the truth, and stopped his son from going to prison," Mayor Marshall said. "Until the day he died, that guy had all of Metro Detroit under his thumb."

"And how did he die?" JP inquired.

"Heart attack—at *fifty*—right in the middle of his morning coffee," answered Vicky. "Again, I'm telling you . . . the Woods family curse!"

As we mulled over the details of Emma Woods's twenty-fifth birthday party, we sat deep in thought, trying to figure out what happened on Halloween night 1997. Jackson chased Clydie Boy across the backyard, their tails wagging wildly. Moto, Phippie, and Rex remained on the sidelines like spectators at a sporting event, barking and yapping as they cheered our boys on.

The dogs seemed to be unaffected by the heavy conversation.

Chapter 14

She was late . . . *again.*

Ursula jumped out of her rental car and scurried up the stone walkway at Woods Hall. "Stupid Starbucks drive-thru! I should've sent Gopher to pick up my latte."

We arrived bright and early on Monday morning, ready to begin our first big project of season three: tackling the exterior of the house. After everyone filled their faces from the craft services table—and both JP and I consumed a couple cups of coffee—we stood on our marks in the grass, alongside the manor.

Ursie shouted out her usual opening line: "Picture's up! Roll sound, roll camera!"

"Speed!"

"Camera's rolling!"

Gopher held up the slate. "*Domestic Partners*, episode three-point-one, scene one, take one."

"Action!"

JP gazed into the lens and flashed his best TV show cohost grin. "Before we can even touch the inside, we gotta fix up the *out.*"

"The stucco here is in good shape," I said, taking my turn. "But the paint is all blistered—*worn out* and blistered, so—" I stopped myself, totally stumbling over my line. "Sorry."

Ursula cued us to stop. "Cut! PJ, you're a little rusty after the hiatus, huh? No problem. This time, you guys make sure to play up the back-and-forth banter. That's what viewers wanna see, okay?"

I felt like saying: *No, viewers wanna see JP Broadway with his shirt off*. Because it was true. But I didn't.

"Back to one!" Ursula bellowed.

This was why movie making (and TV show taping) took so long. Programs like ours were considered (quote-unquote) reality TV, and they were, to an extent. A part of me wished she'd just let Kevin turn on his camera and shoot *everything* we did, nonstop. Then, the editors could fix it all up and put it together in post-production.

"You got this." JP clapped me on the shoulder as we assumed our original positions.

"Easy for you to say. You're the one with the BFA from Carnegie Mellon."

Long ago, I learned when it came to the best Theatre programs, the Yale School of Drama ranked top of the list. New York University also received high marks, as did JP's alma mater in his hometown of Pittsburgh.

"*Domestic Partners*, episode three-point-one, scene one, take *two*."

"Action!"

JP looked at the camera and did exactly what he did moments ago, the exact same way. "Before we can even touch the inside, we gotta fix up the *out*."

"The stucco here is in good shape," I said, taking another crack at my line. "But the paint is worn out and blistered, so . . . Time to break out ye olde power washer!"

"*Ye olde?* I know you're a writer, PJ. But this is hardly Shakespeare." JP smirked directly at the camera, playing up his charm to perfection.

"And cut!"

"That's a cut!" Gopher cried. "Okay, Kev. Let's get a close-up of the worn-out paint over here. JP, shirt off, please."

And here we go!

I wasn't even kidding thinking what I thought about our HDTV viewers wanting to see my partner half naked. It didn't bother me none. I got to see him *more* than half naked. Plus, the attention made him feel good. For an undeniably handsome man, JP Broadway could be surprisingly insecure.

He stood bare-chested on the extension ladder, holding the power-washing hose tight in his hands. He looked like a fireman from a Hot Hunks calendar (minus the protective gear), only not as cheesy. Positioning himself to get the best possible angle, JP hollered down to where I waited below. "Let her rip!"

From his perch high above, he pointed the spray gun at the stucco and squeezed the trigger. A powerful stream of water shot out of the nozzle with impressive force, forcing JP to adjust his grip to keep the hose steady.

I could just picture how the scene would play on the finished episode of *Domestic Partners*, all slow motion, with a sexy music background track.

"Careful!" I called out, steadying the ladder as JP directed the stream at the peeling paint.

The water splashed against the surface, sending droplets flying in all directions. JP remained focused and determined as years of stains were blasted away, revealing the true beauty of the stucco underneath. There was the occasional slip on the wet aluminum ladder, and the need to constantly adjust his position, but quickly he got into a rhythm. He worked steadily and efficiently, making progress with each passing moment, as Kevin captured JP's every shirtless move on-camera.

As he worked his way around the old house, he took care to avoid any delicate features or architectural details that could be damaged by the high-pressure water. Despite the hot morning sun beating down on him—and the wet spray in his face from the occasional gust of wind—JP remained focused on the task at hand.

After a few hours of hard work and constantly having to reposition the ladder, he finally turned off the spray gun, climbed down, and put his shirt back on.

"Good job, hon!" I told JP, pleased with the gleaming end results.

Woods Hall looked remarkably different. The dirty, weathered exterior was now bright, clean, and vibrant. The once peeling and blistered stucco was smooth and uniform. The window frames, eaves, and other decorative features were much more noticeable and prominent. Everything stood out against the clean, cream-colored stucco, adding depth and dimension to the overall appearance of the Arts and Crafts–inspired manor home.

After lunch, Finn and Fiona showed up on-set. They looked ready to work, both wearing coveralls branded with the name of my father's hardware store, a top sponsor of *Domestic Partners*. JP and I slipped ours on as well. It was more about showing off the Jimmy's logo than keeping our clothes clean when we started to paint.

Ursula directed us to where she wanted the next setup. "Guys, grab those buckets and rollers . . . Let's head around back, okay?"

We did as instructed, bringing with us our painting paraphernalia, while Kevin and Dave readied themselves to record us in action.

Gopher marked the slate. "*Domestic Partners*, episode three-point-one, scene three, take one!"

"Action!"

As per the outline I'd helped the HDTV writers come up with, JP handed off a pair of paintbrushes to Finn and Fiona. "Just so you know, the plan is to have you guys work on freshening up the trim. Chippy will handle any framing that needs replacing."

This would involve him removing the old, damaged wood pieces and cutting new boards to fit. But we didn't need to show any of that business at that point. These shots were more about seeing F and F contribute to the renovation of their soon-to-be For-ever Home.

"You guys ready to get your hands dirty?" Immediately I hated the way the words came out of my mouth as soon as I said them.

This was the main reason I avoided watching *Domestic Partners* when it aired. Our next-door neighbor Bob Kravitz, aka Fairway Bob, hosted a weekly viewing party. I made it a point to show up for the season premiere. After that, I conveniently found excuses for why I couldn't be in attendance. JP didn't seem to mind at all the way his voice sounded on camera. Being a professional performer since the age of twenty-two, I guess he was used to it by now.

"I'm ready!" Fiona seemed excited and more than happy to help us out.

Finn, on the other hand, wasn't so enthusiastic. He looked at the paintbrush in his hand with disdain. "Why do we have to do this? We're musicians, not house painters."

JP kept his mouth shut. I could tell what he was thinking from his flaring nostrils. But, with the camera rolling, he wasn't about to call Finn out and make a big scene.

"Come on! This is *your* house," I said, attempting to lighten the mood. "Think about when it's finished, and you can take credit for how awesome it looks."

"I just don't see the point of making us do all the work. It's like you're using us for free labor," said Finn, refusing to budge on his position.

"Cut!" Ursula stepped up from where she'd been observing, off to the side. She remained calm. But we could all tell she'd just about had enough of Finn Lowenstein's attitude. "The point— same as I told you when you complained about giving the free concert the other night—is . . . a bunch of Low-Fi fans and followers will tune in. You don't want them seeing you being a diva, do you?"

"I'm not a diva! And our followers are like in high school. They barely own a car, let alone a house. Why would they watch some lame home renovation show?"

"Easy, buddy . . . I get that you're barely out of high school yourself," JP told Finn, cutting into the conversation. "But don't be knocking what me and Pete are doing here. You don't want help, we'll find another property to work on."

My hero!

Finn took a step forward, putting on his best tough guy 'tude. His dark eyes met JP's baby blues as they stared each other down. "No disrespect, *buddy* . . . You need us way more than we need you. Fiona's got a lot of money now. We can find someone else to remodel this stupid place."

I hated how he used the word *remodel*. JP and I *restored* old houses. There was a big difference, but I decided not to waste my breath on a spoiled brat.

"Please don't call my family's home *stupid*," Fiona said to her fiancé through gritted teeth. "And I do have a lot of money now. But until we're married, it's *my* money. Keep it up and there won't be a wedding in your future."

"You sure you don't want me to roll tape?" Kevin muttered to Ursula. "This is some good TV drama, right here."

"Cool it Kevin! Guys, you all need to quit. JP, no, we can't find another property to renovate. We're on a tight deadline to get this season in the can by Halloween. Finn, you and Fiona signed a legally binding contract. Like it or not, we're stuck with each other for the next two months. How about we make the best of it, okay?"

This was just the third day of taping on an eight-week-long shoot. Despite the long schedule ahead, the energy on set was high, and everyone was eager to bring their best work to the project.

It didn't bode well to be off to such a shaky start.

Chapter 15

The majestic Queen Anne rested on the north side of Fairway Lane.

Just east of Woodward Avenue, opposite the Craftsman Colonial where JP and I resided, the home at number 2 housed the upscale wine pub, Chianti. First constructed in 1898 by William Royce Woods—the cursed lumber baron and Pleasant Woods's founding father—Woods later moved his wife and children into the stately Arts and Crafts–inspired manor located at 13 Woods Way.

The current owners were a Korean American couple, Andrew and Brianna Kim, who acted as chef and manager, respectively, and lived directly above the popular restaurant. Unfortunately, we'd had a recent falling out with Mrs. Kim and her Taekwondo master husband. At one point, it was their hope to purchase the abandoned Tudor Revival next door from the Cash brothers, Tom and Terry. The Kims' master plan was to tear down the old house and, in its place, erect a parking lot. Never mind an historic district like Pleasant Woods possessed strict zoning laws. No elected official at Town Hall would allow an historic home to be razed in favor of a business.

Around us, the sounds of glasses clinking and muted chatter mingled with the soft melodies of jazz coming from a carefully curated playlist. The dim lighting created a warm and inviting ambiance, coupled with the rich aroma of freshly cooked food floating in from the kitchen. The atmosphere was lively but not overly crowded, with patrons sitting in small groups at tables and booths along the sides of the main room. Customers from Pleasant Woods and beyond engaged in conversation, laughing and sharing stories over wines from all over the world.

Dozens of Chianti bottles hung on the exposed brick wall, with signatures scrawled across the straw baskets by the persons who'd emptied them. On the day we first toured the house that would eventually become our home, Cam brought us to the wine pub, and we added our own names to the collection.

I made a mental note-to-self to look and see if our signed bottle remained in its spot.

After dinner, Brianna came back to check on us. "Can I bring you anything else?" The fortysomething woman wore her short dark hair slicked back, a black tuxedo shirt, black bow tie, and black pants.

JP and I intentionally allowed Ursula to do the talking, so we could avoid our neighbor at all costs, in case she still harbored a grudge. I hated it when things got awkward.

Ursie took control of the situation, something she did best. "Hey, can I look at a to-go menu? I wanna take something back for Chippy."

Our contractor skipped out on the break so he could continue fixing up a broken window frame on the back side of Woods Hall, below the third-floor balcony. Ursula kept trying to text him all through dinner but got no reply. My guess was he got into a groove with his work and didn't want to stop. Same thing happened to me whenever I was writing.

"Sure thing." Brianna totally avoided both our gazes as JP and I stood up from our chairs and headed toward the restroom. Guess she was still mad, after all.

"Hey, boys!"

Before we could get very far, someone called out across the wine pub. We halted in our tracks to see Stephen and Evan Savage-Singer, the married queer couple who lived in the mid-century modern two doors down from us. The Drag Queen Queeraoke host (hostess?) and Gulf War vet sat side by side at the bar, sipping on glasses of deep red wine.

The super stylish Stephen wore a linen shirt with rolled-up sleeves, combined with tailored cropped pants and espadrilles. His cocoa skin contrasted nicely with the light-colored fabric. On his dark head, he'd popped an ivory fedora. Evan, more blue-collar, dressed himself in a simple navy T-shirt, khaki shorts, and tennis shoes. A denim jacket hung over the back of his bar stool.

"Hey!" I exclaimed, taking full advantage of the chance to further distance us from Brianna Kim.

Evan apologized when we stepped over to join them. "Sorry we couldn't make it to your open house. Gracie had a dance competition. Took all day."

I smiled at the older man in his early fifties. "No worries, family always comes first. That's what my mom says. How did Gracie do?"

Stephen beamed, the proud co-parent. "Amazing! She got the fly girl moves I taught her *down*! Made Momma Harmony proud, lemme tell ya."

"Following in your old footsteps?" said JP, finally contributing to the conversation.

"She's welcome to *follow*. But child better not come for my Queeraoke hosting gig. 'Course maybe by the time Gracie's twenty-one, I *will* be ret to retire."

Evan held up a big paw to his husband. "In eight years, you'll only be fifty-four. Sorry, babe. You got a long way till retirement."

"Don't you be telling everybody up in this wine pub my age!" Stephen slapped the other Mr. Savage-Singer lightly against his big shoulder. "Ms. Harmony House is forever twenty-one. Same as she was at that Halloween party, the night we first met and fell in looove."

I recalled what Mr. Hank told us at the Woods Hall open house: how Emma's big twenty-fifth birthday bash marked Stephen's very first drag performance. I don't think we ever knew about him meeting his significant other on that same evening. From what I heard (via Bob Kravitz, the self-appointed Yenta Yelena), Evan was once wed to a woman and didn't come out as gay until age thirty. To me, the timeline didn't add up. At Emma's party, he would've only been *twenty-seven*. There had to be more to the story if Stephen claimed they met and fell in love back in 1997, but they didn't officially become a couple until *after* Evan married and later divorced his wife.

Being my overly cautious and considerate self, I chose *not* to ask about the backstory of the Savage-Singers' intimate relationship. Instead, I deliberately changed the subject. "Hey, Stephen! How did your audition for *Top Drag Superstar* turn out?"

Stephen sighed, his face a mix of hope and apprehension. "Once again, I submitted my video, marking the tenth time I've tried my luck."

JP's eyebrows shot up in surprise. "*Tenth* time? Now that's dedication. How do you feel about it?"

A flicker of vulnerability crossed Stephen's expression. "Well, my friends . . . Each year, I pour my heart and soul into those auditions, hoping for that one magical callback. But, alas, silence has been my constant companion."

"I can only imagine how frustrating it must be," I said in sympathy.

JP agreed. "Seriously. You're incredibly talented. It stinks they haven't recognized it yet."

A bittersweet smile graced Stephen's lips. "Thank you, boys. Your words mean the world to Momma Harmony. But, you see, the competition is *fierce*. There are countless queens with immense talent, all vying for the same opportunity. Let me tell you, it's an emotional rollercoaster, to say the least."

I nodded in understanding. "I totally get it. But never doubt your talent, uniqueness, charisma, and kindness. It's only a matter of time before the judges see it too."

Stephen's hazel eyes sparkled with a mixture of gratitude and determination. "Don't you worry. Ms. Harmony is no quitter. Her journey will continue . . . and maybe—just maybe—this year will finally be The One."

With a supportive pat on the shoulder, JP wished our neighbor the best of luck. We all knew the world of show business was cutthroat. But Stephen's spirit remained unyielding, fueled by the hope of finally seeing his dream come true.

"JP and PJ!"

From where we stood near the bar, I spun around at hearing our names, to find Fiona waiting behind us. "Hey! We ran into some friends."

"No worries. Ursula wanted me to let you guys know she headed back to check on Chippy. She tried calling him first, but he didn't answer."

"Okay," I said, before minding my manners. "Evan and Stephen, this is Fiona Forrest. She's the new owner of Woods Hall."

People in Michigan had an odd habit of not introducing people to each other. At least it was my experience compared to when we lived in New York City. I didn't want to be like that, so I made a conscious effort to do so whenever the occasion presented itself.

"Nice meeting you," said Fiona, her usual friendly self.

"Girl, we love your music! Our daughter is a big fan," Stephen confessed. "She'll be thirteen. Totally turned us on to some Low-Fi vibes."

"Thanks so much! Please tell her we appreciate the word-of-mouth. It's how we find new followers."

As Stephen and Fiona chatted a bit more, I noticed Evan's mouth hanging open as he sat listening. "You look just like her . . . Emma Woods."

Stephen tilted his head for a better view of the new Wheeler Automotive heiress. "You do! The clothes might be different, but you got the same piercing blue eyes."

"You guys knew my birth mother?" Fiona asked, pleased to finally encounter someone who did. "What can you tell me about her?"

"Girl, how much time you got?" Stephen leaned forward and playfully touched Fiona's arm. "Kidding! I didn't know Emma all too well. She saw me in an amateur drag show, back when I was just a baby queen. Invited me to entertain at her twenty-fifth birthday party. Lord! I can*not* believe that was almost twenty-five years ago."

JP wasn't nearly as discerning as I was when it came to asking questions. "You guys met on the night Emma Woods died?"

Both Stephen and Evan hesitated a moment before answering.

"We did," Evan confirmed. "Me and Emma were . . . *friendly*, you could say. I went to her twenty-fifth birthday–Halloween party with Fairway Bob, and Tom and Terry Cash."

"You should've seen his costume! Dr. Evil from *Austin Powers*. Even with the fake nose and scary scar, he looked super sexers. But I do love me a bald man!"

Evan's thick hair didn't show a trace of thinning, but I could relate to where Stephen was coming from with his statement. Me, I had a thing for Dwayne Johnson, Jason Statham, and Patrick Stewart . . . and not necessarily in that order.

"I only dressed up like Dr. Evil because Bob wanted to be Austin Powers. Tom and Terry came as Beavis and Butt-Head," Evan explained for the benefit of the rest of us.

"Do I sound like I'm complaining? As I recall that getup got you a big old kiss from Ms. Harmony, did it not?"

Evan's chubby cheeks reddened behind his dark beard. I couldn't tell if the guy was embarrassed by his husband spilling the tea on their private past . . . or was the elder Mr. Savage-Singer trying to hide something?

Just then, JP's cell phone sounded. He pulled out the mobile device and glanced at the on-screen notification. "Excuse me, guys. Message from our producer." He opened the text and read the words aloud: "*OMG! Chippy is dead.*"

My heart sank to the pit of my stomach.

Chapter 16

After JP received Ursula's frantic text, we rushed back to Woods Hall.

A PWPD police car sat parked in the gravel drive behind an ambulance from Detroit General Hospital. As we approached the manor she stepped onto the porch from inside, a look of worry etched across her face. She scampered over to us, her heels clicking on the stone walkway.

"Is Chippy really . . . ?" I couldn't bring myself to say the word.

Relief washed over Ursula. "No! He's not, thank God. But he fell off the ladder. When I got here, I found him unresponsive, so I called 9-1-1. Detective Paczki's out back now."

My partner and I let out a mutual sigh. While the news was still troubling, we were both grateful to hear our friend and colleague was still alive.

The air turned chilly as the sun started to set. Coming closer to the scene of the accident, I could see the aluminum ladder lying on its side, its rungs twisted and bent. A small amount of blood pooled on the ground nearby, my guess being from where Chippy hit his head on a rock when he landed.

Nick Paczki stood by, supervising a pair of paramedics loading our contractor onto a stretcher. He crossed his beefy arms over the front of his blue uniform. At forty-one, he'd been a policeman for close to two decades. Nick briefly dated my sister in high school, when he was a senior and Pamela a sophomore at Madison Park. The eleven-year-old me thought he was totally cute, with his dark blond hair, deep blue eyes, and pale Polish American skin. The hair was turning to gray now, the eyes slightly crinkled around the edges, but he still looked super hunky. Especially with the addition of a fuzzy mustache sprouting above his upper lip.

Chippy's usually vibrant face looked pale and drawn, his dark hair slightly disheveled from the fall. The poor guy groaned, wincing in pain, but he didn't appear too seriously injured. The T-shirt he wore was soiled and his jeans torn at the knee. I noticed a small cut above his right eyebrow. Otherwise, he was breathing and conscious, which I took as a good sign.

Our hearts heavy with concern, both JP and I knew the work we did renovating houses often involved a certain level of risk. But we never expected something like this to happen to one of our own crew.

The ambulance pulled away, sounding its siren as it disappeared down the long and winding gravel drive.

"Good seeing you fellas again. Sorry about the circumstances," said the detective.

"What happened here?" asked JP, his voice strained.

"Well . . ." Nick consulted his notes app, his expression grave as he read over what he took down. "After he came to, your friend Chippy told me a pretty wild story. Said he's up there doing some repair work on a rotted first-floor window frame. He hears a noise, sounds like a music box, he says. You know, you open the lid, a little ballerina girl's dancing inside? He looks up and sees, on the balcony above, what he thinks is a crying woman in a wedding dress."

Ursula inhaled, horrified. "The ghost of Emma Woods!"

Nick pocketed his cell phone. "Whatever he *thought* he saw . . . The guy got spooked, lost his balance, came crashing down hard. Thankfully, he wasn't up very high when he fell. His injuries shouldn't be life threatening."

"You think maybe you should take a look around, see if you can find anything?" JP said. "If Chippy says he saw something—whatever it was—we've known the guy for a while now. He doesn't make up stuff."

"But does he drink on the job?" Paczki asked, his azure eyes narrowing. "Found some empty beer bottles by the ladder your friend Chippy fell off."

"If that's the case, I'll have a talk with him," said Ursula, her tone conveying disappointment.

"They'll test his blood alcohol level at the hospital. But it's quite possible the guy was a little drunk. Maybe he imagined hearing a music box and seeing a crying woman in a wedding dress up there on that balcony?"

"If you want, we can take you inside the house and show you around," JP offered. "Might be a good idea to check out the master bedroom and balcony. Just in case . . ."

Ursula waited for the rest of the crew to return while Detective Paczki followed me and JP inside Woods Hall.

We ascended the grand staircase, off the front foyer. En route to the third floor, Nick stopped to admire the hand-painted portrait hanging on the wood-paneled wall, high above the first landing.

"That's her, huh? Miss Great Lakes 1992! She was a beautiful young woman, Emma Woods." He took a step to one side. "Is it me . . . or do her eyes move?"

Arriving at the master suite, the room smelled musty, although we'd left the windows open for a full week trying to air it out. Detective Paczki brushed his bushy mustache with a thick thumb and forefinger, scanning the space for any signs of suspicious activity. "All right, what do we got?"

I stepped forward and pointed toward the balcony. The French doors were open a crack. "Pretty sure we shut those the last time we came in here."

Nick nodded his graying head thoughtfully. "Let's go check it out." He stepped outside, and JP and I followed. "Hmm . . . Doesn't look like anything's been disturbed, other than the flowerpot that fell off."

Clearly, the detective had seen the story on yesterday morning's *Good Day, Detroit.*

"You think maybe someone climbed up here using Chippy's ladder?" JP asked Nick. "Then entered the house through the French doors."

Paczki considered this for a moment. "Possibly. If your friend wasn't paying attention, somebody might've snuck into the yard and used the ladder. In their haste, they could've forgot to shut the French doors behind them. I'll have forensics dust the ladder rungs, and the door handles . . . see if they turn up any prints besides Mr. Carpenter's."

"Would a ghost even leave fingerprints?" I wasn't trying to be funny. But if what Chippy said he saw on the balcony wasn't of this earthly plane, would it give off any trace of its existence?

As we looked around further, Nick spotted something of interest in the far corner. He walked over to what resembled a small door located on the interior wall. "Hey, what's this?"

"I don't believe it. A real-live dumbwaiter!" said JP, clearly impressed by the discovery. "People used them to bring food up from the kitchen, back in the day."

"You think maybe someone crawled inside there and got up into this room, unseen?" I asked.

"Highly unlikely. It'd be a pretty tight squeeze," said Nick, after inspecting the tiny space more closely. "Someone *your* size might fit, Peter."

Considering my claustrophobia, I didn't even want to think about how it might feel cramming into such a small spot. The inside of the dumbwaiter might've been twenty-five, maybe thirty inches wide and only slightly taller. Even regular old, normal-sized elevators gave me agita.

"What about a woman?" JP said. "Or the *ghost* of a woman, Detective?"

"Just so we're clear, I don't believe in ghosts. But if our so-called ghost was in fact the ghost of Emma Woods . . . I doubt she'd fit inside that dumbwaiter wearing a Princess Di wedding dress costume."

Nick had a point. The gown Diana wore when she married Prince Charles was ginormous!

On the second floor, Detective Paczki popped his head into the bedroom doorways, including the one belonging to Kathleen Anger's young son. We showed him the hole in the plaster wall we covered up with the *Blair Witch Project* poster.

"Don't seem too outta the ordinary." Stepping back into the narrow corridor, Nick took note of the single shut-up room. "Guys, what's in there?" He tried the cut crystal knob, but like the last time, the door wouldn't open.

JP spoke up. "We assume it's another bedroom. I asked Fiona if she had a key, so we could get in and look around. She said she didn't."

Detective Paczki raised an eyebrow. He examined the door more closely, running his hand along the surface. "Locked room, huh? Seems odd all these others are wide-open, don't you think?" Nick raised his voice, calling through the wooden door. "*Hello!* Maybe somebody's inside? Or maybe somebody's trying to hide something from us?"

"No disrespect, but . . . Woods Hall has been shut up for the past twenty-plus years," JP reminded the policeman. "How would anyone get inside to hide—or hide *something*—behind a locked door? And this door was locked, over a week ago, the first time we ever toured the property. It's probably been locked since the day Bill Woods died in 1999."

My partner also had a point. Still, Nick Paczki wasn't taking any chances. The detective reached into his patrol bag and removed a set of what looked like skeleton keys. After selecting one, he stuck it into the keyhole. As he attempted to jimmy the door open, Nick described what he was doing. "This is a special lock-bumping key. With any luck, I can use it to *bump* the pins inside and open the lock."

After a few more goes (and some mild cursing) Detective Paczki gave up. "You fellas got a screwdriver? Might be able to wedge it between the door and the jamb and pry the thing open. Or we can just do it the old-fashioned way and bust her down."

JP hesitated. "Actually . . . I'd prefer not doing either. We've got enough stuff to fix in this house already. A broken door frame isn't something I wanna add to the list."

Paczki considered the request. "Fair enough. I say leave it alone for now. But if you ever do get this door open, I'd appreciate you letting me know what you find."

As we headed downstairs, the creaking of the old wooden steps resonated through the house, adding to the ominous feeling permeating the air. I couldn't help wondering . . .

Why was the door even locked in the first place?

And what about the crying woman in the wedding gown Chippy saw up on the balcony?

If she wasn't the ghost of Emma Woods . . . then who was she?

Hitting the bottom landing, the three of us stopped to catch our breath. We weren't as young as we used to be, that's for sure! I could've sworn the piercing blue eyes in the beauty queen's life-sized, hand-painted portrait were watching our every move.

"Let's check out the living room, since we're here," Nick suggested.

The pocket doors creaked as we slid them open, revealing the dimly lit room with heavy curtains covering the windows. Detective Paczki chuckled at the sight of the huge entertainment center in the corner. "Is that a VCR? Gosh, I haven't seen one of them since I was in high school, back in the nineties."

As we glanced around, looking for anything unusual, our eyes were drawn to the mirror above the stone fireplace. A single word appeared in large, bold red letters . . .

STOP!

Was it written in *blood*?

Chapter 17

A scream echoed through the historic manor home.

We whirled about to find Ursula in the doorway, between the living room and the grand entrance hall. Her eyes widened in shock as she took in the bloody message above the fireplace. I could see her mind working, trying to figure out if this was some kind of prank . . . or if there was a more ominous explanation.

"It's a warning from Emma Woods! She doesn't want us renovating her house!"

"Don't sneak up on us like that," JP told his best gal pal, placing a hand to his racing heart.

"Sorry, guys," said Ursula. "The crew's back from Chianti. Everyone's waiting outside to find out what's going on."

Nick walked over to the mirror. He stuck his finger into the sticky goo . . . and licked it clean. "Corn syrup and food coloring."

"So much for our ghost!" said JP, his voice dripping with sarcasm.

"I'm thinking this is all the handiwork of some neighborhood kids," Detective Paczki told us. "I know just the ones. Probably saw the TV crew filming here earlier and snuck inside the house when your contractor was up on his ladder. My guess is they threw on a sheet, pretended to be the ghost of Emma Woods and scared the guy bad enough to make him fall. Then, they came down here and left us this little note."

"What about the music box and the crying?" I asked, a part of me suddenly wanting to believe in spirits.

"Stuff they played on their phones, maybe? My daughter Nikki's downloaded a bunch of sound effects off the internet. Uses them all the time, making TikTok videos and what-not."

JP, Ursula, and I stared at each other, realizing this could be a plausible explanation for what caused Chippy's accident. Detective Paczki assured us he would go and have a talk with the pesky brats and get to the bottom of the whole incident.

Before we headed out, Nick paused. He turned back to the mirror above the stone fireplace and ran his hand over the sticky surface. "At least we know this house ain't haunted."

We met the others on the patio, a palpable tension gripping the air. Finn, Fiona, Kevin, Dave, and Gopher all wore expressions of worry as they waited for an update. The serene setting seemed at odds with the gravity of the situation, creating an eerie dissonance. The quiet rustling of leaves and the occasional chirping of crickets only served to amplify the stillness of the scene. While the surroundings were indeed idyllic, an uneasiness lingered within me, as if something sinister lurked beneath the surface.

"Any word on Chippy?" Kevin asked, looking expectantly at me, JP, and Ursula. He held his camera at his side.

Detective Paczki stepped forward to give his official report. "Your friend Chip was found at the bottom of a ladder . . ."

The newcomers leaned in closer, eager to hear more of what Nick had to say. Their faces displayed a mixture of anxiety and apprehension. Their postures were tense, with shoulders hunched forward and eyes fixed intently on the detective. Kevin and Dave silently communicated their shared sense of dread. Finn took hold of Fiona's hand. It was as if they were all holding their breath, waiting for the words to confirm or deny their worst fears.

"He's alive. But he's got a bad head injury . . . possibly a broken arm. The paramedics rushed him to the hospital. He should pull through just fine."

The crew's expressions lit up as everyone breathed a collective sigh.

"Thank God! If that guy got killed on our property . . . We're talking a major lawsuit. You need to make sure he's more careful," Finn told Ursula, point blank.

"I will. But it's not all Chippy's fault. He said he saw something up on the balcony . . ."

I could tell Ursula didn't want to repeat what we were told by the contractor, which was exactly what I was thinking, as silly as it seemed.

"What did he see?" Fiona asked timidly.

"He said he saw the ghost of Emma Woods," JP answered, flat out.

Finn's voice rose as he began to rant. "Seriously? This is getting to be a little bit much, don't you think? First, she tries dropping a flowerpot on Fi's head. Now she goes and pushes this Chippy dude off his ladder?"

Nick Paczki rolled his eyes. "There's no such thing as ghosts, Mr. Lowenstein."

"That's what *I* said. But I'm starting to think otherwise, Detective," said Fiona.

"I understand your concerns, Miss Forrest. But Mr. Carpenter wasn't pushed off his ladder. He had a little too much beer while he was working. He got a little tipsy and *thought* he saw a ghost up there." Nick gestured to the third floor of Woods Hall. "He got spooked, and he fell off the ladder."

"Well, you should do some investigating . . . This is *my* house, and I want some answers!" Finn demanded.

Fiona kept quiet as her fiancé confronted the officer of the law.

Nick gestured to me and JP. "Me and the fellas here . . . We already went up and looked around."

"Did you guys find anything?" Fiona asked.

"The French doors to the balcony were open slightly. But

everything outside looked the way it did the other night when we were out there," I said.

Finn howled. "Then who left the doors open? Bro! You're saying some stranger was inside our house?"

"Not necessarily. Mr. Carpenter could've gone up on the balcony—for whatever reason—when he was here working," Detective Paczki replied. "He might've left the French doors open, we don't know for sure. I'll make a note to question him about it. We also got some kids in the neighborhood, like to play practical jokes. When I leave here, I'll go and talk to them about what happened."

Nick waved goodbye and headed off into the night.

"That's a wrap!" Gopher hollered, as per Ursula's urging.

She packed up her Louis Vuitton bag. "I'm heading to the hospital to check on Chippy. Get some rest tonight, okay? I'll text everyone later with the plan for tomorrow."

Finn whipped out his phone and started tapping on the screen. "I need to post about this ghost stuff. Our followers are gonna die!"

Fiona aimed her mobile device at the third-floor balcony. She snapped off some quick pics and posted them, making sure to tag appropriately: *#domesticpartners #woodshall #hauntedhouse*

Seeing the young people using their technology reminded me . . . I needed to check in with my folks. Clyde and Jack were still over at Grandma Patsy and Grandpa Jim's house. My mom didn't mind keeping them longer than usual. She loved taking care of our boys. I did call her earlier, on the way to Woods Hall from Chianti, and let her know about Chippy's accident. But in all the confusion about crying ghosts in wedding gowns, and whether some juvenile delinquents were the actual culprits, I never let her know what time we'd be picking up the boys.

I took out my phone and fired off a text: **_Hello! Finishing up now. Be over soon_** ☺

JP drove while I rode shotgun.

In the SUV, I took advantage of the downtime to scroll through my junk emails. The only messages I ever received anymore were from shopping accounts I signed up for, just to get a discount on my first purchase. Every so often, the online auction site I followed would send out an alert about vintage Mission-style furniture pieces coming up for sale. I desperately wanted to find a matching rocker to go with the signed Limbert armchair given to me for *free* by the antique dealer I bought our Tobey dining room set from.

As we turned onto Viking Boulevard—the main thoroughfare running through my hometown of Madison Park—JP's phone sounded with a notification from Ursula. He leaned forward in the driver's seat and pressed the touch screen on the dashboard console. Siri read the message aloud in a male Aussie accent . . .

Good news: Chippy okay. Bad news: broken arm. Need new contractor ASAP.

"Great!" I said, intentionally acting mildly annoyed.

I knew it wasn't Chippy's fault he fell off a ladder after being startled by the ghost of Emma Woods. Or those nasty neighborhood kids. Unless, of course, he did drink too much beer while he was on the job. But still . . . what's done was done. As co-producers of *Domestic Partners*, we needed to step in and help Ursula solve this unforeseen problem.

"Where are we gonna find another carpenter on such short notice?" JP mused.

After a split second, I came up with the perfect person.

Chapter 18

Corey Regan was the epitome of punctuality.

As the sun rose over Woods Hall on that Tuesday morning, the newly employed contractor stepped out of his pickup. He pulled at the brim of the baseball cap he sported on his sandy-colored head, shielding his sensitive eyes. Morning light spilled onto the lawn, overgrown with weeds and in need of a good mowing. But the golden glow illuminated the grandeur of the work already in progress.

"Hey!" I called from the porch, where JP and I stood waiting to welcome Corey to Team *Domestic Partners*.

Dressed in typical carpenter's attire, he wore a sturdy denim work shirt, the sleeves rolled up to his elbows. His jeans were well faded, and his sturdy work boots laced tight. A wide leather belt fastened around his slim waist held an assortment of tools. A hammer and a set of pliers protruded from one of the pockets, and a measuring tape and pencil from another.

JP extended his hand. "Good seeing you again."

Corey smiled warmly, firmly returning the shake. "I appreciate you guys giving me this opportunity. It stinks being outta work. Gotta keep busy."

I held open the wide front door, with its geometrical cutouts and original brass hardware. "Come on in. We'll give you the grand tour."

We showed Corey around the areas in need of the most attention, including the second-floor bedroom once belonging to Kathleen Anger's young son.

"There's a hole here in the wall," I said, removing the framed poster covering the damaged plaster.

"*Blair Witch Project*. Great flick. I can fix that, no problem," Corey promised.

"You can leave it for now. We're gonna work on the exterior before moving inside," JP explained.

"Ursula is all about making sure the house looks good from the street. In case people stop by and wanna take pics to post to social media," I added.

"Something you guys got in mind for me to work on?"

JP smiled slyly. "We'll show you . . ."

Descending the grand staircase, Corey paused at the landing, halfway down. He gazed at the ornate gold frame surrounding the hand-painted portrait of the twenty-year-old beauty queen, Emma Rose Wheeler. "Too bad she died the way she did. I hear she haunts this place."

"According to the old legend," I confirmed.

Corey kept his attention focused on Emma in her painting. "She made the guy I'm replacing fall off his ladder?"

"The verdict's still out on that one," JP said dryly.

Corey's forehead wrinkled as his eyebrows raised. He tilted his head to one side subtly as he regarded me and my domestic partner on TV and in real-life. The gesture spoke volumes. "Don't tell me you dudes believe in spirits."

"I never said *I* did," said JP, acting all innocent-like.

It bothered me a little to think he didn't take my growing trepidations seriously. Never mind the house we were hired to renovate on national television was supposedly *haunted*. We told the owner of the home we'd help solve the alleged murder of her birth mother. And the one suspect we'd encountered in the past week-plus was the ghost of her dead mom. Unless Emma Woods committed suicide by jumping from the third-floor balcony, we didn't have a clue as to who might've killed the young woman back on Halloween night 1997.

On the side entrance to Woods Hall, hung a vintage screen door made of lightweight aluminum, circa 1940s. It reminded me of the one at my grandmother's house in Royal Heights, with its thin frame, simple profile, and decorative elements.

"What an awesome door!"

"It *is* awesome," I agreed with Corey. "It just doesn't fit with the aesthetic we're going for."

"What you need is a *wood* screen door."

"Too bad we can't just run up to Pete's dad's hardware store and buy one," JP lamented. "It's an odd size. Plus, we need something that's period authentic."

Corey's hands fell to his hips, causing his muscular arms to flex. "Where's the original?"

I could tell that my partner couldn't help noticing the hunk of a man standing there with us. Because I noticed him too! Feeling myself blush a little, I shrugged. "We're not sure."

"I'm thinking maybe someone took it off and put it in storage. Let's go check the garage," said JP.

"Good idea. Garages are like black holes. I knew a guy once, kept so much crap in his, he couldn't park his car inside," Corey said. "One time a bad storm hit, giant tree limb fell right on his Buick."

We headed over to the simple wood structure, with its peaked roof and three large doors. The wheels affixed to the top creaked on their rail as JP and I slid open the first one. The windows were dusty and dark. I could only imagine what we'd find inside.

Cardboard boxes and other discarded items covered the concrete floor. Stacks of old magazines and newspapers sat in piles, reaching up toward the rafters. A vintage Schwinn bicycle leaned against one unfinished wall. A series of pegboards hung on the others, cluttered with rusty tools, equipment, and other miscellanea that hadn't seen the light of the twenty-first century.

After several minutes of moving things around and haphazard searching, Corey called out: "Dudes!"

JP and I hurried over to see what our new colleague had stumbled on. Sure enough, in his callused hands Corey held a rectangular object: the original Woods Hall wood screen door, dating back to 1913. "Found it tucked away in a corner, behind an old washing machine."

"Bummer, it's in pretty bad shape," I said, noticing the worn and battered edges.

It was a sad but true assessment. The dark-stained oak was faded, cracked, and covered in layers of dirt and grime. The copper mesh screen that once kept out insects and other pests was ragged and torn; the decorative hinges now rusted.

Corey ran his thick fingers over the dry wood, examining it closely. "No problem-o. Got a pattern to follow now. I can make a new one just like it. Gimme a few days, I'll have it ready in no time."

JP and I were both thrilled by Corey's offer. "That would be amazing," I said, brimming with gratitude.

Corey smiled down at me and gave my shoulder a squeeze. "My pleasure. I love a good challenge."

If I didn't know the guy had a *girl*friend, I would've thought he was flirting with me! But I was hardly interested in the mixed signals of a hunky straight man. Still, Corey Regan was (to quote Fiona) *def perf obv* easy on the eyes.

"Pete, take a look at this . . ." JP pointed out a narrow alcove, partially obscured by a pile of bald tires and a stack of even more cardboard boxes.

From a distance, it looked like just another storage area, a dead end in the maze of the old garage's interior. But upon closer inspection, there appeared to be a hidden door. The portal blended in seamlessly with the surrounding walls, its faded paint and rusty hinges camouflaged by the jumble of tools, boxes, and debris. Its peculiar shape and texture were unlike any other we could see. The smooth edges suggested age and use. The latch was covered by a small, circular plate, as if to keep it hidden from prying eyes. To anyone who knew what to look for, the door was a tantalizing hint of something hidden beyond, waiting to be discovered.

"Is that . . . ?"

As a kid, I always dreamed of stumbling upon a secret passageway. I searched high and low for clues, looking for hidden openings that might reveal a secret tunnel for me and my own sister to follow. Although I never did find one back then, I never gave up hope. Now, as an adult standing in the old garage at Woods Hall, a thrill of excitement rushed through me at the sight of an actual secret door. My heart quickened as I stared at it, my fingers shaky with anticipation as I reached out.

My hand brushed against the door. A jolt of electricity shot through me, the sensation of wonder and possibility overwhelming. Even without entering, I realized we'd stumbled upon something extraordinary . . . something that might forever change our perception of the world around us.

Gently, I opened the secret door and stepped inside.

Chapter 19

The secret door led to a secret room.

Hidden beneath the depths of Woods Hall, the lumber baron William Royce Woods had overseen its construction during the Prohibition era, once the ban that outlawed the sale, manufacturing, and transportation of alcohol within the state of Michigan had officially taken effect in 1918. Through the hidden portal tucked away inside the old three-car garage, friends and colleagues could enter a secret staircase that would lead them to Paradise.

The staircase was narrow, rough-hewn, and uneven, made of steep stone steps and without a handrail. The distant sound of dripping water echoed off the concrete walls. Descending deeper into the hidden passageway, the atmosphere became damp and cold, the darkness growing thicker. The flight of stairs seemed to go on forever, twisting and turning in a tight spiral, until finally reaching the bottom, where a dimly lit tunnel stretched into obscurity.

The walls here were smoother and more refined than those of the staircase above, made of brick and lined with lanterns that flickered, when lit, casting creepy shadows along the ground. As the tunnel progressed, it began to widen and curve, coming to an end before a brass-studded door with a small peephole set into the wood.

A century ago, this was the spot where one would knock three times—as per the secret instructions—before the peephole slid open, and a pair of scrutinizing eyes peered out. From behind the door, a deep voice demanded the password. Once given, the eyes would nod in approval, and the door swung open . . . revealing a hidden speakeasy.

Inside, the domain dubbed Club Paradise was a sensory-overloading experience, full of the sights, sounds, and smells of a bygone era. The world was a riot of color and motion, with jazz music and the clink of glasses and laughter ringing out. People could be found dressed in elaborate costumes, and the room decorated with Art Deco murals and intricate mosaics. Prohibition era Pleasant Woods was an enchanting vision to behold, a part of something decadent and forbidden.

Unfortunately, all these many years later in the present, the speakeasy had seen better days. With much of its original features obscured by time and neglect, a layer of dirt dusted every single surface. The air smelled faintly of mold and abandonment. The lights no longer worked; the club's former vibrancy plunged into dusky darkness. The floorboards creaked, the walls cracked, and the wallpaper peeled. Cobwebs covered any remaining fixtures and furniture.

The secret Woods Hall speakeasy was a sorrowful place, a haunting souvenir of a lost piece of history.

That afternoon, we popped into the antiques and vintage furniture shop owned and operated by our next-door neighbor, Bob Kravitz. Named for his favorite movie, *Somewhere in Time,* when we first moved to town Fairway Bob invited us over for a private screening of the film, shot at the Grand Hotel on Mackinac Island. Neither JP nor I had ever seen it before . . . since neither of us was alive for the romantic fantasy's premiere back in 1980.

Bob's storefront was small but cozy, with hardwood floors that creaked under browsers' feet. The walls were painted in a warm copper color, which set off the deep, rich hues of the antique pieces carefully arranged throughout the space. The shop was filled with early twentieth-century furnishings, including dressers, desks, chairs, and tables, from Grand Rapids–based makers like Stickley Brothers, Charles P. Limbert, and the Michigan Chair Company. Before moving into an historic Craftsman home, I had no clue of the history our Great Lakes State played in the Mission-style furniture era.

Each piece found at Somewhere in Time was unique and possessed its own special character, with elaborate carvings, polished brass hardware, and richly stained wood finishes. Some of the items Bob, himself, restored to their original beauty. Others showed the wear and tear of their years of use, adding to their charm and history. Vintage light fixtures hung from the ceiling, casting a warm, inviting glow over the space. Old-fashioned paintings and prints lined the walls, creating a sense of nostalgia and adding to the overall ambiance of the shop.

"Well, of course you found a secret passageway!" cried Fairway Bob once JP and I finished telling him of our earlier adventure into the depths of Woods Hall. "That house is full of 'em!"

Today, he paired a light blue collared shirt with khaki pants, and penny loafers, as opposed to his usual heather-gray sweatshirt with the dog silhouette stenciled across the front.

"You're kidding?" I said, marveling at the thought of further exploration.

"No, yeah. Don't ask me how, but I know about a secret staircase leading from the kitchen to the third floor." He pronounced *about* like *a-boot*, owing to his Upper Peninsula accent. He almost sounded Canadian, but not quite like the kids I watched on *Degrassi*.

I reminded myself *not* to copy Bob's Yooper dialect when it was my turn to speak. It was just something I did sometimes. I never meant it as an insult or a form of mockery. It just came *oot*— I mean out!

JP furrowed his brow. "There's a secret staircase inside Woods

Hall? We checked out the kitchen on the first night we did our walk-through. I don't remember seeing any secret staircase."

"That's because it's a *secret*, eh?" Bob described, in detail, the small space at the back of the room. "On the far wall of the butler's pantry, there's a false panel next to a tall, skinny cabinet. Just give it a push . . . pops right open. Then you take the steps all the way up to the third-floor hallway. Right outside the master bedroom."

For the first time in quite a while, JP looked impressed. "That's unreal. Have you ever used it?"

Bob paused. His thin lips slightly parted as he searched for the right words. "*I* haven't used it, but . . . I know somebody who *used* to use it quite frequently, back in the mid-nineties. But please don't ask me to name names cuz I swore myself to secrecy years ago."

Despite the No Pets sign prominently displayed above the counter, Fairway Bob's best friend Willie waltzed through the red velvet drape curtaining off the back storage area and into the shop. The lazy black Lab plopped himself down on a William Morris floral print rug and leisurely licked at his underside.

I didn't dream of asking Bob to break the promise he made to the person who had a habit of accessing Emma Woods's bedroom via secret staircase. Something told me if I waited long enough, the man from Escanaba (Gladstone, really) would spill the beans of his own volition.

"We'll definitely look for this secret kitchen staircase when we're back at Woods Hall," I said, eagerly awaiting the next adventure.

Bob led us to the opposite side of the store, walking and talking as we strolled along. "Hey, so what kind of pieces are you looking for this time around?"

"Pretty much anything that would fit a 1913 Arts and Crafts–inspired manor home," answered JP. He stopped to inspect a solid oak cabinet with clean lines and a rich finish that showcased the natural beauty of the wood grain. Its tall, rectangular shape featured two doors with leaded glass panels adorned with geometric patterns.

Fairway Bob noticed JP's reaction to the fine piece of furniture. "Pretty nice, eh? The doors open. It's got two shelves, perfect for storing books, pottery, or other decorative items."

If Fiona and Finn weren't interested, I definitely was!

Taking out my phone, I snapped a pic of the cabinet and saved it to an album labeled *Low-Fi finds*. The price on the tag ($900!) put the cost at higher than I'd prefer to pay. But Fiona Forrest was a successful rising star in the indie music industry . . . on top of newly becoming an heiress. I assumed she could afford to splurge.

Bob's eyes lit up as he crossed over to where he had some interesting pieces he wanted to show us. "Hey, so I heard about last night . . . when your contractor got spooked and fell off his ladder. I ran into Detective Paczki this morning over at The Depot. He said the guy claimed he saw something up there on that balcony overlooking the back gardens."

I wasn't aware if policemen were bound to a similar doctor-patient confidentiality rule. But Nick sharing the news about Chippy with Fairway Bob didn't surprise me. If nothing else, Pleasant Woods was a close-knit community . . . and people liked to chit-chat.

"Wouldn't surprise me none if it was Emma's ghost," said Bob, blabbering on. "She was wearing a white wedding gown on the night she died. Just like Princess Di's from when she married Prince Charles." He took a breather as he pulled out a set of slat-back chairs that might fit nicely in the finished dining room at Woods Hall. "You guys know I was there that night?"

Remembering what Evan Savage-Singer told us yesterday evening at Chianti, I commented on Fairway Bob's comment. "Yes, we heard that."

"*Waaay* back in 1997. I went to Emma's twenty-fifth birthday–Halloween party with Evan Savage, and Tom and Terry Cash. The four of us were thick as thieves back then. Me and Tom went to Michigan together, I think I told ya, in Ann Arbor." Bob sighed dramatically. "Oh, to be twenty-six again!" Then he scoffed deliberately. "You couldn't *pay* me. I much prefer being in my fifties. I'm older, and I'm wiser. Now, if I could just find me a nice girl to settle down with, eh?"

Both JP and I did our best not to giggle. What Bob said wasn't the least bit funny. We weren't tempted to laugh *at* him. We loved the guy. There was just a bit of confusion among the folks of Pleasant Woods when it came to Bob's sexual preference. He avowed himself a practicing *hetero*sexual. For some reason, most people assumed he was *homo*.

This fact had actually worked in Bob's favor last spring when he auditioned for the role of the lawyer lover of a closeted gay actor, played by JP, in my play *Blue Tuesday*. Of course, he was cast! Regardless of what side he buttered his bread on, he was perfect for the part.

"Gosh, I'll never forget what happened to poor Emma . . ." Bob somberly stared off into the distance. "Such a beautiful girl, she was. Had a bit of a crush on her, I gotta admit."

The memory of that terrible night overpowered the older man, as he traveled back in time.

Halloween 1997

Bob's brain felt all fuzzy.

As the night wore on, the bass from the loud music pounded in his head. Now in his mid-twenties, he wasn't the same kid who could party all night, then get up the next morning and go all day without any repercussions. Glancing around the crowded manor, he watched as people danced and laughed, their energy contagious. He needed to pace himself, to take it easy if he was going to make it through the rest of the evening.

Suddenly, he broke out in a cold sweat. The lace cravat he wore as part of his costume felt too tight. He was a big fan of the International Man of Mystery (*Yeah, baby!*) and the *Austin Powers* movie that came out earlier in the spring. The crushed velvet suit and frilly shirt he procured at Vintage Vibes in downtown Fernridge. While he did wear a shaggy wig, the thick-framed eyeglasses were all his own, as was the peace sign necklace dangling from his neck.

Through blurred vision, he wandered the beautiful home, the buzz of the party swirling around him. Woods Hall glowed with an eerie yet inviting light. The grand façade was illuminated by a hundred flickering jack-o'-lanterns lining the gravel driveway leading up to the historic manor home. The sound of music and laughter could be heard from the street as guests arrived in their costumes, eager to celebrate Emma Woods on her twenty-fifth birthday.

Inside, the ballroom had been transformed into a haunted wonderland, the walls draped in rich, black velvet and adorned with dimly lit chandeliers that cast an eerie glow over the party. The beer kegs flowed with the best brews money could buy: Molson Ice, Pete's Wicked Ale, Sierra Nevada. At Emma's request, an abundant supply of Zima stocked the coolers, a fun throwback to her younger days, before she married Bill Woods and became a mother to baby Fiona.

The alcohol hit Bob harder than expected, and he knew he needed to slow down. Still, the grandeur of the surroundings impressed him. He couldn't believe his luck to be standing in such a magnificent mansion. How did a humble boy from the U.P. of Michigan wind up at the biggest social event of the season?

The intricate details of the house, the festive party decorations, and all the fun Halloween costumes only added to the surreal emotions he was feeling.

There was Mayor Hank Richards and his wife Hennie as Sheriff Tupper and Cabot Cove's resident amateur sleuth Jessica Fletcher. *Detroit Times* society-page reporter LaRena Judge bravely donned a nun's habit for her portrayal of Deloris Van Cartier masquerading as Mary Clarence from *Sister Act*. His best buddies Tom and Terry Cash took the easy way out. The gay twin brothers wore simple Beavis and Butt-Head rubber masks. At least Bob managed to convince his costume comrade-in-arms, Evan Savage, to go all out with his Dr. Evil getup, from the bald cap covering his head down to the light gray Nehru suit he sported. Evan even slipped on a pinky ring, and cradled a hairless (toy) kitty cat, to fully capture the essence of the comic genius.

But it was the hostess—the birthday girl, herself—regally dressed like the dearly departed Princess of Wales, that made the biggest impression on the young Mr. Kravitz. As Bob surveyed the room, his eyes settled on the stunning figure of Lady Diana

Spencer, deep in conversation with President Bill and Hillary Rodham Clinton.

A moment of stunned silence passed, as he stood transfixed,
watching Emma Woods chatting with Quinn and Vicky Marshall.
Gazing at her, he was struck by how effortlessly the former beauty
queen captured the elegance and poise of the late princess, her
every movement imbued with grace and sophistication.

His thoughts raced as he tried to come up with the perfect
words to express his feelings to Emma. But for now, he was content
to bask in her luminance. Bob realized she was a married woman,
completely out of his league even if this hadn't been the case.

Still, a man could dare to dream.

Chapter 20

The Depot Diner was an institution.

Suitably situated right near the railroad tracks, its original proprietress, a cantankerous old woman named June, founded the greasy spoon in the 1960s under her own name. When she passed away a few years back, the owners of The Depot up in Bloomington Hills stepped in to save the classic diner from becoming a nail salon.

Or so the story went.

Inside, the walls were covered in Detroit-themed décor, with vintage metal signs advertising the likes of Stroh's beer and Faygo Rock & Rye, a vanilla-cream soda with a hint of semi-tart cherry flavor that JP dubbed *disgusting*. What did he know? Being from Pittsburgh, the guy put French fries *on* his sandwiches!

The smell of sizzling bacon and brewing coffee wafted into our faces as we entered. Corey and the rest of the crew were busy finishing up the exterior of Woods Hall, so JP and I decided to join Fairway Bob for a late afternoon caffeine pick-me-up.

Our favorite waitress, Olivia, greeted us at the front door, her mousey brown hair pulled back into a ponytail. "Sit anywhere you like!"

I led the way to an empty booth against the far wall, near the windows. The light blue vinyl seats squeaked beneath our bottoms as the three of us sat down. The first thing I did was scope out the table to see which novelty salt-and-pepper shaker set we'd been treated to. That day, it was a kissing Frankenstein and his bride, complete with lightning bolt–streaked beehive hairdo.

As we were about to resume our chat, the train rumbled past. The entire building seemed to vibrate with its power. We paused, waiting for the deafening sound to fade into the distance.

Bob scrunched up his nose in thought. "Now what was I saying? Oh, right! I was about to tell you all about Emma's missing diamond necklace."

Olivia arrived at our table, wielding a hot pot. "Coffee?"

"Yes, please!" I slid my mug over for a filler-up.

"Hey, Liv. How's college treating you so far?" JP asked.

The eighteen-year-old was a freshman Vocal Performance major down at Wayne State, my alma mater. She gazed at my handsome TV show cohost and blushed. "Amazing! It's only been a week, and I feel like I'm learning so much."

Olivia had had a not-so-secret crush on JP for as long as we'd been coming to The Depot. I found it totally cute.

"Are you and Wes still an item, eh?" asked Bob, sounding like the fifty something he was.

"We are! But he's away at State, so we only get to see each other on weekends." Olivia cast her brown eyes down, as she thought of her long-distance love. "What can I get you?"

"I think we're all set with just coffee," JP said.

"No problem!"

Once the waitress was out of earshot, Bob proceeded. "Where were we, eh?" He lifted his cup and blew gently across the top.

"Emma's diamond necklace. You said it went missing after she died," I reminded him.

"Right! When she fell from the balcony, I was out on the patio with Tom and Terry, having a cigarette. I know, it's a filthy habit. But it was the nineties, everybody smoked. Especially when they drank. *Anyhoo!* We heard a scream . . . we looked up . . . seen the whole thing happen."

"That must've been traumatizing," I interjected.

Bob sipped his coffee. "What's even more traumatizing is what I seen next. A face appeared over the rail of the balcony . . . and looked down . . . right at me."

JP cut in, like he didn't have a doubt as to the person's identity. "Let me guess . . . Emma Woods's husband."

"Hey, how'd you know?"

"Fiona read online about Bill Woods breaking the door down after he heard his wife scream."

"So, we're back to square one!" I exclaimed, totally frustrated in our inability to make a dent in this case.

More and more, it was beginning to look as if Emma really did accidentally fall off the balcony on Halloween night. Unless, of course, she jumped. But if that was the case, why would she want to kill herself? Eight months before, she became a new mother. If nothing else, she had her baby girl, Fiona, to live for. The details just weren't adding up.

JP drained the dregs from his coffee cup. "Regardless of whether or not Bill Woods killed his wife, and his rich and powerful dad helped him get away with it . . . what happened to Emma's diamond necklace after she died?"

"That's just it, nobody knows. When the police arrived to examine Emma's body, it was gone. But Bill Woods didn't once question it. He didn't file a report or nothing."

"So, the police never investigated Emma's death as a homicide," I said, summing up what Bob told us. "And they never went in search of her missing necklace."

Something wasn't tracking.

Olivia returned with a fresh pot of coffee and refilled each one of our cups. "Can I bring you guys anything else . . . or just the check?"

There was one more thing I wanted to discuss. But I also didn't want us hogging up a table, so I opted for a chocolate chunk muffin to tide me over till dinner. Of course, I'd split it with JP. That's how we did things when it came to food. We were Sharers, definitely. It made my sister gag how precious we could be sometimes. Just once, Pamela said, she wanted to see us sit down to a meal without going halfsies.

"Was there anyone else at the birthday-Halloween party?" I asked Bob, trying to come up with an alternate suspect in the death of Emma Woods. "Did you guys see anybody who maybe wasn't supposed to be there?"

Bob nervously tore at his paper napkin. "Well, we did do a lot of drinking that night, so my memory's a tad bit fuzzy. Oh wait! Maybe half an hour before she died, I seen Emma across the room talking to Mindee McQueen."

"And who's Mindee McQueen?" asked JP.

"She was Emma's archrival from the beauty pageant circuit."

I pondered Bob's revelation. "If they were rivals, why was Mindee at Emma's party?"

"I've wondered that same question for nearly twenty-five years," said Bob, his sharp features etched with concern. "Mindee came in second place for Miss Great Lakes, the year Emma took home the crown. Ever since she lost to Emma, Mindee hated her. She was always jealous of Emma because she was prettier, more talented, and she married a rich man. Yet for some reason, she showed up at Emma's birthday-Halloween party."

JP's bright eyes flickered with curiosity. "Any idea where this Mindee McQueen person is now?" he asked, folding his big arms across his broad chest.

"Not sure. Back in the day, she worked at the Detroit city clerk's office, I know."

Rather than sit there and wonder, I pulled my phone from my pocket and typed *Mindee McQueen* in the internet search bar. Milliseconds later, I received a slew of results, including photos posted from a social media account belonging to @queen_mindee_mc.

"Is this her?" I asked, showing Fairway Bob the profile picture.

In the pic, a woman in her late forties (maybe fifty?) posed on the great porch of a large log-cabin home overlooking a scenic lake. Her stylish designer dress hugged her curves and accentuated her fit figure. Her chestnut hair was styled to perfection, her makeup flawlessly applied. The passage of time notwithstanding, she retained much of the beauty and glamour of her youth. Her green eyes reflected a wisdom and experience that couldn't be faked.

"Could be her. This woman looks rather well-off. The Mindee McQueen we all knew was a civil servant, struggling to make ends meet. Why d'ya think she entered all them beauty contests, eh? To win herself some big prize money. Hey, maybe she made off with Emma's diamond necklace and hocked it?" Bob teased, as an afterthought.

"Or maybe she just married a rich man," said JP, ever the optimist.

With this additional bit of information, compliments of Fairway Bob, we'd found our first real lead in the case of *Who (Might've) Killed Emma Woods (Other Than Her Husband, Bill)?*

Quickly, my thumbs typed out a direct message.

Hi Mindee!

My name is PJ Penwell. My partner JP Broadway and I host a home renovation show on HDTV called Domestic Partners. At the moment, we're renovating a manor home in Pleasant Woods. The owner is the daughter of Emma Wheeler, Miss Great Lakes 1992. We're wondering if you might be the same Mindee McQueen who was also in that pageant? If so, we'd love to have you on our show as a special guest.

Emma's daughter would enjoy meeting you, and hearing any stories you might share about your friendship with her mother. Please let us know if this is something that might interest you. Thanks so much for your time and consideration. ☺

And send!

Now we just needed to wait and see if the older woman replied.

After finishing off our muffin, we walked along Woodward Avenue, carrying on the conversation re: Emma Woods and her arch-nemesis.

"You don't think Mindee McQueen had anything to do with Emma's death?" I asked Fairway Bob, breaking the silence.

He shook his head slowly. "I don't *think* so. She didn't like Emma, sure. But she never struck me as a murderess."

"Another dead end," said JP, sipping his coffee from a to-go cup.

Bob stopped walking. He leaned in a little closer, his expression serious and almost conspiratorial. "Hey, now you didn't hear this from me . . . but I think somebody else might've killed Emma."

"Way to bury the lead," I said, wondering why he didn't tell us this tidbit sooner. "Who?"

Despite his serious demeanor, there was excitement in Bob's tone. He weighed his words carefully, as if he was about to reveal a dark secret. "Let's wait till we get back to my store, eh?"

It was as if he'd been waiting to share this info with people he could trust.

Chapter 21

We made ourselves comfortable on a Mission-style settle sofa.

Back at Somewhere in Time, Bob pulled up one of the slat-back wood dining chairs he'd brought out to show us earlier. Plopping a squat on the leather-covered seat, he crossed one leg over the other and announced his prime suspect in the death of his dear friend, Emma Woods . . .

Evan Savage-Singer.

"Well, he was just plain Evan Savage in 1997," Bob clarified.

My jaw dropped. "Why would Evan kill Emma?"

I couldn't believe what Fairway Bob was telling us. Well, I *could* believe it. Bob wasn't known for being a fibber. In fact, he was considered a very reliable source when it came to the goings-on in Pleasant Woods. Not that we'd call him a *gossip*, by any means. Anything he might've said about anyone wasn't meant with malicious intent.

"Not many people know this, but . . . Evan and Emma were having a torrid love affair."

"We ran into Evan and Stephen last night at Chianti. He told us he and Emma were *friendly*," JP mentioned sarcastically.

"Oh, they were friendly all right! Remember what I said about the secret staircase leading from the kitchen of Woods Hall, up to the third floor? Emma and I hung out all the time before she died. In fact, she was with me at Glitterbox, the night Stephen first performed as Harmony House. Emma was so impressed, she hired him on the spot to sing at her birthday-Halloween party."

Bob stood up and began pacing back and forth, which didn't bode well with Willie. The black Lab let out a big bark in a show of disapproval. Clydie did the same thing at home to me and JP. Whenever one of us would look up—at an overhead light, or the cupboard above the refrigerator, it didn't matter what—he'd jump up against our leg to let us know he didn't approve of our bad behavior.

"*Anyhoo!* Em told me about her affair with Evan," said Bob, resuming his story about the secret staircase. "He used it all the time to get upstairs and see her."

"How did he do it without getting caught by her husband?" asked JP, intrigued. "Or any of the Woods Hall staff?"

"Easy. Em gave Evan a key. He'd enter through the side door, off the kitchen. No high-tech security cameras or doorbells like everybody's got now, eh? Pleasant Woods was a much safer place to live back in the nineties," Bob remarked.

He didn't reference the pair of murders JP and I helped solve over the past twelve months. Still, we understood his meaning, loud and clear.

"Once he snuck inside, Evan took the secret staircase up to Emma's bedroom. To be honest, if Bill ever caught him, I don't think he would've minded too much."

"Because Bill was having his own affair with Kathleen Anger, the housekeeper," I said, rehashing the information we were made privy to by the mayor and his wife, Quinn and Vicky Marshall.

"And the suspected mother of his son," JP added. For the first time, he seemed to be enjoying himself in this sleuthing game we were playing.

"Exactly!" Fairway Bob confirmed. "That poor girl was so unhappy. Emma and Bill only got married because their fathers forced them. It was nothing more than a business transaction between the two most powerful families in Metro Detroit."

"Why Evan Savage? I mean, he's a handsome enough guy . . ." JP always had a soft spot for a man in uniform. "But Evan's an out-and-proud gay man."

Bob held up a hand. "*Bisexual*. Evan was married to a woman before Stephen, you know?"

When he said this, it reminded me of what Bob told us at some point in the not-too-distant past. "Gracie's mom, right?"

He answered my question in the affirmative. "No, yeah. After Emma died, Evan was devastated. Then he met Stephanie."

JP quickly calculated the math. "But Gracie's like thirteen. Emma died almost twenty-five years ago."

"I'll get to that part . . ." said Bob, snickering. "For almost two years, Evan dreaded facing discrimination in his military career. So, he put aside the part of him attracted to other men. Then, on New Year's Eve Y2K, he reconnected with Stephen at a party. At thirty, he finally found the courage to come out, and he ended his marriage to Stephanie. Evan and Stephen have been a couple ever since."

This I had to laugh at. "He went from *Stephanie* to *Stephen*?"

"Hey, I guess he did!"

JP cocked his head in confusion. "I still don't see how Gracie's birth fits into this whole timeline."

"Stephanie never remarried. But she realized her chance to conceive was getting less and less, the older she got," Fairway Bob said. "Even though their romantic relationship ended, she still cared for Evan. And he still cared for her. So, twelve years after their divorce, she asked him for a donation . . . Nine months later, a new baby was born."

Finally, I understood how Evan, at fifty-two, could be the biological dad of a daughter conceived a little over a decade ago, when he'd been involved with another man for the past twenty-plus years. Though who was I to judge his and Stephen's familial arrangement? For some people, having a child held such importance, they'd do anything to make it happen. JP and I often discussed whether we saw ourselves as parent material. But first, we needed to go from fiancés to legally wedded spouses.

"Hold on! Let's go back a second, will you?" JP asked, determined to make total sense of the scenario. "Before all this business with Stephanie and Stephen and baby Gracie . . . What makes you think Evan killed the woman he was having a torrid affair with?"

Bob sat back down in his chair and prepared himself, mentally, for what he was about to say next. "On the night of Emma's birthday-Halloween party, I see Evan and Emma across the room, having what looks like an argument. Next thing I know, Emma runs upstairs using the front staircase. Evan heads back toward the kitchen. I assume he's planning on using the secret passageway to get up to Emma's bedroom . . . Maybe try and head her off? But the whole thing is none of my business. So, I let it go and step outside for a smoke with Tom and Terry. That's when we hear Emma scream . . . and we see her land on the patio. The diamond necklace was gone."

JP attempted to put together the pieces of this puzzle. "You don't know what Evan and Emma were fighting about?"

"I couldn't hear what they were saying. The music from the live band outside was way too loud. But it was pretty clear the way Emma yelled at Evan . . . he definitely did something to make her mad."

Again, I found it hard to believe local law enforcement would just sweep something like this under the proverbial rug. "Didn't the police ever question Evan about Emma?"

"They didn't question *anybody* at the party that night. The PWPD determined Emma's death was an accident . . . and that was that."

"Seriously? They can't write off something like an automotive heiress dying under mysterious circumstances!" said JP, his voice growing heated at the injustice. "I played a cop on TV, I should know."

"No, yeah. It seemed strange to me too."

"But what about the argument between Evan and Emma?" I said to Bob.

"When I asked Evan what I seen him and Emma arguing about, he wouldn't say. But he swore to me he didn't kill her . . . Now I'm wondering if maybe he wasn't telling the truth?"

"It would make sense. The jilted lover is always the prime suspect," said JP, reciting one of his personal mantras when it came to murder.

"Well, what makes you think Evan is lying?" I asked our next-door neighbor next.

"Cuz of something Stephen told me, years later. Remember how I said he reconnected with Evan on New Year's Eve Y2K? Well, they *first* connected at Emma's birthday-Halloween party, three years before."

Hearing this, I recalled Stephen telling us the same thing when we ran into the Savage-Singers at Chianti on Monday evening. "So, what did Stephen tell you, years later?"

"He told me . . . on the night of Emma's party, she caught him and Evan . . . *kissing*."

"Okay. Well, we've established Evan is bisexual, so . . ." said JP, not seeing the significance of Fairway Bob's disclosure.

I connected the dots. "Wasn't Evan still secretly seeing Emma at that time?"

"He was! I'm thinking maybe after she caught him kissing Stephen, Evan panicked, eh? He was still in the marines, and what with *Don't Ask, Don't Tell*, he couldn't run the risk of being outed. So, what's he do? He follows Emma upstairs to her room . . . and to stop her from telling anyone what she saw . . . he *kills* her."

It was a plausible possibility. Which gave us a potential suspect in Emma's death, other than her husband and his mistress, both also dead. While I didn't want to make waves among our neighbors—or accuse anyone of a crime they didn't commit—I did make a vow to Fiona that we'd help her solve this mystery.

JP and I needed to take further action . . . and quick!

Chapter 22

The sun was starting its descent over Town Hall.

As we drove back to the west side of Pleasant Woods, I could see the darkening silhouette of the white-brick building on the southwest corner of Elmdale Boulevard, its cupola reaching toward the sky. The intricate details of the colonial-style building came into focus as we got closer, the white columns bathed in a warm glow.

A male-female couple strolled past the Grecian fountain in the center of Town Square. Colorful flowerbeds surrounded the terracotta fixture, and in the distance, the clock tower struck five. The man, tall and athletic-looking, pushed a baby in a stroller while the woman walked alongside, holding the leash of an Irish setter. They looked content as the infant cooed and giggled, while the handsome pet wagged its tail and sniffed at the grassy lawn.

If only Jack and Clyde were so well-behaved. God forbid, we should run into another dog during one of our W-A-L-Ks! We couldn't even say the word—we had to spell it out—or they'd go barreling toward the mudroom door in a frenzy. Upon seeing another pooch out in the wild, the boys would go crazy, barking and pulling, and causing a big ruckus. JP kept vowing to enroll them both in obedience class. Me, I worried we'd never get the chance to go. Between renovating an historic house as part of a TV show, and my trying to pen the next great American YA mystery novel . . . to quote from *Blue Tuesday*: *I can't remember the last time I had a day with nothing to do.*

Driving down the winding road toward Woods Hall, I replayed the conversation we just had with Fairway Bob in my head. If Evan Savage-Singer did murder Emma Wheeler-Woods, we needed to uncover some evidence of proof. Or at least find out, in Evan's own words, what happened on that night almost twenty-five years ago. I made a mental note-to-self to reach out to our neighbor two doors down and see if we could stop by for a chat, at some point.

Then, there was our other possible lead . . . Mindee McQueen.

Picking up my phone from where it rested in the cupholder, I opened my direct messages. Still no reply from the Miss Great Lakes 1992 first runner-up. As I tried to calm my racing thoughts, my hand vibrated with an incoming call from Nick Paczki. I contemplated sending him to voicemail. But I remembered what the detective said about checking in with those pesky neighborhood kids, regarding their possible involvement in Chippy's accident.

So, instead, I put the call on speaker. "This is Peter and JP."

Even though I knew who was calling—thanks to the caller's name popping up in bold letters on my phone screen—I never addressed the person when I answered. What if someone else was using said person's phone to make a phone call? The last thing I wanted to do was look stupid by addressing someone as somebody else.

"Hey, fellas. It's Nick Paczki, PWPD. So, I talked to them neighborhood kids I told you about. The ones I thought might know something pertaining to your TV show carpenter's slip and fall off his ladder. Unfortunately, they all denied having anything to do with it."

JP took his eyes off the road for a second, and turned toward the phone I was holding. "Of course, they did."

"JP, these boys are classmates of my daughter. So, I gotta say I believe 'em."

"Of course, you do."

Frank Anthony Polito

"Hey, now. Nikki says they like to get in trouble sometimes. But they wouldn't break into a house, dress up like a ghost, and try to scare a guy to death."

As disappointing as this news was, I wanted to trust the detective's judgment. Still, he kept insisting Emma Woods's death was nothing more than an accident, based on the police report filed back in 1997. If he was wrong about that call, why should we give him a pass on this one?

"Okay, Nick. Thanks for the update," I said, playing at the game of being cordial.

"No problem, Peter. I don't think we need to investigate this any further. It seems like nothing more than an unfortunate incident, plain and simple. Just tell Chip, no more drinking on the job."

"We will do that," I promised, promptly ending the communication.

Around the bend, the new-and-improved Woods Hall came into view. One look and both JP and I could tell Corey and the rest of the crew put in a hard day's work. Immediately, the century-old manor home caught our eye. The rest of the once dull, weather-worn exterior was now power-washed and restored to its original cream color, giving the house a warm and inviting feel. The fully repainted olive-green trim and chocolate-brown shutters provided a stark contrast to the lighter stucco.

The wide front door appeared fresh. The intricate stonework framing the windows and adorning the chimneys looked more defined than ever. The porch and limestone steps were also scrubbed clean, highlighting the woodwork and ornate columns supporting the roof overhead. The overall effect of the power-washing and new paint was a stunning transformation, returning Woods Hall to its original 1913 glory. The restored beauty of the exterior was sure to inspire admiration from passersby and all who visited.

"Wait! I wanna get a shot of your reactions!" Ursula bounded out of the house with Kevin and Dave—and all their equipment—following close behind.

Gopher the PA leapt in front of me and JP, thrusting his slate in front of our faces. "*Domestic Partners*, episode three-point-one, scene five, take one."

"Action!"

"So, what do you guys think?" asked Ursula, from her spot off-camera behind Kevin.

Part of the process of taping a TV show involved the producer asking us questions, to which we would answer as if we weren't being asked but were giving our unsolicited opinions. In post, the other voice was edited out, so viewers wouldn't hear the prompt.

"Everything looks great!" answered JP, raising his voice. "Good job, Corey and the crew!"

"I love the way the front door turned out," I added.

"Kev, get a shot of the door, okay? PJ, keep talking," Ursula ordered.

"Um . . ." I hated having to perform on cue. But it was part of the job, so I sucked it up and played the trick monkey. "The new coat of stain really accentuates the intricate design of the brass door handle and the surrounding woodwork."

Ursula pointed to the lead glass windows. "JP, talk about how clean the windows are now. Go!"

"The windows sure are clean!" said JP, mimicking his commander.

"Not funny, Broadway," Ursula droned.

"Sorry, Urs. Take two!"

Smirking, I could detect my fiancé's frustration. We weren't expecting to be ambushed the minute we arrived at Woods Hall and climbed out of our SUV. But, in trying to keep reality TV *real*, sometimes these off-the-cuff setups would happen.

JP cleared his throat. "The lead glass windows look nice and clean, don't they?"

"They do! Here's a *Domestic Partners* pro-tip for you folks at home," I said, taking an aside to the camera. "Put equal parts white vinegar and water in a spray bottle . . . Spray it on your windows . . . Wipe it off with *newspaper*, you'll get a clean, shiny surface."

"Wanna know why? Tell 'em, Peej!" said JP, grinning broadly as he joined me for this special PSA moment.

We tried to do at least one per show. On the actual episode, we'd cut to what they call in TV-speak, a *lower third*. This was a combination of text and graphical elements placed in the lower area of the screen to give the audience more info. It doesn't necessarily have to occupy the actual lower third of the screen, but that's where the name originated.

BTW, I hated when JP (or anybody) called me *Peej*. Still, I rolled with the punches, being a professional.

"Newspaper is less likely to leave behind lint due to its low absorbency," I explained to our unseen audience. "When you use paper towels, they can cause streaks on the glass. In contrast, newspaper is made with ink that's designed to be absorbed, right into the paper. It doesn't smudge or smear, making it an effective tool for cleaning windows."

"Pretty cool, huh? Thanks, partner, for that *Domestic Partners* pro-tip."

Before we wrapped, Corey took us around the side of Woods Hall and showed us a surprise . . .

As we approached, we could see the brand-spankin'-new wood screen door he built with his own two hands, standing proudly in place of the worn-out one. It was a beautiful—and almost exact—replica of the 1913 version that had been ripped off (for whatever lame reason!) and left in the old three-car garage to wither and dry out. It pleased me so much, I considered soliciting Corey's services and having him make us a new wood screen door for 1 Fairway Lane.

"Wow!" I said, running my hand along the smooth, polished oak.

JP clapped Corey on the shoulder in a show of manly affection. "Amazing! You pulled it together."

Corey beamed with pride. "Thanks, guys. I really wanted to do justice to the original." He pointed out the various features of the door, from the carved panels to the stained glass accents. "Check out the screen," he said, tugging on the mesh. "Copper, just like the other one."

Impressed, JP and I admired the incredible attention to detail and craftsmanship Corey put into the door's design. "This is a work of art," I said, feeling grateful to see the lengths our new team member went to in recreating the historic door and delivering on his promise.

The good luck we had in meeting the guy the other night at Top Dog astounded me to no end.

Corey grinned. "I'm just glad you dudes gave me a job. It's my pleasure to help preserve a piece of history. And get rid of that crappy aluminum screen door from the forties!"

What were the chances of a total stranger entering your life, right when you needed them?

Chapter 23

Downtown Fernridge bustled on that Friday night.

With only six days left until the autumnal equinox, I was bound and determined to get out and enjoy what little warm weather we had left. In Michigan, it could be a balmy seventy degrees one day, and the next we'd have a blizzard.

The sign above the frosted glass doors announced the night-club's name in a vibrant and eye-catching display. Featuring a black rectangular backing with neon letters mounted on top, the word *Shout!* was written in a bold font, with the *S-H* crafted in brilliant white neon letters, and the *O-U-T-!* illuminated in striking hot pink. The sign glowed brightly and was visible from a distance, tempting patrons in to enjoy the lively, LGBTQ+-friendly atmosphere.

"I'm so glad you guys invited us!" Fiona shouted over the high-energy dance music blasting from the DJ booth.

JP and I met up with the Low-Fi duo around ten o'clock. It felt nice to have a night free after putting in a close to sixty-hour work week over at Woods Hall. What felt even nicer was to be on our own without a camera crew following us around . . . and without Ursula Boss barking out orders. Earlier that evening she flew back to NYC and wouldn't return to PW till Monday.

"We're so glad you could come!" I said, going in for a round of hugs. TBH, I wasn't much of a hugger, but the situation seemed to call for it, so I went with the flow.

Drag Queen Queeraoke took place within a separate, semi-private performance space. Seating could be found in limited supply at one of a dozen candlelit cocktail tables set up before a small platform stage. Peeking inside, I spied a vacant four-top, down front. "Shall we grab a seat and put our names on the list?"

As we moved into the cabaret room, the legendary Detroit drag queen known as Harmony House strutted over to greet us. Sporting her usual '90s-inspired emcee attire and long beaded braids—a look she referred to as *Fly Girl couture*—the Black beauty made a grand entrance. I'd seen the outfit before: backwards Day-Glo suspenders over a studded push-up bra worn with cutoff jean shorts, fishnet stockings and slouchy socks. But I didn't dare mention it to Ms. Harmony. That would be rude.

"Hello, hello! I cannot tell you how much it pleases me to see you boys. And who do we have here?" Stephen, as Harmony, stretched out his slender arms to behold our companions. "Well, if it ain't Miss Fiona and Master Finn of Low-Fi! My Harmonizers are in for a special treat tonight. You must honor us with a song. I will *not* take nay for an answer."

Finn looked a little anxious, speaking up. "Sorry, no can do. Me and Fi are pros. We don't sing for fun . . . or for *free*."

Ms. Harmony stared down at Finn from her oxblood-red Doc Martens. "Oh, honey. The only thing you're getting paid tonight is *attention*. And you won't earn a dime with that attitude." The sassy drag queen gave Finn and Fiona a wink, then turned back to me and JP, ready to kick off the night's festivities. "I know you won't sing, JP, you old stick-in-the-mud. Peter, I'm putting us down for our usual duet. Be ret to rock the mic when I call you up."

Like it or not, I'd be slaughtering Starship's "Nothing's Gonna Stop Us Now" (from the classic '80s rom-com *Mannequin*) before the evening was over.

"All right! All right!"

Promptly at ten thirty, Ms. Harmony stepped onto the stage to a round of thunderous applause. She daintily held the silver microphone, taking care not to muss her fake nails as she greeted her adoring minions. "Now listen to Momma, my children"—Stephen lifted an index finger to his overly painted lips and made eye contact with the audience—"because she is about to blow your mother-tucking minds. I am beyond excited to tell you about the VIPs we have gracing us with their presence this evening."

The hoard of Harmonizers leaned forward, focusing their short attention spans on the stage in anticipation of the impending proclamation. A few shouted out guesses while others expressed their excitement with cheers and whistles.

"These indie darlings are breaking barriers with their unique sound and fearless attitude. My daughter Gracie loves them, almost as much as I do. They're the hottest new band on the scene right now . . . Low-Fi!"

A collective gasp filled the cabaret room, followed by a raucous round of clapping. Phones flashed from every direction. Ms. Harmony waited for the clatter to die down before continuing. "That's right, Harmonizers! Finn and Fiona promised us a song or *three*, so be on your best behaviors, children. Mmmkay?"

The crowd went wild, screaming and cheering as Finn and Fiona smiled and waved back. I could tell Finn wasn't too pleased to be put on the spot like that. What choice did he have but to comply with the drag queen's promise? With so many cameras documenting their every move, F and F couldn't afford to risk turning off their Low-Fi followers by refusing to sing a little Queeraoke.

Around midnight, the show broke for intermission. This was when things went from uncomfortable to just plain awkward. A statuesque figure pranced into the cabaret room, dressed in a stunning, tight-fitting sequined gown and a sky-high wig.

The glamorous Latinx drag queen stood tall and confident in her stiletto high heels. The slit in her long skirt accentuated her even longer legs, the plunging neckline showing off her ample breastplate. Her makeup was bold and fierce, with exaggerated lashes, arched eyebrows, and bright coral lipstick that popped against her caramel skin. Her platinum hair was styled in a voluminous bouffant that added to her towering height—she had to be at least six-foot-five—and her long nails were painted to match her pouty mouth.

"Guys, I need to put you on the spot for a second," said Stephen, dropping his voice half an octave as he spoke as himself. "Come meet my drag daughter, Miss Melody Mansion."

The young queen strode toward us, extending a hand like a Southern belle might when greeting a potential suitor back home on the plantation. "Gentlemen! Momma Harmony's been raving about you all week long. I just had to come by and see you handsome devils for myself." She leaned in and air-kissed both me and my partner.

"Didn't I tell you, Melody, dahling? These boys are H-A-W-T, *hawt!*"

JP wasn't buying the flattery. "Sounds like somebody wants something. Huh, Pete?"

"Oh, child. You know me all too well! Me and Melody wanna talk to you both about something special we got coming up. The Haus of Houses is putting on a little charity Extravaganza up at Glitterbox . . . and we would looove for you fabulous boys to take part."

As domestic partners (lowercase) and *Domestic Partners* (capped and italicized to indicate the name of our TV show), JP and I exchanged a lot of glances, be them *curious* or *anxious* or *furtive*. In that moment, standing in the cabaret room at Shout! before a pair of scheming drag queens, the looks we gave each other couldn't be described by Roget himself and his thesaurus.

"You what?" I asked, still trying to wrap my head around Stephen's invitation.

"You heard Momma Harmony," said her drag daughter, Melody. "The Haus of Houses is raising money for Affirmotions, the queer youth center right here in Fernridge. We need to make this the biggest and best show of the season. We've got a whole lineup of girls: Kadence Kondo, Carol Cottage, Fermata Flat . . . As local queer celebs and members of this rainbow-colored community, we'd love for you both to join us on stage. Say hey to Tempo Tenement and Adagio Atelier!" she proclaimed, pointing at me and my partner.

I wasn't sure how to respond, and from the expression of horror on his handsome face, I don't think JP was either. The thought of doing drag (for the first time ever) in front of such an important and potentially *huge* crowd was nerve-racking, to say the least.

"I don't know, ladies," said JP, picking up on my telepathic signal. "We're right in the middle of another home renovation. Plus, Pete's not much of a performer."

Harmony, ever the optimist, chimed in. "Now hold on just a minute. Me and my husband saw *Blue Tuesday*. PJ, you held your own on stage with everybody else. And JP, we are constantly blown away by everything we've ever seen you do!"

We stared at each other, pondering over the proposition. We were flattered by the drag mom and daughter's compliments, but still unsure about performing in a show as their equals.

"We appreciate the offer, ladies, but I don't think it's for us," said JP, shaking his head.

"Come on, boys!" Melody pleaded. She took hold of JP's face with her hand and gave his head a gentle turn, inspecting him like a piece of meat in a supermarket display cooler. "Look at the bone structure on this side of beef! And this little cutie-pie . . ." She stared down at me coyly. "The crowd is gonna eat you right up! Just imagine how fierce you'll both be, all dragged out and ready to slay on the runway!"

"What do you say? We'll make sure you both get the full-on treatment. Hair, makeup, the works!" Ms. Harmony promised, before going for the jugular. "Think of all the queer youth you'll be helping out."

For a moment, I stopped to consider the dilemma facing us . . .

On the one hand, the idea of appearing in drag in front of a large audience was daunting, and the prospect of being in the literal spotlight—yet again, and so soon—terrified me. On the other hand, I think both JP and I recognized the importance of having a safe and supportive space for queer youth. I knew from personal experience how much it can mean to have a community of people who accept and affirm you.

Growing up in Madison Park in the early aughts, I didn't have access to such a center, so I struggled with feelings of isolation and loneliness. This opportunity presented me with a chance to use my time and talents to make a positive impact. By agreeing to participate in the charity Extravaganza, we could help raise funds for a cause that was close to our hearts, while making a meaningful difference in the lives of young queer people in Metro Detroit.

"It's for a good cause," I said, still feeling unsure but wanting to do the right thing. "We're in."

JP gawked at me. Clearly, he did *not* appreciate my answering on his behalf. But he couldn't possibly back out now since I already committed our time and our talents.

The drag queens squealed with delight, hugging us tightly. "We knew you boys would come around!" Harmony announced.

With that, our journey into the fabulous world of drag was set to begin. Surely, I'd hear more later about the way I opened my big mouth, speaking for us both as if we were one single entity.

But it wasn't the first time . . . nor would it be the last.

Chapter 24

Mom cleared away the dirty dishes.

JP pushed his chair back and stood up, in a show of chivalry. "Can I give you a hand?"

"That's okay. I got it," my mother insisted.

Since moving to Michigan, we'd taken to coming by my folks' house on Sunday evenings. With baseball season still in full swing (pun intended), we usually arrived in time to catch the tail end of the Tigers game. Or as my mom would say: *To watch the Tigers lose . . . again!* Then, we'd sit down for dinner in my parents' eat-in kitchen. This was a feat not-so-easily accomplished, since the ten-by-eight-foot room could barely fit a dining table, let alone four adults sitting around it, and two dogs down on the floor below.

Mom stood at the narrow countertop, directly behind her seat. Recently, she stopped coloring her hair, and the light above the sink reflected off her silvery locks. "So, the renovations are going good?" she asked, filling the single basin with warm water.

"They are." I slipped Clyde and Jack a piece of the chicken breast I'd brought along for them, before Mom snatched away my plate.

For dinner, she made her famous spaghetti Bolognese. But this time, she remembered JP was a vegetarian, so she swapped out the ground hamburger for a plant-based protein. My father wasn't too thrilled about the substitution, but at least he made the effort to try it.

Dad sat at the table in his sleeveless T-shirt, bare shoulders on display. He stirred a heaping teaspoon of Cremora into his coffee. "You guys want some?"

"No, thank you. I take it black," JP politely replied. He couldn't stomach the thought of the non-dairy powdered creamer local to Michigan.

Dad helped himself to another scoop of the off-white powder. "More for me. Hey, how's your contractor guy doing? Mom said he got drunk and fell off a ladder."

My mother grabbed the dish towel and gave her husband a whack. "I didn't say he was drunk, Jim! I said he was *drinking*. There's a difference."

"You see how she treats me? Spousal abuse!"

Mom raised her hand, as if she were about to strike the man she married over four decades before. "I'll show you spousal abuse!" Then, she leaned in and softly kissed his cheek.

So went the game they played.

My parents liked to pretend they were arguing by talking in angry tones. It was something they did for amusement and to keep things interesting at their age. I didn't doubt for a minute they loved each other. I prayed my and JP's partnership would remain just as strong in the coming years.

After Mom finished dealing with the dishes, she poured herself a hot cup of coffee. "Any more ghost sightings, Peter?"

"Not since Chippy fell of the ladder."

"So, that's why he fell? He saw a ghost. Maybe he *was* drunk," said Dad, giggling.

My father had an infectious, high-pitched laugh that never failed to make me smile. His eyes got all squinty and crinkly at the corners, as his face stretched into a wide grin. The more he laughed, the higher the pitch got until only the dogs could hear him.

"Jim! Stop saying that poor man was drunk. You want him to

lose his job?" Mom reached down and gave Clyde a gentle pat on his big noggin.

The show of affection awoke the green-eyed monster in Jackson Russell. God forbid someone should pay attention to his big brother! Within seconds, Jack crawled out from under the table . . . and jumped right up onto my mom's lap. She fumbled to catch the little dog, and to keep herself from falling off her chair.

"Easy, Jackson!" Daddy JP called. "How about asking? Sorry, Grandma. That dog knows no boundaries, I swear."

"It's all right, my little granddog," my mother said in baby-talk, as she stroked the puppy's wiry coat.

"How's the new guy working out?" asked Dad. "The one who replaced the drunk?"

There was no way of stopping him once he was stuck on a subject, so I answered my father's question, flat out. "Corey? He's good."

"Did you show your folks the screen door he made for us?" asked JP.

Mom beamed. "Yes, we saw it on Facebook! It turned out nice. I'm glad you guys found a replacement for Chippy so soon. You met him up at the brewery in Royal Heights?"

"We did. Talk about a random coincidence, huh?" I said.

"*Everything happens for a reason*," my mother told us, quoting one of her favorite philosophies. "It's like I always say: *When one door closes, a window opens.*"

Ever the bubble burster, my father couldn't resist pitching in his two cents. "What do you even know about this guy?"

JP pushed aside his empty coffee mug. "Not much. Other than he's good with his hands. That's all I care about in a carpenter."

"You didn't ask for references, or run a background check? You can't take a person on their word, nowadays. Not with all the crazies out there. People stalk you online, get ahold of your info, then the minute your guard is down . . . they rob you blind!"

"Give me strength," Mom muttered. She locked eyes with me

and JP, across the tabletop, then broke into a fit of laughter at my father's expense.

Don't get me wrong, I loved my dad. But he was a bit of a worrier. Over the years, his anxiety had become more specific and almost obsessive. His latest paranoia revolved around the smart speaker me and my sister got him and Mom last Christmas. Dad swore up and down the thing was listening in on their conversations. Pam and I tried telling him, that's how a smart speaker works . . . it *listens* for you to ask questions, so it can answer.

"It's okay, I did my research . . . I checked Corey out online," I assured my parents.

"How do you even know that's his real name?" Dad demanded.

"Um . . . Well, I found him on IMDb."

JP gawked at me like I just revealed something secret. "Corey has an IMDb page?"

I internalized a sigh, knowing full well I already relayed this information to my fiancé. It would do no good to argue or remind him he was probably scrolling through his phone in search of cute pet videos at the time.

Instead, I played the opposite; something I learned when acting with my real-life partner on stage this past spring. "I didn't tell you I found Corey on IMDb? Apparently, he's a filmmaker."

"What kind of films?"

"Mostly short horror movies. I asked him about it the other day when we were working. He said he's trying to save enough money to make a feature."

JP rolled his eyes. "Good luck! He won't come up with that kinda cash doing carpentry work for HDTV."

"Dad recorded a horror movie the other night and made me watch it," Mom said, through with listening to her son and his partner debate over something she had no knowledge of or interest in. "Sooo stupid! And then he goes and falls asleep halfway through the show."

Dad started giggling again. "Not my fault I was tired! Spent twelve hours working at the store that day."

"I keep telling him he needs to retire," said Mom, tossing her silver shag haircut.

"I'm only seventy! Who's gonna pay all our bills if I retire? Plus, who'll give these guys a discount on their home renovation TV show stuff?"

Instead of informing my father that HDTV could probably afford to pay full price for paint and such, I resumed the conversation with JP. "Low-budget stuff I've never heard of. Oh, and guess who starred in all of Corey's films? Ashley, his girlfriend."

"Surprise, surprise. She did say she's an actress." JP pulled up the IMDb app on his iPhone and navigated to Corey Regan's profile. "This one sounds like a real winner," he scoffed. "*A genetically modified breed of mosquitoes escapes from a research lab and starts attacking a small town, spreading a deadly virus in their attempt to take over the world.*"

My dad leaned forward in his seat, ready to add the title to his must-see list. "Sounds good, what's it called?"

"Take a guess, based on that stellar logline," said JP.

Giving it a stab, I answered. "*Attack of the Mutant Mosquitoes?*"

"If only. Try *Skeeters*. It gets a two-point-eight rating on Metacritic."

Mom looked at JP curiously. "Is that bad?"

"It's not great. Corey should probably stick to being a contractor," he said dryly. "At least he's good at it."

Before we packed up the boys and headed home to Pleasant Woods, my mother made a startling announcement; one that would forever alter the dynamics of our family—hers and mine. After over a decade of being without, my parents decided to adopt their own dog.

Houston, we had a definite problem.

Chapter 25

The word *begging* does not describe it.

When I was a wee little lad, not quite ten years old, I pleaded with my parents to let me bring home a puppy. Hysterically, I wept literal tears in a desperate attempt to get my own way. Even back then, I was a bit of a Drama Queer.

The black-and-white doggie, I first saw on the day she was born, down the street from our house, on the opposite corner of the next block. Her mother was a German shepherd named Heather, her father some sort of border collie, judging by the look of her. When full-grown, she was a dead ringer for Fly from *Babe*, the dog who became the tiny pig's surrogate mom.

I called her Lucky, after the runt in Disney's *101 Dalmatians* who nearly died at birth. I promised to love her and walk her and pick up her poop, each and every day, with no complaints. Sadly, as I grew into a busy teenager, it was my mother who became Lucky's primary person. Mom was the one who opened the can of food twice daily, let her into the yard, cleaned up her messes, and carted her to the vet . . . including the very final trip.

Just six short weeks after I headed off to forge my way in the world as a writer, my poor Lucky Dog left us forever.

In my defense, the twenty-four-year-old me didn't realize . . . a dog's life is short. At almost fifteen, Lucky was an old girl. No longer was she the playful puppy I'd placed inside a wicker basket and pedaled around the block on my sister's bike. I honestly believed, in my naïve young mind, the next time I returned for a visit I would see my little Lucky asleep under our kitchen table, the way I'd always found her every other time I ever left.

I was wrong.

On the car ride home, as per usual, JP drove. I sat in the passenger seat, splitting my focus between checking my DMs for a reply from Emma Woods's archnemesis Mindee McQueen (still none!), and keeping an eye on the boys in back. Before we adopted Jack, we weren't concerned with buckling Clyde into a seat belt, so much. He just sat and relaxed or lay down and napped. But Jackson Boy . . . he was all over the place!

Mostly he stood and pressed his tiny nose against the window, smudging it with his doggie snot. But then it got to a point where he crawled between the two front seats and tried sitting on Daddy JP's lap while he was driving. Regardless of how cute he looked doing it, we both knew it couldn't be safe. What if JP had to suddenly slam on the brakes or something? We didn't want our little doggie boy to go flying through the windshield.

But what sealed the deal—and forced us to invest in a harness with seat belt attachment system—was the day I drove with the boys out to Metro Airport this past spring. JP just finished shooting a queer holiday rom-com called *A Very Marry* (M-A-R-R-Y) *Christmas*, costarring with influencer-turned-actor Jayden Jaymeson, for a major streaming service. As I waited in the loading zone for my partner to pick up his luggage, I took out my camera and started shooting a vid to post on @TheDailyClydeandJack. As if on cue, with his furry front paw Jackson flicked at the levered door handle . . . and totally opened the car door! After that excursion, we made darn sure the child safety locks were activated at all times.

"I can't believe your mom wants to get her own dog," JP said, disappointed by my mom's big news.

"I can't believe my dad is gonna let her bring another animal into their house."

The whole time we had Lucky, Dad did nothing but complain about what a nuisance she was. On top of the expense of owning a pet, and having to feed it twice a day, there was the whole issue of shedding. To combat the unwanted pet hair, my dad put up a gate that stayed shut, twenty-four seven. Lucky lived in our kitchen. She spent most of her life lying on the cold tile floor. She never even had a blanket, let alone a bed to sleep on. She never had a toy to play with. Rarely was she given a treat or taken for a walk. For all intents and purposes, she was an animal. She was *not* a member of our family.

This isn't to say that we didn't love her, but back in the day, dogs were simply dogs.

"What are *we* gonna do?" asked JP, as if the concept of my parents having their own pet would totally inconvenience our lives.

TBH, it kind-of-sort-of would, since Mom was our primary dog sitter. Voluntarily, she took care of the boys on a regular basis. But JP and I both knew the sad reality of the situation.

"Try not to worry. We'll figure it out."

JP snorted. "She's gonna regret it once she realizes how much work a dog is. And what if her dog doesn't get along with Jack and Clyde? Then we're stuck without someone to watch them."

"They can stay home alone. It's not like they're kids. They don't have to be under constant supervision, hon."

"I know. They just like going to Grandma's house." While he tried making it seem like Clydie and Jackson would be the ones to suffer over this latest development, JP wasn't hiding his frustration at how it personally affected him.

"Well, I can't tell my mom she can't get her own dog," I said, raising my voice slightly. "And we can't just assume her dog won't get along with the boys. Clyde didn't like Jack when we first adopted him. Now they're best buds."

Looking over my shoulder, I caught a glimpse of the puppy brothers, all cuddled up in the back seat of our SUV. They looked so content and peaceful, with Jack's head resting on Clyde's back, and Clyde's tail wagging softly against Jack's side. The car was filled with the soothing sound of their breathing, and it gave me a sense of comfort and joy knowing they were both happy and safe, after being rescued.

"I just don't wanna deal with having to find someone else to watch them," JP the spoilsport complained. "What if we both need to go out of town? I thought you wanna go to New York and meet with your editor about your new novel."

He was right. For months, Sabrina hounded me about the follow-up to my *Murder High* young adult mystery series, in which queer teen detective TJ Inkster graduates high school and goes off to college. She even gave me a title full of whimsical word play: *Murder U.* But between producing (and acting in) my own play, and renovating an historic home on TV, when was I supposed to find a chance to get any writing done?

"We can't go anywhere for an extended period of time and leave the boys home all by themselves," JP reminded me.

There *had* to be a solution.

"We could always ask Fairway Bob to come by and let them in and out. Clyde and Jack love Willie. Bob would probably even walk them if we asked him to. Or Cam. He's right down the block."

"Cam's hardly ever home. He can barely take care of Snoop. He's always off trying to sell some house and putting him in doggie daycare."

"I guess we'll cross the bridge when and if we come to it. Maybe we can help my mom? We can make sure she finds a dog that gets along with Jack and Clyde."

We crossed the border from Madison Park into Fernridge, passing by the neighborhood rec center. Behind the mid-century brick building with a flat roof, the sky was tinted a warm golden hue as the sun set. The bright lights of a baseball diamond lit up the field where an adult-league softball game was in progress. The park around the baseball field was bustling with activity. Families scattered around the edges, enjoying the game and each other's company. Kids played on the playground equipment, while couples strolled along the paths meandering through the park.

Smiling fondly, I recalled how my dad used to play on a team up at Softball City, back when I was in fourth grade. I used to go with him all the time, appointing myself as his team's official batboy. I even made a fancy BATBOY badge, decorated with glitter and sparkles, so everyone was aware of my important position. In retrospect, I'm sure all Dad's baseball buddies could tell what a little queer boy I was. But, at the time, I totally didn't care, so long as I looked fabulous!

As we drove past, I couldn't help but feel nostalgic for those simpler days. Being the daddy to two little doggies—on top of being an author *and* the cohost of a home renovation TV show—could be tough. But I wasn't complaining. I had everything I ever wanted: a fiancé who loved (and supported) me unconditionally, a home to call our own, and two beautiful fur babies to shower with affection.

Peter "PJ" Penwell was the luckiest guy in the whole wide world.

"How are we gonna do that?" JP asked, bringing me back to reality.

"Do what?"

"Help your mom find the right dog."

Oh, that.

"I'll email Margot from Home FurEver. Maybe she's fostering a dog, and we can bring my mom to meet it? We can take Clyde and

Jack with us to see how they all get along. Then we'll know right off if it's a good fit."

"I guess we can give it a try."

We drove the rest of the way home in silence, lost in our own thoughts. In back, Jackson and Clydie remained snuggled up, their warm bodies radiating comfort and security.

If only their Daddy JP could be so relaxed.

Chapter 26

On today's episode of *Domestic Partners* . . .

After two full weeks of nonstop work at Woods Hall, the plan was to shoot us in action as we freshened up the first-floor half bath. Like most of the other rooms in the old manor home, the original 1913 design was completely masked over by a contemporary mid-'90s look.

Located on the ground floor, just off the grand entrance hall, the formerly grand powder room had fallen into a state of disrepair. The walls, once covered in expensive marble tiles, were now cracked and peeling, the grout stained and discolored. A classic white pedestal sink lined one side of the small room, opposite a traditional two-piece toilet with a white porcelain tank and elongated bowl. The polished brass flush lever that perfectly matched the sink fixtures, towel bars, and toilet paper holder were covered in a thick layer of dust and grime, with rust and decay visible on the metal components. The edge of the sink was chipped, and the basin cracked, with the pedestal base discolored from decades of neglect. The toilet bowl was stained and filled with stagnant water, with the tank lid falling off.

The large oval mirror that used to hang above the sink lay shattered in pieces on the floor, a sad and broken reflection of its past self. The metal frame, once an elegant and opulent feature, was now bent and twisted, with sharp fragments of glass jutting out at odd angles. The gold finish, once so bright and gleaming, was now tarnished and dull. The formerly clear and flawless surface of the mirror appeared cloudy, with cracks and fissures spiderwebbing across it.

The Carrara marble tile, imported from Italy, was a classic choice for upscale homes like Woods Hall, due to its soft white and gray veining that created a timeless look. The tiles were arranged in a diamond pattern and polished to a high shine to evoke luxury and sophistication. But the years had taken their toll, with the effects of time and abandonment eroding their beauty and elegance.

"Like with everything else in the world of home renovations, this small room comes with big challenges," JP told our viewers via Kevin's camera lens.

I stood in the doorway of the half bath with Finn and Fiona, the three of us dressed in our JIMMY'S HARDWARE coveralls, waiting to pick up with my line. "Every guest you ever have over is gonna see this bathroom. So, we wanna be sure it makes an impression the minute they step inside."

"Sounds good!" cheered Fiona, the picture of positivity. "Where do we start?"

Kevin panned to his left for a shot of our *Domestic Partners* plumber-in-residence, Yannick, whose last name just so happened to be (what else?) Plummer. He came highly recommended to us by my brother-in-law, Mason, as a hardworking and dependable man. At forty, he had a thin and wiry build, with light brown hair he pulled back into a man bun.

"That toilet can go," Yannick told us, staring down in disgust at the piece of porcelain in the corner.

"Okay. Go where?" asked Finn, fearful of being put to work, as always.

Yannick sneered. "To the trash dump for all I care!"

Fiona admired the solid wood door with two recessed panels situated below a single window. "I love this!" The frosted glass,

with its abstract pattern, added a touch of privacy, while still allowing some natural light to pass into the otherwise windowless room.

"The problem is . . ." Corey stepped into frame, as our new
master contractor, to offer his expert opinion. "The door won't
shut." He gave a quick demonstration.

The eighty-inch piece of painted-over wood creaked on its
rusty hinges as Corey pushed and pulled. When he attempted to
close the door all the way, the outside rubbed against the frame,
preventing it from moving any further.

"Now, this is to be expected in a hundred-year-old house.
Normally to fix the sticking, we'd just sand it down, make sure it
closes, then paint over the spot where we sanded." Corey touched
the door on the exterior side, facing the foyer. "But this door here,
we're not gonna paint. What we're gonna do instead is"—he fully
opened the door and took out his screwdriver—"we're gonna fix it
here on the *inside*."

In a matter of seconds, Corey loosened the screws on the upper
hinge. Next, using a chisel, he gave a few scrapes to the wood at the
hinge point, beneath where the hinge lay. Then, he replaced the
three screws on the hinges and . . . *voilà!* The bathroom door closed
tightly.

Corey turned to Kevin's camera. "And that's how you fix a
sticky door, the *Domestic Partners* way."

He sure was a charmer!

"Kevin, cut to PJ now for his close-up," Ursula instructed. She
reached out and pretty much manhandled the guy to get him to do
what she wanted. "Peej, it's all you. Go!"

Struggling to recall the copy I wrote for this bit, I paused, ever
so briefly.

Ursula snapped her fingers in my face. "PJ! Wake up!"

"Sorry," I said, trying to remember my line. Once I got it, I
took a deep breath and smiled broadly. "The powder room doesn't
look so great right now. But it's just a matter of cleaning everything
up and making it shine again."

JP joined us back on-camera. "Now we'll just take off the door completely and send it out for dipping and stripping. When it comes back, it'll look just like it did when Woods Hall was first built."

Finn grumbled, raising a hand to get Kevin's attention. "How much is that gonna cost?"

Kevin panned over to where Finn stood by Fiona's side. I could tell he was ready to go off on another one of his rants, so I intervened. "Should only be a couple hundred dollars, Finn." Last time he got all heck-yeah, we had to stop the scene and start all over.

"I don't see why we gotta fix all the old stuff. It's a total waste of money," Finn said, launching into another tirade.

"Dude. A brand-new door'll cost you double. And it won't be solid like this one," Corey bluntly told the kid. "So, how about letting JP and PJ do their thing?"

Finn took a step toward the carpenter. "Don't *dude* me, bro . . . This is Fiona's house. She can have whatever kinda bathroom door she wants. Babe, what do you think of this janky old thing?" he asked Fiona amiably.

"I really like it," Fiona admitted. "We probably couldn't find a new one with a window, huh?"

JP answered. "Not like this . . . Finn, you wanna save money? Better to restore the original door, okay?"

Finn let out a huff. "Fine! Reuse the crappy old door. But for the new toilet, can we get one of those Japanese jobs? Babe, I saw the coolest post . . . said they come with heated seats and even a bidet if you want."

Again, I felt the need to jump in and save the day. "Finn, those smart toilets are nice. But they're super expensive. Like *thousands* of dollars."

"Bro, it's not like we're broke. We can afford to treat ourselves."

"If you want a smart toilet, baby, we'll get one," Fiona lovingly told Finn. "Guys, what do you think?"

JP explained to Fiona exactly what he thought of her fiancé's harebrain idea. "A Japanese smart toilet doesn't go with a 1913 Arts and Crafts–inspired manor. Sure, they're super cool and all high-tech. But you two need to keep in mind, this is a historic house. You might not be the last owners. Potential new buyers will want this place because of the historic features."

Finn crossed his arms, shoulders slumped. He stuck out his lower lip, pouting like a two-year-old. "So, I can't get my Japanese smart toilet, is what you're saying? Well, that sucks!" He stomped his foot on the marble-tiled floor and stormed off set. A second later, he stopped and called out, "You know, I can't wait to get away from here for a few days! It'll be nice to be back onstage, making music again."

I almost forgot; Low-Fi booked a mini tour, and they were heading out of town in the morning. The Midwest-college-town circuit consisted of stops in Bloomington, Columbus, and Pittsburgh. When we first heard the news, JP and Ursula weren't too thrilled to learn F and F would be unavailable, should we need their help with a project. At this point, I think we were all grateful to get them—well, at least Finn Lowenstein—out of our hair for even a little bit.

"Sorry, guys. Pick out whichever toilet you think will go best in here," said Fiona thoughtfully. "If it's okay, I'll go with Finn back to his parents' house now. We need to start packing for our trip."

JP and I wished Fiona well. I promised we'd check in about anything important, pertaining to the renovation. Otherwise, we'd leave them alone for a few days. Hopefully, when the couple returned home to Pleasant Woods, Finn's bad attitude would be a thing of the past.

"That's a wrap!"

Once Gopher gave us the all-clear, Yannick tore up the old toilet. Corey removed the bathroom door and hauled it out to his truck. We had a guy Down River who could submerge the entire thing in a stripping solution, then sand it down to remove any rough spots or bumps so we could apply a new finish. It was a heck of a lot quicker than trying to DIY it. Plus, attempting to sand off the oil-based paint was next to impossible.

JP gathered his things. "Wanna text your mom and tell her we're on our way?"

"Hey, would you mind going to pick up the boys on your own?" I asked, coming up with an impromptu plan. "I wanna stick around and do some work on the powder room."

"You sure, Pete? Remember the last time you stuck around somewhere?"

The incident my partner referred to occurred earlier in the spring, one night after *Blue Tuesday* rehearsal. Vicky Marshall wasn't feeling too good after eating some bad sushi, so I volunteered to stay in her place and put away the props. Little did I realize, I wasn't all by myself in the Royal Heights Playhouse. Someone (who shall remain nameless) hid themselves backstage and—after JP and the other actors all left for the night—they proceeded to drop a hundred-pound stage light from the grid, nearly hitting me directly on my head.

Fortunately, I escaped the attempt on my life, unscathed. But I was, in fact, more than a little shaken up by the encounter. So much so, it made me stop and reconsider my desire to want to continue working while *completely alone* in the allegedly haunted manor. Yet, despite all the hesitancy, I was eager to get started on this project. So, I sent JP to fetch Clyde and Jack from my parents and, like a big boy, I stayed behind.

Crossing my fingers, I prayed I wouldn't run into Emma Woods . . .

Or her *ghost*.

Chapter 27

The ring light glowed like a spooky spirit.

Taking my spot in front of the camera, I checked to make sure I could see myself on the phone screen. Using the selfie-mode was never my first choice. Something about the feature always made my face look too long and too thin. As a gay man, looking *skinny* was never a good thing. We were meant to be well-muscled. Hence the reason JP and I spent more hours per week than I cared to, chained to the machines at the PW community center gym.

"Hey, guys! It's PJ Penwell from HDTV's *Domestic Partners*, live-streaming from Woods Hall. My cohost, JP Broadway, and I recently started renovating this 1913 manor home for our show. Now, I won't give too much away. We want you to tune in when season three airs next summer. I know, June is sooo long from now! But here's a little sneak peek . . ."

I hated making reels for our social media pages. It was bad enough we spent much of our work days being recorded. The last thing I wanted to do in my so-called free time was shoot even more content. But The Boss, aka Ursula, insisted. So, here I was at nine o'clock on a Monday night, doing just that.

I will admit, I thought I looked fairly decent in that moment, at least on-screen. For a non-professional performer, I was camera friendly enough. The LED light helped give my aging skin a smooth glow. With the drab coveralls removed and wearing a tightish sleeveless T-shirt, I realized all the side lateral raises were starting to pay off. For the first time in my almost thirty-five years, it looked like I finally had me some shoulders.

"I'm about to start working on this powder room. As you can see, it's definitely in need of some TLC, but I'm pretty psyched to get started. First things first, we gotta get rid of this old sink . . ."

With that, I picked up a sledgehammer and got ready to dive into the demo. As I raised the heavy hammer overhead, I stole a glimpse at my phone. A fierce determination reflected back at me. My eyes narrowed slightly, the muscles in my face tense in anticipation of the impact. As I prepared to strike, the glint in my eyes intensified, like a spark of fire. It was a moment of pure concentration, as though I was willing myself to succeed through sheer force of will.

Taking a deep breath, I steeled myself for the impact as I brought the massive hammer down with all my might, against the old porcelain. The first blow landed with a resounding *clap*, the sharp crash echoing through the empty room. The sink's glossy surface splintered, and a spiderweb of cracks appeared.

"Time for something new and fresh," I explained to my unseen audience, chuckling to myself as I continued smashing the old basin to bits.

Triceps flexing, I brought the hammer down again. This time the sink shattered into a hundred different pieces. The ceramic fragments flew in every direction, bouncing off the marble-tiled walls and floor with a clatter.

Quickly, I double-checked for any residual damage. Thankfully, there appeared to be none.

A cloud of dust rose up in the room, causing me to hack and cough. "Always make sure you wear a mask, guys," I told my loyal viewers. Heeding my own advice, I pulled a KN95 over my soiled face, mocking my own forgetfulness. "Nice job, Penwell."

The sink was now a pile of rubble at my feet, nothing more than a memory as the white porcelain mixed with chunks of dark metal plumbing. I took a step back, panting, and examined the mess of broken shards and debris, and the destruction wrought by yours truly. The room felt different, emptier somehow, as though the sink held some kind of weight that was now lifted. I took another deep breath, oddly satisfied in knowing the old broken fixture had been cleared away, making room for something new and better.

"All right, all right!" I said, sounding like Stephen Savage-Singer doing his drag act as Harmony House. "What should I destroy next? Send me your ideas in the comments."

As I waited patiently for my followers to submit their suggestions, somewhere deep within Woods Hall . . . a door slammed.

Startled by the sudden noise, my entire body went tense. My eyes widened, and my eyebrows shot up. Without consulting my phone screen, I could tell the expression on my face was one of both shock and terror. The sledgehammer slipped out of my hands, causing me to jump a second time as it clattered against the marble tile. My heart rate rapidly increased, as a rush of adrenaline prepared my body to fight or flee.

Of course, it totally embarrassed me to be caught on camera in such a vulnerable position.

"Okaaay, what was that?" I asked, addressing the phone still held by the holder on the ring light. My mind went to the dark place. The first thought I had was the possibility of someone else being in the house.

Someone like the ghost of Emma Woods!

Or it could've been as simple as a gust of wind. I couldn't recall leaving a window open somewhere. Maybe one of the crew guys forgot to lock up everything when they left for the night? Taking yet another deep breath, I did my best to calm myself down. I reminded myself to stay focused. I realized I should probably investigate the cause of the noise, for my own safety as well as my mental health.

Lifting my phone from the ring-light holder, I held it in front of my face. "Change of plans, guys. Come with me while I go see what's up. And if for some reason we get cut off, call for help, okay? Hopefully I'm just being paranoid when I say that. But Woods Hall is rumored to be haunted, so you never know *what* we might find."

Walking slowly through the grand entrance hall, my eyes darted from side to side in search of the source of the slamming door, as I continued with the live stream. "JP, if you're watching, I'm okay . . . for now, at least. Anybody else watching this, feel free to comment if you see or hear anything unusual. I don't wanna freak out, but . . . I kinda feel like something's not quite right here."

At the base of the grand staircase, I stopped to take in the expansive entryway, phone still in my grasp. Suddenly, a sweet and haunting tinkling noise caught my attention. "Whoa, do you guys hear that? It sounds like a music box."

Distinctly, I recalled what Mayor Marshall told me and JP the other afternoon: *Emma Woods collected music boxes.*

"Pretty sure it's coming from the second floor," I said into my phone. "Guess I'll go take a look."

Before I could make another move, the antique wall sconces started to flicker, the same way they did on the night of the Woods Hall open house when we brought my sister inside to show her around.

"I *thought* Sparky fixed that short," I said, voicing my anxious thoughts aloud.

The flickering continued for a few more seconds before all the lights completely went out. Fortunately, my phone remained on, now the only source of illumination in the old manor home. The sudden darkness and uncertainty caused my pulse to skyrocket, as I braced myself for what might come next.

The most logical thing to do was turn on my phone's flashlight, which is exactly what I did. With a click of my thumb, the function activated, and a bright beam of light lit up the grand entryway. As I swung the light around, silhouettes danced on the wood-paneled walls, creating an eerie atmosphere that, TBH, sent shivers down my spine. The light revealed the intricate details of the ornate molding on the ceiling. But it also cast deep shadows into the corners of the room, hiding any potential threats from view.

"I should *probably* look for a light switch . . . I know there's one here somewhere," I said to whoever might be observing on their own mobile devices, wherever they may be.

Frantically, I scanned the walls, hoping to restore some sense of normalcy to the situation. As the flashlight beam swept over the wood paneling, my eyes locked onto a familiar shape . . . the outline of an antique brass switch plate.

Without a second thought, I rushed toward the switch, my hand fumbling to reach out and flip it up. I felt a sense of relief as the switch clicked into place, and the bright glow of illumination chased away the cold dark shadows as the lights fully came back on.

The practical part of me thought I should walk directly toward the front door and go home, immediately if not sooner. The inquiring part wanted to uncover the source of the tinkling sound.

Against my better judgment, I slowly made my ascent up the grand staircase, the music box sound growing louder and louder with each step. A sense of unease crept over me, like someone was watching my every move. Glancing up, I stared suspiciously at the hand-painted portrait of Emma Rose Wheeler, Miss Great Lakes 1992.

"Is it just me . . . or are her eyes moving?" I asked anyone who might be listening via my live stream.

Reaching the top of the landing, I peered down the narrow corridor at the walnut-stained doors of the different bedrooms. All were wide-open—except for one—same as on the night we first toured

Woods Hall with Fiona and Finn. Tentatively, I approached the closed door. I knew it was locked, from before, so why did I bother trying it?

To my surprise, when I gave the cut crystal knob a gentle turn . . . the solid wood door swung open with ease. The hinges groaned as the door squeaked ajar, revealing a dark and dusty room beyond. Forgetting to share my inner monologue with my at-home audience, I hesitated, unsure of what I might find inside.

Curiosity getting the better of me, I took a step forward.

Chapter 28

Moonbeams seeped in through the tattered lace curtains.

A spooky glimmer washed over the small bedroom, cobwebs dangling from the plaster ceiling. Faded paper adorned the walls, the once beautiful patterns barely visible from decades of direct sunlight. The floorboards creaked under my feet, as I gingerly made my way inside.

The space was empty, except for a few pieces of furniture. On one side, an old rocking chair swayed slightly on its own, as though someone unseen was still sitting in it. In the far corner, I approached an antique dresser. The cracked mirror above reflected a distorted image of the room (and of me) as I peered into it.

Atop the bureau rested the most beautiful music box, carved from mahogany with mother-of-pearl inlay. The dainty figure of a ballerina twirled around as the mechanical instrument played a haunting melody.

The thing totally creeped me out!

Quickly, I closed the lid to silence the music and took a closer look at the vintage dresser. The piece was made of dark, rich wood, worn down by years of use. The edges were rounded and smooth, showing signs of the hands that had opened and closed its drawers so many times. The knobs were fabricated from brass, and although they'd lost their shine, they still added a touch of elegance.

As I inspected the dresser more closely, it reminded me of a chest from my grandmother's house in Royal Heights. Only hers had a special secret drawer. What were the odds this one would too?

Sure enough, along the bottom I located a small latch. Giving it a firm push, a hidden compartment down below revealed itself. Inside, I found an old leather-bound journal, which I opened and started to read . . .

This is the private diary of Emma Wheeler-Woods.

Right when I turned the first page, the lights in all of Woods Hall suddenly went out again.

From the dark, the music box resumed its melancholy tinkling. Two blackouts in the span of five or so minutes couldn't be coincidence. Try as I might to keep calm and carry on, I needed to get out of that bedroom . . . and out of that house!

With the old diary tucked under my arm, I sprinted into the hallway and dashed toward the flight of stairs at the far end. I don't even know if I was still documenting my experience for all the world to see. Live streaming on social media was the furthest thing from my mind in that moment.

Upon safely reaching my destination, I swiftly began my descent, taking the steps two at a time. On the fourth tread, I tripped. Down the wooden staircase I tumbled, feeling the impact of each stair as I fell. Desperately, I tried grabbing hold of the banister, but my efforts were futile.

Landing at the bottom with a loud *thud*, a sharp pain stabbed at my side. For a few seconds, I lay in the silence trying to catch my breath, wondering if I simply lost my footing . . . or did someone intentionally *shove* me?

Although shaken, I was bound and determined to get up and keep going. But first, I needed to find my phone. I let out a frustrated sigh, my mind reeling with thoughts of where it could be. It must've fallen out of my pocket, and I failed to notice it in my haste to escape. How was I going to find the missing object in total darkness? I had to get ahold of JP and have him come to my rescue.

Pushing myself to my feet, I gritted my teeth against the pain in my hip. As I staggered toward the staircase, my eyes surveyed the surrounding area, searching for any sign of my missing mobile device. But everything was a blur, my vision still hazy from the tumble I just took. Stumbling forward, I leaned against the wood-paneled wall for support.

And then I heard it . . .

The faint ringing of my phone resonated through the dark and silent house.

Filled with hope, I searched around for the source of the sound. My eyes landed on a faint glimmer of light across the room. I squinted to make out the shape of my phone lying on the marble-tiled floor near the staircase. With renewed determination, I limped toward the set of steps, my body still sore from the fall.

Finally reaching the spot, I bent down and picked up my mobile, wincing. As I looked down at the screen, a simultaneous surge of relief and anxiety filled me, brought on by the image of my handsome fiancé. On one hand, I was grateful to see a familiar face and know that someone who cared was trying to reach me. On the other, I felt a sense of dread at having to explain how I found myself in another potentially dangerous situation.

My fingers hovered over the *answer* button. I knew I needed to pick up the call, to let JP know I was okay, but the words were caught in my throat. Finally, I summoned the courage to press the button and bring the phone to my ear. "Hey, hon," I said, my voice cracking with emotion.

There was a pause on the other end of the line. Then JP's voice came through, sounding both relieved and concerned. "Pete! Are you okay? I saw your live stream."

I breathed deeply and tried to steady myself, comforted by his call. "I'm fine."

"Okay, good. I'm on my way with the boys to pick you up. Be there in five minutes."

With great relief, I reignited the flashlight feature on my phone and shined the beam around the grand entrance hall. Cautiously, I began moving, scanning the darkness as I crept along toward the marble-tiled foyer and wide front door, beyond. Logically, I knew I needed to be careful. But I also knew I couldn't stay trapped in the dark for much longer . . .

Not with the ghost of Emma Woods lurking about.

A cool breeze blew across the grounds of Woods Hall.

Standing on the porch, I waited (im)patiently for JP to arrive with Jackson and Clydie. I shivered in the chilly evening air, tucking my hands into my jeans pockets. Suddenly, showing off my shoulders in a sleeveless T-shirt didn't seem like such a good move.

A moment later, I heard wheels rolling across the gravel driveway and turned to see our crystal-black SUV coming to a stop in front of the historic manor home.

"Hey, guys!" I called as JP stepped out of the car with our boys. Intentionally, I tried keeping it casual, in spite of the pain inflicted upon me after falling down a flight of stairs.

As JP got closer, he took a gander at me and my bruises and balked. "Pete! You look terrible. Seriously, we need to get you over to urgent care and have you checked out."

"I'm okay," I lied. "Come on, I wanna show you something."

With the lights still out, the atmosphere inside Woods Hall was just as scary as before. JP suggested we try the fuse box. But locating the panel and flipping the switches didn't do much to remedy the problem.

"Forget about the lights and follow me . . ." I turned on my phone's flashlight and led the way toward the grand staircase.

JP guided the boys along on their leashes, and we climbed up the steps to the second floor. I was eager to show him the unlocked room and the vintage dresser with the secret door and creepy music box on top. Unfortunately, when we arrived, the walnut-stained portal was all locked up once more.

JP placed a reassuring hand on my shoulder. "I saw the room on your live stream. What was that book you found inside the dresser drawer?"

"Emma's diary! I totally forgot about it. Shoot, now where did it go?"

JP and I tiptoed back to the staircase, our flashlight beams casting shadows on the walls. The dogs followed closely beside us, their paws clicking softly on the wooden floorboards. Little Mr. Fuzzy Face scurried along as fast as his long legs could carry him, while Mr. Clyde trotted leisurely, taking in his new surroundings.

As we proceeded down the flight of stairs, Jack began to whimper slightly, the darkness and unfamiliarity of the space making him nervous. I reached down and scratched him behind his left ear, reassuring him everything would be okay. Clyde, on the other hand, remained calm and collected, walking down the steps with the confidence of an old soul.

"Let's check over there by the wall," I said, my voice a hushed whisper.

We headed over to the spot where I landed after my earlier fall. Jackson and Clydie stayed by our side, sensing the tension in the air around us. I knelt and shined my flashlight on the marble tile in search of the missing diary. There, lying facedown on the dusty floor, was the old leather-bound book. I reached out to grab it, my hand brushing against cobwebs. A gust of wind blew through the foyer, scaring the bejesus out of me.

Like a hot potato at a child's birthday party, I handed the diary off to JP, feeling a sense of relief over finding it. He looked at the old journal skeptically. "We shouldn't read this. We need to give it to Fiona. Emma was her mom. She should be the first one to see what's written inside."

"But what if it's full of clues? Maybe Emma wrote something about the person who killed her in there!"

JP sighed, clearly conflicted. He opened the cover, its one corner bent back, and began flipping through the yellowed pages. Before we could get too absorbed in Emma's private diary, Clyde started to bark loudly, breaking our concentration, causing Jack to run off down the hallway.

The little dog stopped a few feet away and scratched at the wood-paneled wall.

"What's your dog doing?" JP asked me. He had a habit of referring to Jack as *mine*. Especially when he misbehaved.

"Oh, Jackson!" I cooed, following after the Parson Russell terrier.

Like the RCA dog on the record label, Lord Jack Strohein sat on his little bottom and stared inquisitively at the wall, slightly above where an antique Mission-style armchair rested. Meanwhile, Clyde's barking fit grew even more ferocious.

"Guys! What's wrong?" I asked, shining my light at the wood paneling.

Then, as if he were a professional agility animal, we watched Jack jump up onto the seatback of the Mission-style armchair. At which point, an entire section of the wood paneling spun halfway around, revealing an identical Mission-style armchair on the opposite side . . . and yet another hidden tunnel.

"Wow," said JP, staring in amazement. "It's like something out of a movie."

Jack jumped off the chair and disappeared behind the wall. Without a second thought, Clyde followed his baby brother into the chasm.

"What's *your* dog doing?" I asked, taking a rule out of JP's proverbial playbook with my teasing.

"Guess we're going exploring," he said.

With caution, we entered the secret passageway.

Chapter 29

Using our cell phones as lanterns, we navigated the dark and winding tunnel.

The walls were rough and uneven, the air damp and musty. The only sound we could hear was our heels clicking against the cold cement floor. Despite the unknown lying ahead of us, we were both excited and terrified.

"It's okay, Clyde," JP told him quietly.

The poor beagle-bull slinked along at our side, his head lowered, tail tucked, trying to make himself as small as possible. His body language clearly communicated his unease. His stocky frame was noticeably hunched, and his ears were pressed back against his big head. He made a valiant effort to keep up with us, but Clyde's movements seemed slow and labored. His stubby legs moved hesitantly, as if he was afraid to take a step too far. His soulful brown eyes, which were usually bright and full of sparkle, looked dull and glazed over. He appeared to be in a state of shock, struggling to process everything happening around him.

"Jaaack!" I called into the silence.

No response came back.

"Hope he's not in any danger," said JP, his words echoing off the damp walls.

We continued to walk along the secret passageway when sud-

denly my partner stopped. "What's wrong?" I said, worried by
what he wasn't telling me.

JP pointed to a decorative piece of wood placed at eye level on
the stone wall. "Look!" He walked over and lifted a small, hinged
flap to reveal a pair of oval-shaped circles. With the flick of a small
lever, the holes opened, and two beams of bright light penetrated
the dark of the hidden tunnel. He bent forward and peeked
through.

"What do you see?"

"It's the landing on the staircase off the front foyer. I bet these
holes are cut into Emma Woods's beauty pageant portrait."

"Just like in *The Private Eyes*! Remember that scene where
they're drinking poisoned tea in that room, and the eyes in that
painting start moving back and forth, watching them."

JP stared at me sideways. "What's *The Private Eyes*?"

Was he seriously asking me this question?

"The movie with Don Knotts and Tim Conway from *The
Carol Burnett Show*."

In this comedy murder-mystery from 1980, Knotts and Conway play two bumbling detectives, Inspector Winship and Dr. Tart,
who are hired by a wealthy man named Upton to investigate a series of murders at his haunted mansion. The previous investigators
have all met with mysterious deaths, so Winship and Tart are tasked
with solving the case while avoiding a similar fate.

As they explore the mansion and interview the various suspects,
Winship and Tart meet a range of eccentric characters, including a
mute servant, a grumpy chef, and a seductive maid. They also discover several hidden passages and secret rooms, which add to the
creepy atmosphere of the old home. While piecing together the
clues, Winship and Tart become increasingly convinced that Upton
himself is the murderer. However, they must first survive several
dangerous encounters with the various traps and pitfalls the manor
has to offer.

In classic Don Knotts style, the movie combines slapstick humor with spooky thrills and chills. When I was a kid, I used to watch it with my dad on DVD, all the time. I found it hard to believe my own fiancé had never seen such a classic film.

"If you say so," said JP, sort of blowing me off. But I tried not to take it too personally.

Suddenly, we heard a muffled cry coming from the far end of the hidden tunnel. It sounded like Jack, whining. Either he was asleep and having a bad dream . . . or he was hurt.

"Jackson! Stay, boy. The daddies are coming!" JP cried out to our little lost puppy.

Down the dark, creepy passageway of the old manor home we crept, our phones' flashlights guiding the way. Clydie, our trusty canine companion, followed us closely. His cold wet nose sniffed wildly against the cold, hard floor. His focus was intense, as he seemed completely absorbed in the task of picking up Jack's scent.

"Find your brother," I commanded, hoping the beagle-bull would lead us to our missing Jackson Russell.

JP aimed his light toward the far end of the corridor. "There he is!"

Poor little Lord Strohein! The whimpering pup cowered in the corner, his eyes fixed on something in the distance. We followed his gaze and couldn't believe what we saw at the end of the secret passageway . . .

The ghostly figure of a young woman in a white wedding dress and diamond tiara, accompanied by the tinkling melody of a music box. The ethereal apparition glowed in the darkness, her gown billowing as it dragged across the cold ground, where a dense fog hovered.

"Did you see what I *think* I saw?" I whispered to JP, my heart pounding.

"I sure did."

"Did it sound like she was *crying?*"

"That much I couldn't tell. Let's follow her and see where she goes."

Scooping up my little Jackson, we set off after the ghostly fig-ure, trailing her down yet another tunnel, an offshoot of the origi-nal hidden one. The sound of the music box grew louder, and the fog grew thicker as we drew closer to our target.

At the end of the long passage, we came to a door in one of the stone walls. JP pushed it open and stepped through with Clyde, so I followed them with Jack held tight in my arms.

The space was small and cramped. The smell of old wood and mothballs filled my nostrils. Long coats hung from a wooden, hori-zontal bar in front of us. The setting seemed familiar.

"Are we inside that old wardrobe?" I wondered, remembering the one we saw in the second-floor bedroom belonging to Kathleen Anger's young son.

Sure enough, as we opened the door, we found ourselves stand-ing in the very same spot.

JP and I looked at each other in shock, but we knew we needed to keep moving forward. As we headed toward the exit, my partner noticed something. The *Blair Witch Project* movie poster had been taken down, revealing the crevice in the plaster wall that it once covered, even bigger than before.

"Aw, man!" he wailed in annoyance. "Look at the size of that hole! What happened?"

Moving closer, I took a peek. The hollow was now large enough for me to put my small hand inside. "Corey mentioned he tried fixing it. Guess he made it worse. I'm sure he'll take care of it when he gets a chance. Don't worry."

JP shook his head. "He better take care of it! We don't have time to deal with this mess on top of everything else we've gotta finish by Halloween."

Gingerly, I placed Jack down on the floor, and we exited the bedroom with the two doggie brothers leading the way. As we stepped into the hall, we looked around. There was no sign of the ghostly figure, or the fog that accompanied her, or the tinkling tune of the music box.

The house was quiet once again.

"Guess we should go home, huh?" JP said, breaking the silence.

I nodded in agreement. "I guess. Nothing we can do here with the power out."

As we tromped back down the staircase, the scent of the mysterious woman we followed out of the secret passageway seemed to have dissipated, at least as far as the dogs could detect.

Suddenly we heard a loud sound, almost like a crackle, as the electrical circuits in the house returned to life. It was as if the power was impatient to be restored, and made its presence known in a sharp and startling way. The lights flickered briefly, and then all at once, they came back on with a powerful surge. The sharp noise echoed throughout the historic manor home, bouncing off the wood-paneled walls and filling the stale air with an almost electric energy.

It was a jarring reminder that the old manor was still very much alive.

Pausing, we glanced at each other in confusion. Then, our eyes were drawn to the living room fireplace, where not only did a raging fire burn, there was yet another message waiting for us on the mirror above . . .

LEAVE THIS HOUSE!

"Seriously? We're going! Finn and Fiona should probably install an alarm system in this place to keep out the riff-raff," JP joked.

Even though the so-called blood was probably another batch of corn syrup and red food coloring, the sight still gave me chills. To think some unknown entity was there inside Woods Hall with us— with *me*, before JP and the boys arrived—I didn't know how much more I could take of *Domestic Partners: Haunted Mansion Edition.*

"Who do you think wrote this? If it wasn't the nasty neighborhood kids, I mean."

"No clue. But we need to go," JP replied, his voice low and serious.

"Home, boys!" I gave Jack's leash a firm tug to indicate it was indeed time to return to 1 Fairway Lane.

Crossing the marble-tiled foyer, we headed out the wide front door without stopping to turn off the lights or put out the fire in the fireplace. That's how freaked out we were! The whole time, I couldn't shake the sensation of being watched. It was as if the house itself was trying to tell us something; I just couldn't quite put my finger on what. Before we departed, I almost checked out the eyes of Emma Woods's Miss Great Lakes 1992 portrait, but . . . I feared I might see a pair of actual eyes staring back.

Outside on the porch, we both breathed a sigh of relief. Jackson waited patiently for his daddies' next move, and I gave him a reassuring pat of praise. "Good boy!"

Walking toward the car, I couldn't help but feel a sense of unease. Something wasn't right about Woods Hall.

I knew we couldn't ignore the fact for much longer.

Chapter 30

The room was quiet and peaceful.

With only the soft *whoosh* of a white noise machine in the background, I lay in bed thumbing through Emma Woods's old diary, propped up on a plush pillow. JP stretched out in his spot beside me, his face illuminated by the soft glow of his phone screen. He scrolled through in search of new *likes* on his latest @TheDaily-ClydeandJack post, a super cute pic of the boys strapped into their car-seat belt harnesses, taken before we drove home from Woods Hall.

Clydie plopped his chunky beagle-bull body between JP's long legs, with his big head facing the opposite end of the bed, snoring away. Jackson, aka White Shadow, burrowed under the blanket, cuddled up against my sore hip as my own personal heating pad. He was like his Daddy PJ in this regard. I couldn't sleep a wink unless I had at least my ear covered. I'd even taken to wearing a lightweight hoodie to bed—with the hood pulled up—to combat this very fact.

As I read, Emma's personal and private thoughts transported me back to the end of the last millennium. The old leather-bound book was a fascinating glimpse into the life of a former beauty queen and model . . . and I felt compelled to keep turning the pages.

9/1/97
SoHo Grand Hotel

Dear Diary,
*   I can barely find the words to describe the sadness that I'm
feeling in this moment. After a lovely Labor Day weekend by
myself in Manhattan, I woke up this morning to the tragic news
of Princess Diana's death. It feels surreal to even write those
words.*
*   I can't help but feel a sense of sadness and loss today, all
alone in this big city. It's hard to comprehend that someone <u>so full
of life and compassion</u> could be taken from us so suddenly. I can
only imagine how her family and loved ones must be feeling right
now. Poor William and Harry! To lose their mom when they're
both so young. I don't know what I'd do if I were in their shoes.
And if I were to die sometime soon, and leave my poor baby
Fiona without a mom, it would be <u>the worst thing ever</u>.*
*   Today, I will take a moment to reflect on Princess Diana's
life and the impact that she had on the world. She may be gone,
but her legacy will live on, and she will <u>never</u> be forgotten.*
*   Rest in peace, Diana!*
*   xoxo*
*   Em*

Judging by this journal entry, I understood why Emma chose to
embody the then-late member of the royal family at her twenty-
fifth birthday celebration.

Turning the page, what I found next totally shook me.

9/2/97
Café Luxembourg

Dear Diary,
I've just come from a reading with my personal astrologer. It

was a long overdue meeting, and the main reason I came on this
trip to NYC. I was anxious to hear what she had to say about
the upcoming events in my life. As always, Miss Zelda did not
disappoint.

Seriously?

My favorite astrologer was Emma Woods's personal zodiacal
guru?

#quellesurprise #mindblown #holycrap

"Hon, listen to this . . ." Excited beyond belief, I turned toward
JP. "Emma mentions Miss Zelda in this entry. She even met with
her for a tarot card reading in September 1997, right after Princess
Diana died."

Beneath the blanket, Jackson let out a low grumble. He did this
on a regular basis. We couldn't tell if it was his not-so-subtle way of
letting us know he was there, so don't squish him . . . or if he was
just plain annoyed by the sudden movement.

"Easy, killer!" JP warned the little dog. "You need to stop reading that old journal."

"But it's sooo good. And what if we find something important?"

He set his phone down in his lap and looked at me. "Something
important like . . . ?"

"I don't know. Like something about the night Emma died," I
countered. "Then when Fiona gets back from the tour, we can surprise her with some good news."

JP ran a hand through his thick hair. "I don't know, Pete. It just
feels like we're being nosy."

Considering his words, I paused for a moment. "I get where
you're coming from, but . . . I think we owe it to Fiona to crack
this case. Maybe Miss Zelda is the key?"

JP still seemed unsure, as he went back to his scrolling. "You're
gonna do what you want anyway."

"I know I am," I said, smiling impishly.

With that, I resumed reading the diary entry dated 9/2/97 . . .

During our tarot card reading, Miss Zelda drew the Page of Wands. She told me the card signifies "a bright, enthusiastic child who is full of spunk but easily bored and even naughty at times." Hearing this made me wonder if it could be a message about Fiona. At only six months, she is already developing her own personality. Every day with her is such a joy! I look forward to all the changes that she'll go through the older she gets.

Or maybe Miss Zelda was referring to our housekeeper's son in her reading about the "naughty" child?

I can't shake off a feeling of unease that's been troubling me for some time. He's only nine, but something about Royce just isn't right. He's always lurking about Woods Hall, staring at me and making me totally uncomfortable. It's like he's some demon boy or something and he wants me gone.

I know it's not his fault that he was born into this life, and he has to grow up in someone else's home. I also realize that he lived in Woods Hall long before I married Bill and moved in. Maybe I'm just being paranoid?

Back to Miss Zelda's tarot card reading. The most concerning card that came up was the Death card. She explained that it doesn't always mean a literal death. Sometimes it's just an end, possibly of an interest or a relationship (ES?)—but no matter what, it should lead to an increased sense of self-awareness.

I'm trying not to worry too much. As Miss Zelda said, "Sometimes we need to let go of things to make way for new opportunities." I'm so grateful for her wisdom and guidance, and I'm super excited to see what my future holds.

xoxo

Em

ES!

The initials could only stand for one person . . . Evan Savage.

#loveaffair #secret #quelscandale

"Hon, guess what I just now read? Emma mentioned Miss Zelda drawing a tarot card indicating the end of a relationship . . . and the initials ES."

JP kept staring at his phone screen. He moved on from checking the comments on our dogs' social media to perusing the latest post on the official *Domestic Partners* page. I could see the reflection of the screen in his eyes as he scrolled through. His fingers moved deftly, tapping and swiping as he read. "Who's ES?"

"Duh! Remember, Fairway Bob said Emma and Evan Savage were having a torrid love affair before she died?"

JP furrowed his brows. "Oh, right. So . . . ?"

I shrugged. "I guess this confirms it in Emma's own words. That's all."

JP nodded thoughtfully, before finally shutting off his phone. After placing it on the nightstand beside the bed, he rolled over and turned off his light. "Night, hon."

He didn't even bother giving me a kiss.

#sad

I stared up at the cracks in the plaster ceiling. The silence in the room was heavy, broken only by the soft sound of Clydie's heavy breathing.

I knew I should *probably* roll over and go to sleep myself. Instead, I picked up my own phone and checked, yet again, for a response from Mindee McQueen to my direct message. Still nothing, but this time there was promise. The word *seen* now appeared in the bottom righthand corner, below the bubble.

With renewed hope that I might soon hear from the Miss Great Lakes 1992 first runner-up, I returned to the pages of Emma Woods's private journal . . .

9/26/97
Detroit

Dear Diary,

I'm on a modeling assignment for Renaissance Advertising. It's been a long day, and I'm totally *wiped out. But I have to admit it's been exhilarating to be back in front of the camera. There's one thing that's been bothering me, though. One of the marketing execs from the agency has been getting a little too flirty, and it's starting to make me uncomfortable. While I appreciate the flattery, it's becoming a bit* too *much.*

It all started during a break when we were both standing outside, smoking. This person came up to me and started complimenting me on my looks. "You're even more beautiful in person than in the pictures" and "I can't believe someone like you exists on this planet." Talk about cheesy!

I laughed it off at first, but they kept going, telling me how much they wanted to take me out—even though they know I'm married—and how they couldn't stop thinking about me. I tried to politely decline the advances, but this person didn't seem to take the hint.

Now, every time they look at me, I feel like I'm being undressed by their eyes. I'm not sure how to handle the situation. At first, I thought this person was just being friendly. Now I'm worried they might be obsessed with me. I can't shake off the feeling that they might do something rash *or try to* harm *me in some way.*

Okay. I found *three* odd things about the journal entry I just read.

1. Emma didn't conclude it with her usual *xoxo*, followed by *Em*.

2. She didn't name the marketing exec who flirted with her shamelessly, and who she thought might do *something rash* or try to *harm* her in some way.

3. Emma referred to the marketing exec as *this person* and *they*. I had a feeling, twenty-five years ago, while being nonbinary probably existed as a gender expression, it wasn't a thing the way it was in the second decade of the twenty-first century.

Emma also didn't refer to the person as *he* or *him* . . . so maybe the person was, in fact, a *she* and a *her*? There was *one* person JP and I both knew who fit both these descriptions . . .

Cheri Maison.

Promptly, I reached for my phone and pulled up her contact info. We first came to know the rising Realtor after we finished taping *Domestic Partners* season two. Cheri was hired as the listing agent for the newly renovated property, a stab in the back to her archnemesis, my bestie Campbell Sellers.

I should've known the call would go directly to voicemail, being after ten p.m. I know *I* wouldn't answer if somebody had the nerve to bug me that late at night!

"Hey, there! It's PJ Penwell," I said, waiting for the beep. "Might you be free for brunch with me and JP in the morning? There's something we'd like to talk with you about."

If her house-showing schedule was anything like Cam's, chances are she *wouldn't* have time to meet with us. But we needed to figure out the identity of the unnamed marketing exec referenced in Emma's diary entry.

Hopefully, Cheri would hold the key.

$\mathcal{H}$alloween 1997

She admired herself in the mirror.

Although she was African American—and not a white woman from New Zealand—dressed in leather armor and a long black wig, the marketing executive bore a striking resemblance to the popular warrior princess from television, Xena. More than anything, she wanted to impress the party's hostess with her outfit.

For months, Cheri had been nursing a crush on the former-beauty-queen-turned-model, and she hoped to finally catch her attention. She couldn't wait to see the younger woman's reaction when she strolled through the wide front door at Woods Hall.

She arrived, fashionably late, to find the soirée already in full swing. Excited to show off her costume and mingle with the other guests, she strutted through Woods Hall. She felt fearless in the battle gear she'd donned for the occasion, like she could take on the world. Or at least find the nerve to make known her true feelings for Emma Woods.

Immediately, she spotted the Cash twins, Tom and Terry, dressed as animated TV brothers Beavis and Butt-Head. She wasn't a fan of their cartoon antics but found the rubber masks a perfect choice for the pair.

She didn't have a lot of gay male friends. As an out lesbian, Cheri kept to her own kind. The LGBT crowd in Metro Detroit was odd in that regard. There were boy bars like Shout!, the one Tom Cash recently opened down in Fernridge, and there were girl bars like Nexus in Royal Heights. But rarely did the clientele of either mix, at one venue or the other.

Still, she couldn't help but feel a sense of camaraderie with the Cash twins. They were both open about their sexuality, and she'd admitted to hers only a few years earlier. It was nice to be around people who understood her. Sometimes, she felt so alone in the world.

Three glasses of Dom Pérignon later, the thirty-year-old commanded her courage and went in search of the object of her affection. She cornered the birthday girl in the hallway, just off the kitchen, relieved to find no one else around to interrupt their private moment.

Emma greeted her warmly. She leaned in for an air-kiss, placing a soft hand on the slightly older woman's shoulder. The touch from Renaissance Advertising's top model sent shockwaves through Cheri's aching body. Emma looked stunning in the white wedding gown and diamond tiara she wore as the recently deceased Lady Diana Spencer. But a pang of jealousy poked at Cheri as she reminded herself of a cold hard truth: Emma was married to Bill Woods, a man who didn't love his wife the way she did.

Taking in Cheri's outfit, Emma questioned the costume.

Cheri's face fell at having to explain the identity she'd assumed for the party.

Once clarified, Emma completely understood. She confessed to not watching the TV show that served as Cheri's inspiration.

Her disappointment was profound. After going to so much effort to impress, the fact that Emma didn't even know the character she'd worked so hard to personify was more than just a letdown. She hoped the twinge of embarrassment on her dark face wasn't too evident.

Emma apologized, then she at last complimented Cheri's appearance.

Lightheaded and tipsy from all the alcohol she'd imbibed, she decided to make her move. She brushed a lock of Emma's honey-blond hair, styled to perfection to resemble the late princess. She wished the young woman a *happy birthday* . . .

Before leaning in to kiss her.

As she closed the distance between herself and Emma, a nervous excitement overcame Cheri. But as their lips met, she was suddenly filled with a sense of dread.

What if Emma didn't feel the same way?

What if this ruined their relationship forever?

As the kiss ended, she pulled back slightly, looking into Emma's piercing blue eyes for any sign of reciprocation. Emma stared back at her, a small smile playing at the corner of her lips. Cheri Maison's heart leapt with hope.

Maybe this could be the start of something new?

Chapter 31

We sat in stunned silence.

As the former marketing executive recounted her experience, JP and I listened intently. Around us, the sights, sounds, and smells of The Depot Diner faded away. Fully understanding the severity of the situation, we found ourselves completely engrossed in the fifty-five-year-old woman's tale from when she was just thirty. All we could do was focus on the sound of her voice and the expression on her pretty face.

Her short hair, dyed a vibrant blond, framed her warm smile. She always wore minimal makeup, allowing her natural beauty to shine through. Her clothing was always stylish but professional. Today, she sported a cream-colored blazer over a simple white blouse, worn with sleek black slacks and black suede pumps. Her accessories were tasteful and understated, a gold watch and a pair of pearl stud earrings that complimented her dark skin.

"So, what happened after you kissed Emma at her birthday-Halloween party?" I asked, utterly entranced and needing more details.

Cheri's hazel eyes sparkled at the memory, a surge of emotions flooding through her. "Surprisingly, she kissed me back."

"That's good, I guess," said JP, joining in after sitting silent for so long.

Her blissful expression spoke volumes. As she talked, Cheri gestured with her hands, emphasizing the points she was trying to make. "I'm telling you guys, I was flying. I don't think I ever felt like that before. It was a mix of joy, excitement, and disbelief all rolled into one. After the kiss, I pulled away and just stared at Emma. She stared right back, not once breaking eye contact. I told her I hope she didn't mind what I did . . ."

The words caught in Cheri's throat, causing them to trail off, and in their place leave a painful lump.

"How did Emma respond when you said that?" JP inquired, picking at a lone home fry left on his plate.

Cheri's cheeks flushed with emotion, and her body tensed up as she struggled to hold back a sob. She looked down at her tightly clenched fists and took a few deep breaths, trying to regain her composure. "Not good."

"Oh no!" I had a bad feeling this story of unrequited love was about to take a turn for the worst.

As the sadness took hold, Cheri's posture slumped, and she appeared defeated and broken. Her normally bright and engaging personality vanished, replaced by a deep sadness. She blinked rapidly as her eyes welled up. "Emma told me, in no uncertain terms, she was *straight*. She reminded me of her marriage—to a *man*—and when I tried explaining, she told me to save my breath. It hit me like a punch in the gut to hear her talk that way. She was so . . . cold."

Trying to put myself in the place of a lesbian woman living in the mid-1990s, shortly after Ellen came out publicly, I said the only thing I could think to say. "Wow, Cher. I'm sorry."

"I told Emma, I made a mistake. I thought there was something between us. When I said it, she practically laughed in my face and told me I thought wrong. Our relationship was purely professional. Nothing more. We weren't even friends."

"You're kidding? She invited you to her birthday party," said JP, amazed by this new picture being painted of the deceased beauty queen and model.

"She invited everyone from the ad agency. Guess I was just another name on the guest list."

As I processed Cheri's account of Emma Wheeler-Woods's cruel intentions, I felt a mix of shock, disappointment, and betrayal. Up until then, I'd given Emma the benefit of the doubt and assumed she was an innocent victim in the events leading up to her downfall. However, this revelation shattered that perception and left me reeling.

Maybe Vicky Marshall was right in her negative opinion of the young woman?

But Fairway Bob counted Emma among his closest friends.

Evan Savage apparently cared for her as well, based on the extent of what we'd come to learn of his personal past with the automotive heiress.

But then Bob said he suspected Evan of lying when he swore he didn't kill Emma.

I didn't know *what* to think anymore. Other than being frustrated and angry at someone I never even met, for her callous response, and for the way she seemingly used Cheri's feelings as a means of manipulation.

"I realize she had a lot to drink that night. If Emma was sober, maybe she wouldn't've acted the way she did. Then I started to panic," Cheri confessed.

"Why? It was an honest, drunken mistake. Happens to the best of us queers," I teased, attempting to lighten the mood. "You didn't do anything wrong. Not in the grand scheme of things."

"Sure. But Wheeler Automotive was one of Renaissance's biggest clients, and Emma was the face of her father's company. If my actions caused the agency to lose out on all that business, all that billable income . . . Quinn Marshall would've fired me faster than white on rice."

"So, did you apologize?" JP asked, fully invested in the way things played out a quarter of a century prior.

"You bet I did! I humbled myself right there in that hallway. I said: *Please, forgive me. I didn't mean to overstep my bounds, Miss Wheeler. You wanna know what she said to that? My name is Mrs. Woods."*

"Talk about a slap in the face!" I proclaimed.

Granted, Emma was twenty-five years old at the time of this altercation. I needed to remind myself that—no matter how much prestige she'd gained as a beauty queen and fashion model, or how much money she'd been born into—she was practically still a child. I know *I* could never handle the pressure and responsibilities she faced at such a young age. Or that Fiona was facing now, as one half of a Grammy-nominated musical duo.

Sure, I was a (quote-unquote) bestselling author, with deadlines to meet, and a successful television show to cohost, but . . . no matter what level of notoriety I achieved in my career, I still felt like the same old Peter James Penwell who grew up in humble Madison Park, aka *Madisontucky*, the son of a small-business owner and homemaker-slash-daycare provider.

Cheri laughed in spite of herself. "You can bet I spent the rest of that party hiding out in a dark corner with a drink in my hand. *Mortified* doesn't even begin to describe the way I felt for kissing Emma."

"You didn't see anything strange after that?" I said, remembering the reason we asked Cheri to meet with us for breakfast that morning.

"Anything strange, like . . . ?" Cheri signaled for our server to bring over more coffee. Had it been after five p.m., I bet she'd request something stiffer.

"What Pete's asking is . . . Do you have any idea who might've killed Emma Woods?" said JP, intervening. "Presuming she didn't fall from the balcony at Woods Hall . . . or jump off on her own."

Cheri's fingers fidgeted. She twisted the sapphire ring on her left hand. She avoided eye contact as she avoided answering the question posed to her. Glancing around the diner, she struggled to conjure the correct response. "See? That's just it. I barely remember being at the party after that point. Guys, please believe I am *not* proud of myself when I say this . . . When Emma rejected my advances, I sought solace in the bottom of a bottle. Zima, to be exact," she said, pulling a sour face. "Be thankful they got rid of that stuff before your time. Talk about nasty!"

"Aw, man! I always wondered what it tasted like. Was it like Sprite? Because I heard it was lemon-lime flavored," I said, wishing I could live vicariously through Cheri Maison's youth.

"Maybe if they added an entire five-pound bag of sugar to a single bottle," she said bitterly. "All I can say is . . . when they brought it back in 2017, Zima was the last blast from my past I wanted."

JP tapped his fingers on the tabletop, showing his impatience at my going off on a '90s-infused tangent. "Okay, Cheri. Well, we're asking if you know what might've happened to Emma Woods because Pete found her old diary from 1997."

Cheri's wideset eyes grew even wider at the mention of the old journal I discovered in the secret drawer at Woods Hall. "Did you guys read it?"

Reaching into my black leather Shinola messenger bag, I removed the object now up for discussion. "I did."

"Show her September twenty-sixth," said JP, with a thrust of his dimpled chin.

Obeying the order, I opened the leather-bound book to the entry in question and read aloud one phrase . . .

"I can't shake off the feeling that they might do <u>something rash</u> or try to <u>harm</u> me in some way."

Cheri's dark face grew pale. She looked uneasy and unsettled at the words written by Emma Woods. Even though she wasn't mentioned by name, she wore her guilt like an albatross. Around us, all we could hear was the clinking of silverware and dishes as she stopped to consider the magnitude of the accusation.

After a few beats, Cheri cleared her throat and broke her silence. "I can't believe Emma wrote that about me," she said, her voice quivering slightly. "I loved her . . . I would never harm her in any way. But here's the thing . . ."

She paused briefly, as if weighing the consequences that might come from disclosing her next statement.

"It's like I said," continued Cheri, albeit reluctantly. "I have zero memory of the rest of that night. In fact, I'm pretty sure I blacked out. I woke up early the next morning in my own car, parked on the side of Woods Way. I started the engine to drive home, and the radio turned on. That's when I heard the report . . . Emma Woods was *dead*."

"Okay . . . So?" said JP, failing to see where Cheri's story was leading us.

"So . . . I have no idea if I killed her or not."

The server arrived at our table with a steaming pot of coffee.

Chapter 32

JP and I stayed behind at The Depot.

After Cheri left, we waited for the check to be dropped off at our table. We'd offered to pick up the tab, since she gave up her morning home showings to meet with us.

While we weren't any further in our quest to catch a killer, we did learn some valuable info: Emma Woods had a mean side. I found it interesting that the victims in most murder mysteries weren't the nicest of people . . . and, often, they *deserved* to die. But was that also the case in the case we were now trying to solve?

"I don't know what to do next," I said, running a hand through my hair, exasperated. "Another dead end."

JP nodded, his expression grim. "It's so frustrating. We've gone over all the evidence, but nothing's adding up."

"It's like we're missing a piece of the puzzle, but we don't even know what the puzzle looks like."

JP tapped on the table, lost in thought. "Maybe we need to start thinking outside the box? Look for connections to Emma Woods we haven't explored yet. Or maybe we could talk to some of the people at Emma's birthday party again, see if they remember anything else?"

Hearing this, I felt a renewed sense of determination. "I definitely think we should ask Evan about what Bob told us."

"I don't know," said JP, suddenly sounding less optimistic.

"We need to find out if he lied to Bob."

"Even if he did, he's not gonna admit he killed Emma Woods. The guy's got a husband and daughter. He'll go to prison for a very long time if he confesses."

I nodded, understanding the gravity of the situation. "I know. But we have to try, at least."

JP leaned back in his chair, a thoughtful look on his handsome face. "Maybe we can talk to Stephen? He's been with Evan for over twenty years now. By this point, he's gotta know about the affair his husband had with Emma Woods."

"Yes. But if we do talk to Stephen, he might not tell us the truth. You know, that whole thing about spouses not testifying against each other and all that?"

"Good point. If someone asked me about something *you* did, and you didn't want anyone knowing, I wouldn't rat you out either."

I drummed my fingers on the Formica, trying to think of a new angle we could pursue. Then, an idea struck me. The diary lay on the table in front of us. "Maybe we should read another entry?"

"We shouldn't be reading that thing at all. Save it for Fiona, she'll be back on Monday. Let *her* read it and figure out who killed her mother . . . if anyone even did."

I picked up the old leather-bound book. "Hon, this is the only real lead we've got. These are Emma's own words in here. I used to keep a journal when I was younger. I wrote down all my most personal and private thoughts. It was the one place I could be honest about my life at the time. If somebody wronged me—or I thought they wanted to *kill* me—I, for sure, would write about it."

JP looked doubtful. "But you've already read so many of those entries. What makes you think there's anything new to find?"

"You're right. It's probably more of the same," I admitted. "But it's not gonna hurt."

JP sighed and leaned back in his seat. "Okay, fine. But promise me something, Pete. If we come across *anything* in that diary—any-thing that points to anyone as Emma Woods's killer—then we give it to Nick Paczki. *Do not pass Go, do not collect two hundred dollars.*"

I couldn't see how Monopoly had anything to do with the price of chai at Starbucks, a paraphrased line from *Blue Tuesday* we often quoted. But still, I agreed with my partner's proposal to let the authorities take over our unofficial investigation.

Flipping through the diary, I stopped at an entry dated a week before Emma's death. As I began to read, JP leaned forward, his eyes focused on me as mine skimmed the page. "What's it say?" he asked eagerly.

"Believe it or not, it's about Mindee McQueen . . ."

10/24/97
Woods Hall

> *Dear Diary,*
> *Today I met up with Mindee at the city clerk's office, down-town. It was* <u>*sooo*</u> *good to see her again after* <u>*five*</u> *long years. It felt like no time had passed since we had our little tiff. And guess what? She was* <u>*more*</u> *than happy to help me out with my prob-lem.*
> *Now that this terrible ordeal is finally behind me, I can* <u>*fi-nally*</u> *get on with my life. But I keep wondering, will I ever truly be happy? I hope so!*
> *xoxo*
> *Em*

A waitress bustled by, carrying a tray loaded with plates of pan-cakes, eggs, and bacon. In her haste, she bumped against our table. JP and I were so engrossed in the pages of the old diary, we hardly noticed the disturbance.

He glanced up from his coffee and raised an eyebrow. "What *problem* do you think Emma needed help with?"

I chewed on my lower lip, trying to picture the possible predicament referenced in the diary entry. "Good question. I'd say we could always ask Mindee . . . if she'd ever respond to my message."

Call it *fate* or *coincidence* or, as my college Playwriting professor used to say (still not sure why), *call it asparagus*, but . . . when I begrudgingly picked up my phone to habitually check my DMs, I made a surprising discovery in the form of a reply from Mindee McQueen!

Hi PJ,

Please forgive my delayed reply to your message. Yes, I was a contestant in the Miss Great Lakes pageant back in 1992. Emma was my very best friend at the time. All these years later, I still can't get over losing her.

As for your offer, I'm a big fan of your TV show. I would love to be a guest on an episode and to meet Emma's daughter, all grown up. But first, there's something important you should know. Please give me a call at your convenience. My number is 248-555-9840.

Thanks, Mindee

I couldn't believe our good luck. I knocked back the ice from the bottom of my water glass and crunched on it. "What should we do?" I asked JP, even though I already knew the answer.

"Call Mindee and see what she says."

The thought of speaking to a stranger made me more than a little anxious. Rarely did I call anybody on the actual phone, other than my mom. Or maybe if I had an author interview and it was the interviewer's preferred method of communication. Then, I'd have no other option. But I kept complaining about not hearing from Mindee McQueen. Now that I had, I needed to take advantage of any light she might shed on the mysterious death of her dear friend Emma Woods.

"Well, I really don't wanna talk to her in the middle of the breakfast rush," I decided.

So, we paid our bill at the counter cash register and stepped outside into the midmorning.

A gentle breeze brushed against our faces, carrying with it the scent of autumn leaves that were just starting to turn orange and yellow. Soon, it would be perfect weather for a trip to Yates Cider Mill with Clydie Boy and Jackson. Never did we attempt going in September. Too crowded . . . and far too many bees! But an October day—midweek while the kids were all still in school—made for a nice escape from the suburbs.

I could just picture the afternoon we'd spend out in the rural countryside, among the rolling hills and meandering river, the trees ablaze with fall colors and the smell of woodsmoke and ripe apples in the air. The rustic red mill, with its gigantic wood wheel, always reminded me of high school. On weekends, Cam and I would make the thirty-mile drive from Madison Park with our drama club friends, and we'd eat way too many donuts and drink so much cider that we'd all end up with bellyaches. JP hadn't ever been to a cider mill before we moved to Michigan. I guess they weren't a thing where he grew up in Pittsburgh. Instead, when he was a kid he went apple picking with his parents. To me, that sounded like *work*, and not something I'd ever consider a fun time.

As I dialed the number Mindee McQueen gave me, my heart began beating faster with anticipation. The phone rang a few times before I heard a female voice in my ear.

"Hello?"

"Hi, is this Mindee?"

"Yes, it is," she answered tentatively.

"Hi, Mindee. This is PJ Penwell from *Domestic Partners* on HDTV. I just saw your direct message . . ."

The woman on the other end of the line paused slightly. "Of course! Sorry it took me a while to get back to you. I was out of the country, traveling."

This explained the recent posts on Mindee's page, taken amidst the ancient temples and gardens of Bali and Bangkok, with their colorful roof tiles and lush greenery.

"No problem. You said there's something important we should know," I said when I couldn't think of anything else to add.

Mindee McQueen paused again before responding. "There is . . . Could you and your partner come out to my lake house in Clarkstown? I'd rather not discuss what I need to tell you over the phone."

After we hung up, she texted me the address. With the old diary in tow, JP and I headed home, ready to pursue our newest lead. Maybe Emma Woods's former best friend and archrival would be our key witness?

Before getting on the road, we let Clyde and Jack outside for a quick potty break. Then, we slipped the boys a chicken-flavored edible dog bone, hopped into our SUV, and headed north on I-75.

On the drive up the interstate, we both felt a glimmer of hope for the first time in days.

Chapter 33

My pulse quickened the closer we got to Clarkstown.

As JP navigated the winding highway, I stared out the passenger side window, taking in the picturesque scenery. The golden leaves of the trees lining the road shimmered in the autumn sunlight. October was officially here, which meant we had a little less than four weeks left to finish the renovations at Woods Hall . . . and to keep the promise we made to Fiona.

Hopefully whatever Mindee McQueen wanted us to know would help us in our hunt for Emma Woods's killer.

"So, what do you think?" my partner asked, disrupting the hush between us.

"It's a nice place to visit, but I wouldn't wanna live all the way out here."

I couldn't imagine feeling comfortable residing in such a rural community. While the natural beauty of the area was undeniable, the worries about our safety as a same-sex couple outweighed any desire I might've had to own lakefront property.

JP turned to me, a hint of a smile on his lips. "I meant, what do you think about meeting Mindee McQueen?"

The whole ride out to her lake house, I couldn't shake off the angst I felt since our earlier phone call. She sounded so cryptic and cagey. Her insistence on discussing what she knew about Emma Woods in person had only fueled my curiosity. Yet at the same time, it filled me with anxiety.

As an author, I'd always been drawn to the mysterious and the unknown. Now that we were on the cusp of uncovering something potentially significant, I couldn't help feeling concerned over what that something might turn out to be. But JP's presence beside me in the SUV was a reassuring reminder that I wasn't in this thing alone. Together, we'd face whatever challenges came our way.

"Thar she blows!" my fiancé joked, gesturing through the front windshield.

Towering pine trees and a serene-looking lake greeted us as we drove up the dirt driveway to the two-story cabin. The structure was made of sturdy logs and had a steep pitched roof that gave it a cozy and inviting feel. The wraparound porch was wide and welcoming, with a row of rocking chairs facing the stunning view.

"Wow," I murmured when we pulled up in front of the house. "This is amazing."

"Nice, huh?" said JP, putting the vehicle in park.

Stepping out of the car, the clean country air filled our lungs, as if we were breathing in nature itself. The mix of pine needles, wildflowers, and the fresh lake water reminded me just how toxic living in suburbia could be.

Suddenly, the front door to the cabin opened, and a slightly older woman with chestnut hair and emerald eyes stepped out. She resembled the pictures posted on social media closely enough, so we had no problem identifying her. Her outfit that day consisted of cream-colored capri pants, a button-down blouse in a bright coral, and off-white sneakers. Around her neck she draped a pale pink cashmere shawl to ward off the late morning chill.

She waved excitedly. "Hello! You must be PJ and JP. I recognize you from your TV show. I'm Mindee."

We ambled over to the wraparound porch. "Thanks for meeting with us. Your home is beautiful," I said, paying due props.

Mindee smiled humbly. "Thank you. It's not much, but I do adore it."

If a two-story log cabin on a private lake wasn't much, I'd hate to see Mindee's version of opulence.

The interior of the log cabin had a rustic and welcoming feel, with warm colors and raw materials that blended in perfectly with the surroundings. As we entered, we found ourselves in a cozy living area with hardwood floors and walls made from actual logs. The lumber varied in size, with natural knots and grains visible throughout. The spaces in between were filled with a light gray mortar to create a tight seal and helped insulate the home. Left in their natural state, there was no paint or finish on the wood. Instead, the organic appeal of the original texture created an inviting atmosphere, making it the perfect place to curl up with a good book or enjoy a hot cup of tea on a cold day.

The rugged yet elegant look of the cabin's wood logs also gave the lake house a quaint charm, enhanced by the addition of carefully chosen furnishings and décor. A pair of supple leather armchairs flanked the large stone fireplace in the center of the room, while a woven rattan chair with a plaid cushion added a lighter and airier feel.

This was where we sat with Mindee McQueen as she began to share her story . . .

"I never married. Instead, I spent the past twenty-five years enjoying life, traveling, and taking it easy," she said with a contented sigh.

"In her diary, Emma mentioned you worked at the city clerk's office down in Detroit," I said, attempting to guide her toward the topic we'd come to discuss.

"I did. But I . . . came into some money, so I quit working altogether."

The way Mindee hesitated mid-remark piqued JP's interest. "That sounds like the dream. Not that I don't enjoy what Pete and I do on *Domestic Partners* . . . But what's your secret?"

Mindee crossed her long legs, shifting uncomfortably in her seat. Her fidgeting seemed to convey an uneasiness, as if she was reluctant to share more about her personal windfall. "No secret, really. More like some unexpected good fortune. But I didn't invite you guys here to talk about me."

Sensing her discomfort, I followed Mindee's lead and switched back to our original subject. "Emma also mentioned in her diary you helped her with a problem. Can you tell us about that?"

Mindee's expression turned serious. "That's *exactly* what I brought you here to talk about."

She went on to explain that the journal entry dated 10/24/97 was related to correcting the identity of baby Fiona's father on her birth certificate.

Neither JP nor I could believe the unexpected twist. But we both understood the meaning behind Mindee's disclosure.

"We already know about the affair between Emma and Evan Savage," JP said, trying to keep his tone gentle, so as not to insult our hostess.

Mindee's green eyes widened in surprise. "Oh, I see," she said softly, taken aback. "Let me guess . . . Bob Kravitz told you."

The three of us shared a laugh. As we partook in the moment of camaraderie and connection, our bodies relaxed, and our shoulders dropped. We sat in comfortable silence for a few minutes, basking in the warmth of the fire and the joy of our newfound friendship.

"So, Evan is Fiona's biological father? Not Bill Woods," I said, just wanting to be sure. "Okay. But why did Emma decide to change the name on her daughter's birth certificate a week before Halloween?"

Mindee took a deep breath before resuming her story. "All I know is . . . Emma showed up at the city clerk's office, looking like a complete mess. She asked me to fix Fiona's birth certificate to say Bill wasn't her father. I was shocked, to say the least. Emma told me about the affair with Evan Savage, and how he was Fiona's real dad."

JP leaned forward in his seat, his face becoming grave. "Did you go through with it?"

"I wasn't gonna . . . at first. But Emma begged me. She told me she planned on telling Evan the truth at her birthday party. She wanted to run away with him, and she needed to make sure Bill had no legal claim to Fiona when she did. So, I helped her."

"Did Emma offer you any sort of proof . . . or did you just take her word for it?" I asked, not meaning to sound skeptical, but wondering about Mindee's mindset at the time she agreed to do something totally illegal.

"I didn't need any proof. No matter what went down between me and Emma, she was still my best friend. She'd never lie to me about something so serious."

"So, you made the change on Fiona's birth certificate. Then what happened?" JP casually asked.

"As a show of thanks, Emma invited me to her birthday party. She said she wanted us to be close again. When I arrived at Woods Hall, Bill was *not* happy. He demanded to know why I was there and told me to get out. But Emma stood up to him. She informed Bill it was none of his business who she invited to her own party. They argued, and I excused myself. It was the last time I saw her alive."

Her voice shaking slightly, Mindee continued with her tale. "After Emma died, I knew something was off. I suspected Bill had something to do with her falling off that balcony. So, I confronted him. He denied having anything to do with it, of course. He informed me he already knew all about Evan being Fiona's father. But if word got out Bill Woods's wife had another man's baby, it wouldn't look so good. So, he offered me a large sum of money to keep my mouth shut."

I took this as being the unexpected financial good fortune Mindee mentioned before.

She paused, her eyes locking onto ours. Her voice was low and somber as she wrapped things up. "All these years, I've regretted taking that money. I didn't know what else to do. Bill threatened to turn me in for tampering with Fiona's birth certificate. At the time, I thought it was right to keep quiet. She seemed better off being the great-great-granddaughter of a lumber baron. But it's time for Fiona to learn the truth about her real father."

Nodding in agreement, the significance of this latest development weighed heavy on my heart. It was going to be a tough conversation with Fiona and Evan that JP and I would soon need to have.

I hoped they could both handle the consequences of Emma Woods's past actions.

$\mathscr{Halloween}$ 1997

Evan watched intently from across the ballroom.

In front of all their costumed guests, Emma's husband, Bill, presented her with a lavish diamond necklace. Upon receiving such a fine piece of jewelry, the former beauty queen's piercing blue eyes pooled with tears.

The twenty-seven-year-old marine sergeant knew the young wife and mother wasn't crying out of joy, but out of sorrow. The marriage between the automotive heiress and the lumber baron's great-grandson was nothing but a sham. Bill didn't love Emma, and she didn't love him . . . and Evan was aware of both these facts.

Over the course of the evening, he tried getting close to her, so they could sneak off somewhere and be alone together; so he could comfort her and shower her with the love and affection she so rightly deserved on that special night. He knew she wasn't intentionally ignoring him. As the Halloween party hostess and birthday girl, Emma Woods's attention was in high demand. Evan understood this.

By the time for the evening's entertainment arrived, he was two sheets to the wind. The young drag queen known as Harmony House strutted her stuff across the ballroom floor, putting on a spectacle of a show. Evan got a kick out of the name she chose for her alternate persona, after the popular Metro Detroit record store

chain. As she sang live to an oldie but a goody ("Waterfalls" by
TLC), to his surprise, the twenty-one-year-old with the cocoa-
colored skin caught Evan's eye.

But it wasn't the first time he felt this sort of desire.

For many years, he struggled to come to terms with his bisexu-
ality, after being raised in a conservative household. At the age of
nineteen, Evan joined the United States Marine Corps as a means of
escaping his attraction to other men. He knew being openly gay
was not accepted in the military, and he thought by joining, he
could suppress his attraction to men. He was looking for a way to fit
in, to belong, and to be part of something bigger than himself. Evan
believed the structure and discipline would help him control his
longings and conform to the expectations of society.

It might've been all the beer he consumed at the party. It
might've been Emma's unintentional slight. But before Evan knew
what was happening, he discovered himself being dragged into a
dark corner.

He insisted it was all a misunderstanding. Somehow, Ms. Harmony misread the looks of admiration he gave her during her
performance. He felt a rush of conflicting emotions: confusion,
embarrassment, and a strange flutter in his stomach that he couldn't
quite explain.

To silence his protests, the drag queen placed a finger to Evan's
full lips . . . and she kissed him.

A blood curdling cry rang out.

Emma appeared just in time to see the man she loved in the
throes of passion with another man. His spirit sank at the sight of
her standing there, her expression a mix of shock and devastation.
He could feel the weight of his infidelity bearing down on him, the
crushing realization that he'd betrayed the person he cared about
most in the world. He realized she'd caught him in the act. He
knew he couldn't make excuses or apologize enough. He was a
cheater, no better than Emma's own husband. He'd have to live
with the guilt and shame of his actions for the rest of his life.

She ran off toward the front staircase in the grand entrance hallway.

Quickly, Evan headed to the kitchen and slipped into the secret passageway leading up to the third floor of Woods Hall. As he scaled the stairs, his mind raced with regret and guilt, his heart pounding in his barrel chest. When he reached the master bedroom, he found the door locked. He begged Emma to allow him inside. He needed to explain what she just saw. But no response came from within.

He could hear her muffled sobs, and his heart broke. He told her how much he loved her. He didn't mean for the kiss to happen. He was a fool, and he got caught up in a drunken moment.

Emma remained silent, refusing to hear him out.

Chapter 34

The nutty aroma of fresh coffee filled the house.

As JP and I settled ourselves in the sunken living room, Evan Savage-Singer emerged from the kitchen. He held a clear carafe in one hand and three cups in the other.

"Here we go!" Evan said with a smile. He set the pot down on a glass-top table and began pouring steaming liquid into our ceramic mugs.

Taking a sip, I savored the rich, bold flavor of the hot beverage and gazed about the mid-century modern home.

The living room was a beautiful space that effortlessly blended classic style with contemporary design. It featured high ceilings and large windows, allowing in plenty of natural light, making everything feel bright and open. The main seating area centered around a low-slung sofa with clean lines and a solid gray fabric, flanked by a set of matching armchairs with angled legs.

A large wooden console table spanned the length of one wall, offering ample storage for books and decorative objects. Opposite, an abstract piece of artwork hung, its bold shapes painted in vibrant shades of blue, green, and yellow. A pair of vintage floor lamps with geometric shades provided additional lighting and served as eye-catching accents in the room.

Evan settled into one of the armchairs, across from me and JP on the sofa. The khaki shorts he wore revealed a pair of rather hairy legs, as he crossed his feet at the ankles. "So, what's up? You sounded pretty desperate to talk when you called, Peter."

"Sorry, I didn't mean to . . ." I took a deep breath, trying to steady my nerves. "You sure we shouldn't wait for Stephen?"

Evan leaned forward and perched on the edge of his seat. "He might be a while. He's out shopping with Melody, his drag daughter. They got some charity Extravaganza coming up at Glitterbox. Heard they asked you guys to perform in it."

"They did," I said once I realized JP wasn't about to speak up, trying to pretend the whole encounter was just some bad nightmare. "And it looks like we're going to."

"Awesome! Can't wait to see you both in full-on drag mode."

Neither could we!

"Well, if this is about my affair with Emma Woods," Evan continued, "maybe it's better Stephen's *not* here?"

I could totally sympathize with the older man, hearing his statement. While I recognized the importance of being truthful with one's partner, I understood how difficult it might be for Evan to talk openly about a past relationship in front of his husband.

"We discovered something about Fiona . . . Something we think you should know," said JP, forging ahead.

Evan stared at us, attempting to read our faces for any sign of trouble. "Is everything okay?"

Carefully, I placed my cup on the coffee table. I took another deep breath and looked back up at Evan. It was time to have this difficult discussion, no matter how uncomfortable it might be.

"Do you remember a friend of Emma Woods's named Mindee McQueen?" I said, before rehashing the conversation we had earlier that morning with the Miss Great Lakes 1992 first runner-up.

The one in which she informed us Evan Savage-Singer was Fiona Forrest's biological father.

"Fiona . . . is my daughter?" Evan leaned back in his armchair, as if trying to physically distance himself from the news, his gaze shifting between JP and me.

"Mindee McQueen confirmed it," my fiancé assured our neighbor. "I mean, you might wanna take a DNA test. But Mindee says she believed Emma when she told her."

"Fiona doesn't know yet. But we wanted to give you a heads-up before she finds out," I said, thinking it the least we could do.

Evan slowly nodded. "I appreciate that. And I've gotta say . . . I'm *not* surprised. The timing from when me and Emma first got together . . . it all adds up."

They met during the summer of 1996. After being stationed at a marine base in California, Evan returned home to Michigan. One afternoon while he was out for a jog near Woods Hall, he turned to see a sleek sports car screech to a stop. The Porsche 911 halted mere inches from where he was crossing the road. As Evan looked up, he noticed a gorgeous woman emerge from the car, her honey-blond hair whipping in the wind.

Right away, he recognized the twenty-three-year-old former beauty queen, Emma Woods.

She felt awful for almost hitting him with her luxury vehicle. She explained how she was distracted by a call she'd gotten on her car phone. As a gesture, she offered to make up for the unfortunate incident over a drink . . . or a few.

The bar they chose was off the beaten path, on the north side of Detroit, just south of Fernridge. A neon sign flickered above the entrance. The dimly lit interior smelled of stale beer and cigarette smoke. The patrons were a rough-and-tumble crowd of old-timers, as well as a few young locals looking for a cheap buzz.

No one recognized the automotive heiress sitting close beside the Gulf War vet.

As the alcohol flowed, Emma began to confide in her drinking companion. She revealed the details of her unhappy marriage to the great-grandson of a lumber baron. She confessed to Evan how she felt trapped in her privileged but lonely life . . . and how she longed for excitement.

Evan had always been drawn to adventure. He felt an immediate connection with the slightly younger woman. Soon, he found himself opening up to her about his experiences in Iraq, and about his own struggles with loneliness and isolation. As they talked, a bond began to form between the pair, and before parting ways, they exchanged phone numbers.

Despite their different backgrounds and social circles, the pretty model and the handsome marine found a deep connection in each other. In the months that followed, they began dreaming of a life together, free from the constraints of their pasts. They met up whenever they could steal a moment away from their respective lives, be it at a secluded park, where they could sit and talk without being disturbed, or a downtown hotel room, where they finally made love.

Nine months later, on the fourteenth day of February, baby Fiona was born.

"I asked if I was the father . . ." Evan's eyes glistened with unshed tears as he recalled the long-ago memory. "Emma said no. I could tell she was lying, but I didn't force the issue. Bill Woods was a powerful man. I'd never do anything to put Emma, or her daughter, in danger."

He sucked down the rest of his coffee, then continued with his story. "A few weeks before her twenty-fifth birthday party, Emma called. Bill was out of town on a business trip, and she invited me over to Woods Hall. It was the first time I got to see Fiona since she was born. One look at her, I knew she was mine."

JP politely interrupted. "Can you tell us *why* Emma wanted to meet up with you?"

"Sure. She told me she was leaving her husband. She said she wanted us to run away together. She couldn't take it anymore . . . the way Bill treated her. The way he lied about his affair with their housekeeper. Emma knew Bill was the father of Kathleen's son. It was part of the reason she ever got involved with me, to get back at him for cheating on her the whole time they were married. She said she loved me, and she wanted us to be a family: her, me, and Fiona. It made me so happy. But then I messed it all up. I got drunk at that party . . . and I kissed Stephen."

The second he said this, Evan's face flushed, and he walked back his last remark. "Don't get me wrong, I love the guy. That's why I ended up marrying him. But on Halloween night 1997, I was totally in love with Emma Woods."

The armchair creaked under his weight as Evan stood up. He lumbered over to a two-tiered, chrome-plated bar cart and poured himself a shot of bourbon from a crystal decanter. "What the heck? It's five o'clock somewhere," he said, swallowing down the warm brown booze.

JP and I sat in silence, allowing Evan to process the past few minutes. There was something else I wanted to ask him about, but I feared coming off as insensitive or rude if I acted too swiftly.

Leave it to my partner to keep the ball moving forward. "What happened after you pounded on the door to Emma's bedroom?" JP asked, with no concern over being too blunt.

Evan's hands began to shake slightly, betraying the intense emotions he was feeling. "I begged her to let me in. I said I could explain. She called me a closet case and told me to go away. For a second, I thought about breaking the door down. But I saw Bill coming up the hallway, so I snuck back into the secret passage. When I got downstairs, I stepped outside to look for my dudes . . . That's when I heard Emma scream. Then, she landed on the patio, right in front of me."

I couldn't imagine being a witness to such a horrible incident. "So, do you think it was all an accident? Emma drank too much at the party, she was upset over seeing you kissing Stephen, and she just slipped?"

"No! I think Bill Woods got into that locked bedroom, and he pushed Emma off the balcony. There was a whole slew of people out on that patio with me. We all saw Bill looking down over the railing after Emma fell."

"What about the housekeeper? She probably had a key to every room in Woods Hall," JP said. "What if Kathleen followed Emma upstairs and they fought? She could've stolen Emma's necklace and pushed her off the balcony. She was Bill's mistress. He would've totally covered for her."

The crease between Evan's eyebrows wrinkled as he stopped to consider. "I guess it could've been Kathleen, maybe?"

"Too bad she died in that plane crash with Bill Woods," I said.

It would be nice if we could speak to the dead couple and get their sides of the story.

Chapter 35

Margot emailed me on Friday.

Hi PJ,

I have some good news! I think I might have a dog for your mom. Her name is Bella, and she is a beagle-feist mix. She is still young, and she loves to play. She's got a lot of energy, so an environment without young children is preferred. As playful as she is, she also likes to cuddle. She is house and crate trained already, also spayed and UTD on vaccinations, and microchipped.

Overall, she is a very healthy and happy puppy. I know she'll make for an amazing companion, which is why I thought of your mother. If she'd like to put in an adoption application, I will hold off on posting about Bella until I get a chance to look it over.

If you have any questions, just let me know.

Best, Margot

The next morning after breakfast, we loaded Clyde and Jack in the car, stopped by Madison Park to pick up my mother, and drove fifty miles out to Orion Oaks. Being a good son, I allowed Mom to sit up front with JP, and I squeezed myself in back with the boys.

Jackson seemed more than happy to have his Daddy PJ sitting by his side. The little dog stood up on his hind legs and perched his front paws against my shoulder, panting away. Whereas Clyde just gave me the side-eye, looking all confused, like he had no idea why I wasn't riding my usual shotgun.

As we pulled onto the highway, Mom turned around to face me in the back seat. "I'm so excited to meet this little Bella. I hope she'll be a good fit for us. I told Dad he should come today. What if Margot won't let me adopt her without meeting him first?"

"I doubt it'll be a problem. Margot's pretty laid-back," I reassured her.

Based on our past experiences adopting Clyde and Jack, JP and I found the process fairly simple. With Clydie, we had to schedule a home visit with Margot, so she could see where we lived and make sure our home was puppy-proofed. We did worry slightly since we didn't have a fenced-in yard yet. But Margot acted more interested in talking about the man who lived in our house before us, Whit Voisin, who went to high school with her older brother. She also droned on, for a bit, about how she used to date Tom Cash, which caught both me and JP by surprise considering Tom was gay. But the '90s were a totally different time, so it wasn't totally unheard of for a girl to go to prom with a closeted queer guy.

When we rescued Jackson, we drove out to Margot's McMansion with Clydie, and the four of us had a little meet-and-greet inside the garage. Of course, all Jack wanted to do was hump his soon-to-be big bro, and Clyde wanted no part of it. But after all of maybe ten minutes, Margot informed us we were more than welcome to take the little orphan terrier home, so long as we paid the two-hundred-dollar adoption fee.

"The bigger issue is whether Bella will get along with Jack and Clyde," said JP, adding his two cents to the conversation. He still wasn't totally onboard with Mom adopting her own dog. Especially if it was going to negatively affect our boys in any way.

As much as I loved my partner, he could be a total pessimist sometimes!

Mom smiled and reached between the two front seats to pet

Jackson and Clydie in back. "I hope they get along with her too. It's been so long since we had a dog at our house, I'm a little nervous."

"Don't worry. If it doesn't work out with Bella, Home FurEver has tons of dogs they need to find homes for," I said, feeling confident.

Mom nodded gratefully and settled into her seat for the rest of the ride.

Forty-five minutes later, we pulled into Margot's driveway. The house was a sprawling, two-story home with a grand entrance, a perfectly manicured lawn, and a two-car garage. By no means did it appeal to my taste—it was far too contemporary and cheaply constructed—but there was no denying it was nice, by modern-day standards.

"Good morning!" Margot waved to us from the front porch. She stood waiting with a cute little canine tethered to the end of a long leash, her wild red hair blowing in the breeze about her pretty face.

The little doggie by her side had short brown fur and droopy ears that hung down from her head, giving her an endearing and expressive appearance. Her body was compact, with sturdy legs and a cropped tail that seemed to have a mind of its own, wiggling to and fro. As we approached with Jack and Clyde in tow, the pup peered at us with round dark eyes, her glossy black nose sniffing inquisitively.

"Good morning!" I called back to Margot, keeping a strong hold on Jackson as he pulled me toward the porch. Anytime he got the chance to meet someone (even if he already knew them), he was all about it.

As we got closer to Margot and her canine companion, Jack's excitement reached a fever pitch. His long legs pumped frantically as he tried to hurry me along. Meanwhile, Clydie could sense his baby brother's enthusiasm in making a new friend, so he had to get right in there and protect him as he did.

"Easy, Clyde!" Daddy JP commanded, attempting to draw him back, but to no avail.

When we finally reached the top step, Jack leapt forward with a joyful bark, practically dragging me with him. His tail wagged eagerly as he greeted Margot and Bella, his nose twitching as he inhaled all the new scents.

"Nice to see you again," I told the dog rescue woman, although it was only a month since the Woods Hall open-house fundraiser. "This must be Bella."

"This is her," she confirmed with a smile. "Why don't we all go out back and get better acquainted?"

Margot led us around the garage and through a gate in the privacy fence, into her spacious garden. The neatly trimmed grass gave both me and JP immediate backyard envy. A large oak tree in one corner provided ample shade for the pups to play under, while we humans sat and chatted at the wrought-iron table set up on the patio.

"So, tell me a little bit about why you're interested in adopting a dog," Margot said, addressing my mother.

Mom hesitated for a moment, gathering her thoughts. "Me and my husband were down in Pennsylvania visiting his cousins. They've got a miniature beagle. She just laid on the couch next to me and let me pet her. Ever since I started taking care of Jack and Clyde, it made me think it might be nice having my own dog."

Margot nodded. "That's great. And do you have any specific qualities you're looking for?"

I could tell Mom was feeling a bit on the spot and unsure how she should respond, so I jumped in. "It's been a while since she's had a dog. I think one that's already housebroken and knows some basic commands would be good for her."

Margot nodded again. "Totally understandable. Bella *is* housebroken, and she knows how to sit and stay and lay down."

Mom glanced over to where her prospective new pet was busy sniffing away at one of Margot's flowerbeds and totally ignoring her potential new playmates. "That's good. She doesn't seem very interested in Jack and Clyde, though."

Instead of engaging with their new doggie pal, Jackson and Clydie were roughhousing with each other. Jack barked and lunged at Clyde, trying to mount him and take him down. Clyde's response was to bite at Jack's fuzzy face, grabbing onto his muzzle and antagonizing him even further.

"You get 'em, Clydie!" Margot cried across the yard, before commenting on Mom's remark. "It's natural for Bella to be a little shy around other dogs. It'll take a while for her to get to know them and establish her boundaries. But if it turns out, for some reason, she isn't a good fit, we can always find you another dog who is."

"That's exactly what I told her," I said to Margot as JP kept his opinion on the matter to himself.

Mom thought it over, silently weighing the decision in her mind. "Bella seems like such a sweet girl. I think I'd rather take my chances than wait for another dog. If that's okay."

"It's perfectly fine. Remember, if things don't work out, you can always bring Bella back. Just give it some time, same thing I told PJ and JP when they first adopted Jack. Now look at the two of them!"

Across the yard, the brothers Broadway-Penwell continued to circle each other, tails wagging as they engrossed themselves in their playful tussle. Jackson Boy jumped back and forth, nipping at Mr. Clyde's floppy ears, while Clydie dodged and weaved, skillfully avoiding the attacks.

Mom nodded, taking a deep breath before continuing. "I know, it's just been so long since I've had a dog of my own. I'm excited, but also a little anxious."

"Don't worry. Bella will fit right in with your family in no time," Margot assured us.

On the drive back to Madison Park, Mom held Bella tightly on her lap. Seeing them riding together, it reminded me of the night we first rescued Jack, and he did the same thing in the car with me, the entire way home. On this outing, however, Bella appeared to be totally indifferent toward my mother. I felt terrible, knowing how much Mom wanted a puppy of her own. She was fine being a grandma to both Clyde and Jack, but it wasn't like being a mommy.

Unfortunately, the situation only seemed to worsen once we got Bella back to my parents' house. The minute Mom guided the little girl inside, she took one look at Dad chilling on the couch watching TV . . . and jumped right up next to him.

Immediately, she turned over onto her back and looked at my father with her big, brown eyes. Whimpering softly, the beagle mix puppy began licking at the strange man's hand, trying to get his attention.

"Hi, Bella!" he sang in a high-pitched baby voice, causing JP to stop dead at the silly sound.

Personally, I couldn't ever recall hearing that hilarious noise come from my father before. But I wasn't about to say anything, watching in awe as Dad gave the doggie an affectionate belly rub.

Bella emitted a low purring sound of contentment. There was no denying, she finally found her person . . .

And it did *not* appear to be my mom.

Chapter 36

Finn and Fiona returned on Monday.

We met up outside Woods Hall, excited to hear all about Low-Fi's out-of-town trip. As we approached each other, I noticed Finn looked a bit tired. Fiona, on the other hand, was bouncing with energy, practically buzzing with excitement.

They both looked polished as ever on that cool early morning during the second week of October. Finn wore a black leather jacket over a white T-shirt, paired with slim fit jeans and high-top sneakers. His dark hair was messy, but intentionally so, and his dark sunglasses added to his rock star appeal. Fiona wore a vintage plaid dress with a black leather jacket draped over her shoulders. Her honey-blond hair was styled in a half-up, half-down fashion, and she carried a small crossbody bag.

Me, I felt like a total schlub in my usual navy hoodie and jeans, my Tigers cap covering my head. But the last thing I wanted to do, working outside, was wear something nice. As for JP, he looked handsome, as per usual. Today, a tight-fitting light blue sweater paired with tan canvas work pants showed off his fit physique.

"Hey, guys!" said Fiona, grinning from ear to ear as she greeted us.

I leaned in for a hug. "Welcome back! How was the tour?"

"Amazing! We played some great gigs and met some fun people," said Finn, still half asleep. "We're pretty wiped out. But it's all good."

"I bet. How was Pittsburgh?" JP asked, curious about his old stomping grounds. Supposedly, Shadyside was unrecognizable now, with all the trendy new bars and restaurants popping up everywhere.

"Pittsburgh is the best! We played this awesome venue in Millvale called Mr. Smalls," said Fiona, gushing at the memory. "It was one of our favorite stops on the tour."

"The scenery was beautiful too, bro. All the bridges and the view of the city from Mount Washington," added Finn, beaming. "You're lucky you grew up in such a cool place, man."

JP smiled, happy for the favorable report on his hometown turf. "The Burgh definitely has its charm. Glad you guys enjoyed it."

Fiona gazed around the grounds of the manor home, taking in the recent additions. "I can't believe how much the place has changed in just one week."

In the homeowners' absence, Corey and the crew kept themselves busy filling in the old beds with fresh flowers. At that moment, our carpenter-slash-gardener was working on planting a row of boxwood hedges alongside the front porch.

"I can't wait to see what it looks like with everything in full bloom," said Fiona, pleased, before turning back to me and JP. "Anything else we need to know?"

After careful consideration, I concluded it wasn't our place to reveal what we learned from Mindee McQueen. As her birth father, it was Evan Savage-Singer's responsibility to decide when and how to approach the personal matter. I didn't want to risk damaging his chance at having a relationship with Fiona by interfering. We needed to trust he'd do what was best for both him and his eldest daughter when it came time to tell her the truth.

While I didn't like lying, I felt it best to keep my answer to Fiona's question vague. "Nothing right now."

Corey leaned his shovel against the edge of the porch. He strolled over to us, wiping his hands on his overalls. With a gentle nod, he greeted our group. "Happy Monday! How was the tour, kids?"

Fiona's face lit up. "The tour was awesome!"

"You guys went to Cleveland . . . Did you get to the Rock and Roll Hall of Fame?"

Finn jumped in bitterly. "Bro! We went to *Columbus.*"

Corey raised his eyebrows, chuckling at his own error. "Cleveland, Columbus . . . It's all Ohio, right? So long as you guys had fun."

"We did! Everything's looking great here, by the way," Fiona said in praise of the progress. "You're doing a great job with the landscaping,"

Corey glanced down at his work boots, shuffling them slightly in the grass. His sandy hair fell over his forehead, partially obscuring his bright eyes as he blushed.

Out of nowhere, JP tossed a random question at the contractor. "Hey, did you get a chance to fix that plaster hole in the upstairs bedroom yet?"

Corey looked up, caught off guard. "I have *not*. Unfortunately, it's proving to be quite the challenge."

JP's face fell at hearing this news. "Seriously?"

Corey held up his big hands in a show of shame. "I know, I know . . . But I'm working on it, I promise."

"It's okay. How long do you think it'll take?" I asked easily.

"Not very. I just need to pick up some more plaster to finish the job."

I didn't mean to downplay the frustration JP was feeling or let Corey off the hook in any way. But I also didn't want the guy getting mad for accusing him of being incompetent.

JP folded his arms and rocked on the balls of his feet. "Well, could you do it ASAP? That bedroom is the last one we need to finish on that floor."

My partner could be so serious about making sure everything

was completed on time. But sometimes, his worries could be a bit excessive. TBH, I think JP was more scared of what Ursula would say if she found out we were behind on finishing a project. While it was important to stick to a schedule, I always felt we could be a bit more flexible, given the unexpected curveballs that were sure to come our way during any renovation process.

"I'll get on it right now," Corey replied, before hopping in his pickup truck.

As he drove off, Ursula's rental car rolled up the gravel drive. The sleek black sedan seemed to purr as it slowed to a stop, and The Boss stepped out. She closed the car door with a soft *thud* and walked over to join us, dressed in all black, same as every other day. That morning, the weather took a turn toward the chilly, so she traded her lightweight joggers for thicker sweatpants and an actual jacket instead of a hooded sweatshirt.

"Welcome back, you two! How was the tour?" she asked Finn and Fiona, covering her brow with a hand against the bright sun.

"The tour was good," answered Finn, sounding only mildly annoyed at the prospect of having to relay yet another recap.

Fortunately, Ursula didn't care to hear any details. She had an important announcement to make. "Okay, guys . . . I've got some big news." She paused for dramatic effect, practically bouncing with anticipation. "I heard from HDTV this morning. The crew from *Ethereal Encounters* is confirmed. PNN is one hundred percent coming to film at Woods Hall on Halloween night."

JP's blue eyes sparkled at finally hearing something positive. "No way! Urs, that's incredible!"

"I know! And wait, there's more . . . We've also got Emma Woods's personal astrologer on board to lead the séance. Isn't that crazy?"

Fiona turned toward me, and we pretty much squealed in unison. "OMG! Miss Zelda!"

"The one and only. We're hoping to contact Emma's spirit and find out what really happened to her on the night she died."

Finn grew quiet. "Guys, I already told you how I feel about this whole séance business."

Ursula placed a hand on the young man's arm to ease his anxiety. "Relax, okay? The whole thing's a big publicity stunt. Miss Zelda is a total fraud, from what I've heard. The PNN producer told me they plan on rigging the séance. It might look like the ghost of Emma Woods shows up, but no way is it gonna be real."

Hearing these words, my exhilaration for shooting the upcoming *Domestic Partners* season finale dwindled into disappointment. I couldn't believe what our executive producer was saying. Was it all just a trick and a less-than-honest way to attract new viewers to the show? Ursula's confident tone made it clear she believed the whole thing was a setup, and Miss Zelda—a woman I trusted daily for celestial guidance—was nothing but a common con artist.

Still, I looked forward to meeting the astrologer in person and asking her about the readings she gave Emma Woods, once upon a time. Fingers crossed the aging woman could recall the events of twenty-five years ago. I wasn't even forty, and I could barely remember what happened yesterday!

"Hey, guys . . ." Gopher the PA sauntered over to us, his hands in his pockets and a concerned expression on his young face. He cleared his throat before speaking his piece. "Me and some of the crew were cleaning up the back garden just now. We found something kind of strange hidden in the bushes."

JP placed his hands on his hips and calmly addressed the PA. "What kinda something strange?"

From behind his back, Gopher revealed some sort of gadget. The bright red color and blinking lights gave it a menacing appearance. He held it up, displaying it for all to see.

"A fog machine?" said Fiona, sounding surprised at the discovery.

Ursula's brow furrowed as she came closer for a better look. JP's eyes narrowed as he took in the object, his mind already racing with possibilities.

"Yeah, I thought it was kind of strange. I mean, it's not like we're planning any kind of fog effect or anything for the show," Gopher replied, scratching his head. "And it doesn't really seem like something you'd find laying around in a garden."

I looked at Ursula, still standing nearby. "Did you set up a fog machine to use during Low-Fi's concert on the night of the open house?"

Our executive producer shook her head. "No, I had nothing to do with it. As much as it's a great idea, I'm afraid it wasn't one of mine."

Fiona fiddled with the strap of her crossbody bag. "Why would someone do such a thing?"

JP grinned mischievously. "Easy. To try and make us *think* Woods Hall is haunted."

Finn's temper rose as he remembered the terra-cotta planter that almost took out his fiancée. "Fi almost got killed that night! What kind of person would go through all the trouble just to try and spook us?"

Gopher nervously glanced around the grounds. "I don't know, man. But it's kinda freaking me out. I mean, what else do they got hidden around here?"

Ursula reached out and touched the PA's shoulder. "Relax, okay? We'll keep an eye out for anything suspicious. In the mean-time, let's just focus on making sure everything is ready for the PNN crew when they get here in three weeks."

I admired the positive attitude. The discovery of a strategically placed fog-making device only added yet another layer to the al-ready strange events occurring at Woods Hall. But if nothing else materialized over the next twenty-one days . . .

I feared we'd never solve this mystery.

Chapter 37

It was time to do some investigating.

JP couldn't stop thinking about the fog machine Gopher found buried in the bushes out back at Woods Hall. To quell any fears anyone might have about someone trying to intentionally spook us, we returned to the secret passageway where we last saw the ghost of Emma Woods.

Creeping down the dark and dusty tunnel, using our phones' flashlights for guidance, our hope was to uncover any clues that could help us figure out who—or what—was behind the supposed haunting of the old manor home.

"Any idea what we're looking for?" I asked, sticking close to JP's side.

Always the brave one, he led the way, his footsteps echoing softly against the stone floor. "I don't. But we'll know it when we find it," he answered, keeping his focus on the narrow path ahead.

Feeling a chill, I knew in my bones JP would protect me, should we run into anything supernatural or otherwise. Still, it didn't take much to get my mind going with negative thoughts of what could possibly go wrong.

We walked for what felt like hours, turning this way and that, searching for any sign of a hidden room or an offshoot of the original passage. Suddenly, I heard JP gasp.

"Look at this," he whispered, shining his light on a small, intricately carved door set into the stone wall. It was barely visible, several feet from the floor, and made of a dark, polished wood.

I moved in for closer examination, my heart thumping in my chest. An ornate carving of a tree with twisted roots and gnarled branches decorated the surface. "What do you think it's for?"

"I don't know. But I bet it's something significant." JP reached out and touched the intricate object.

The portal wasn't large enough to lead anywhere, measuring ten-by-twelve inches, maybe? I was never good at guesstimating, but the sight of the small door filled my mind with curiosity and confusion.

Why did someone install a door that small, so high off the ground . . . and what purpose could it serve?

I couldn't imagine anyone being able to fit through it, so it must've been intended for something else entirely. Despite my confusion, I was eager to investigate and see what secrets the door might be hiding. However, I couldn't shake the feeling of unease I felt, wondering what could be waiting for us behind it.

We tried pushing and pulling the door, but it wouldn't budge. Frustrated, I started tapping on the wood, trying to find a hidden latch or catch. Suddenly, I heard a faint clicking sound, and the small door swung open with an audible creak. Our flashlights cast eerie shadows across the passageway as we discovered something concealed within the wall.

Tucked away inside was a compact object with a glossy black finish, a lens at the front and small control panel on the side. "Looks like a video projector," I said, remembering the one used to show the outtakes reel at the end-of-season wrap party.

As we further examined the machine, we could tell it was expertly installed, with cables and wires carefully tucked away inside the wall to avoid any tangling or damage. Clearly, whoever hooked up the device was highly skilled and experienced.

"The plot thickens," said JP, taking a page from one of my young adult mystery novels. "Strange place to hide a projector."

"I'll say," I said, in complete and utter agreement.

The discovery of this unexpected piece of technology added another layer to the already complicated puzzle JP and I were trying to solve. My thoughts raced with questions . . .

Who put it there, and for what reason?

Was it related to the mysterious occurrences at Woods Hall?

What would happen if we turned it on?

"Is there a power button?" asked JP, feeling around the projector's panel for a switch he could flip.

As if by magic, the machine whirred to life. A bright beam shot out from the lens and lit up the opposite wall of the tunnel. Unfortunately, the ethereal image we saw before us appeared to be of no significance.

"It looks like a bunch of nothing," I said sadly.

A series of small squiggles, almost like white noise or static, danced and swirled around in the beam of light, creating an almost hypnotic effect. It was difficult to discern any specific shapes or patterns, as they seemed to be constantly shifting and changing. Were they the result of dust or debris in the air, or perhaps a glitch in the projector's lens or image processing?

"What the heck is this?" JP stared hard at the stone wall, muttering under his breath. He stepped forward, waving his hand in the light, trying to disrupt the strange squiggles. Then, he shouted at me. "Pete! Go get a sheet!"

"What kind of sheet?"

"Something light colored if you can find one. I wanna see something, okay?"

I hesitated for a second. "You can't stay here all by yourself." Again, my thoughts raced . . .

What if the ghost of Emma Woods reappeared when I was gone?

Or the person who hid the video projector in the wall returned to retrieve it?

How could I help JP if he needed it, and I wasn't there?

"I'll be fine, just hurry back."

Despite my trepidation, I wasn't about to argue. So, I kept my mouth shut and headed off to look for a sheet . . . or something resembling one.

The sound of my footsteps echoed against the ancient stone walls as I tore through the passageway. Rushing back to the Mission-style armchair that marked the secret opening, I could feel the cold, damp air on my skin. Soon as I got there, I sat down and held on tight, bracing myself. The section of wall behind me did a complete one-hundred-eighty-degree turn, dumping me out in the hallway located on the opposite side.

Now where would I find a sheet?

Earlier that afternoon, Corey and the crew were working on painting the dining room. Fiona decided she wanted to go with something dramatic for the color, so we opted for a deep blue that also added sophistication and elegance to the design.

Bursting through the wide archway, the strong and distinct odor of fresh paint fumes hit me. I scanned the scattered remnants of this latest project, spotting a clean drop cloth on the floor among the chaos of buckets, pans, brushes, and rollers. Not bothering to fold it neatly, I snatched up the canvas and hightailed it back to the hidden tunnel.

In my rush to return to JP, I tripped over a half-empty paint can left carelessly in my path and tumbled to the hardwood floor, twisting my foot. A sharp jolt shot through my ankle joint, causing me to yelp like a wounded puppy. Momentarily stunned, I sat absolutely still, unsure whether I should try to get up or not. I thought of poor JP, down in the secret passageway, all by himself. I needed to get back to him. But I also needed to make sure I wasn't hurt.

As I cradled my throbbing appendage, a sudden wave of dizziness hit me. I pressed my free hand to my forehead. Was it just a minor twist, or was it something more serious? I tried to move my foot, wincing at the pain creeping up my leg. The idea of putting any weight on my injured ankle made me waver. But I couldn't just stay there in the dining room all night. The overpowering smell of paint fumes was causing my eyes to water and my nose to sting.

All of a sudden, I felt lightheaded. The fumes were so strong they seemed to permeate every corner of the dining room. If I wasn't careful, I feared I might pass out.

Slowly, I shifted my weight and tried to stand up. I let out a low groan as a fresh wave of agony hit me, causing me to wobble unsteadily. "Easy," I told myself, sounding the way I did whenever one of the dogs pulled too hard on his leash.

Grabbing onto a nearby ladder for support, gingerly I took a step forward, testing my weight on the hurt foot. It was painful, but bearable. With a deep breath, I took another step forward, determined to push through the discomfort and make my way back to my fiancé with the drop cloth bunched up under my arm.

Hobbling back into the secret passage, it took me nearly twice as long to reach JP as it did when I left him. He raised his eyebrows as I reappeared. "Pete, what's wrong?"

"I twisted my ankle," I said, wincing as I shifted my weight.

JP frowned. "You need to be careful."

"I'll be fine," I assured him, producing the drop cloth I procured from the dining room.

After wrapping himself in the large piece of fabric, JP moved to the far end of the tunnel, opposite the video projector. He instructed me to turn on the machine. As I did so, the white light filled the passageway once again. When projected onto the canvas cloth, the ethereal image flickered, making it appear as if JP were an actual apparition.

"Look," he said, gesturing to where the moving picture played atop his corporal body. "It's not real."

I squinted my eyes, attempting to see what he was pointing at. "What do you mean?"

"Somebody's trying to make us *think* Woods Hall is haunted."

Now, I understood. Using the video projector, someone could

shine the squiggling image at someone else, making them appear to be a ghost floating about. Someone dressed up as Emma Woods—dressed up as Princess Diana in a white wedding gown—on the night she died!

"But why would anybody wanna do that?" I asked, feeling a knot in my stomach.

JP removed the drop cloth from around his shoulders and turned off the video projector. "That's what we need to find out."

"Well, should we let Ursula know about this?" I wondered what she'd think when we informed her the spirit we'd all seen was nothing more than some squiggles projected against a backdrop.

"Not yet. Right now, we need to keep things quiet."

"Okay. I don't get it."

"Think about it, Pete. Who knows about all the hidden passageways in this house?"

I considered JP's question for a second. There was Fairway Bob and Evan Savage-Singer, from back in the day. But neither of those guys had personal access to the property. That only left Fiona and Finn, the homeowners, and the *Domestic Partners* crew, who all had their own keys and could gain entry, any time night or day.

Which meant *one of our own* was responsible for the mysterious goings-on at Woods Hall.

"We don't want them knowing we're on to them," JP said cautiously. "Whoever they might be."

I sighed, feeling uneasy about keeping secrets. But I trusted his instincts and knew he was right. To unveil the truth behind the haunting of the old manor home, we needed to tread carefully. There was no knowing who, exactly, we were dealing with . . .

Or just how dangerous they might be.

Chapter 38

The tradition of Devil's Night dated back to the 1930s.

A synonymous term in Metro Detroit to describe Halloween Eve, October 30th had a notorious reputation for being a night of arson, vandalism, and other criminal activities. Early on, young people would engage in harmless tricks, like soaping windows or toilet-papering houses. But in the 1970s, the pranks became more destructive, and soon arson became a major problem.

In the 1980s and 1990s, Devil's Night became infamous for the hundreds of fires set across the city. The highest number on record occurred in 1984, totaling well over eight hundred. In response, the city of Detroit implemented various initiatives to combat the problem, including volunteer patrols, curfews, and community events. The efforts paid off, and by the early 2000s, the number of fires had decreased significantly.

On Devil's Night in present day, the fears once associated with the unofficial holiday were pretty much nonexistent. In fact, I almost forgot the significance of the date on the calendar, as we prepped on that Sunday evening to shoot yet another *Domestic Partners* big reveal.

After almost three weeks of work, the newly renovated dining room of Woods Hall was a fabulous display of period-appropriate elegance, craftsmanship, and refinement. First, the room was meticulously painted by Corey and his crew, then exquisite pieces of early twentieth century furniture from Bob Kravitz's antique shop were bought and brought in. The mahogany dining table was no doubt the centerpiece of the room, surrounded by matching chairs upholstered in a luxurious velvet fabric.

Above the table a magnificent chandelier hung, drawing the eye up toward the high ceiling. It was a vintage fixture, with dozens of delicate arms extending outward and upward, each adorned with glittering droplets of crystal. When illuminated, the chandelier was sure to cast a warm, golden glow throughout the room, reflecting off the crystal prisms and creating a dazzling display of light and shadow.

A stunning buffet lined one wall, complementing the rest of the décor. Made of rich, dark wood, the vintage piece featured intricate carvings along the edges and legs and boasted drawers with ornate handles, providing ample storage for silverware and table linens.

The hardwood floors gleamed with a deep polish, while natural light flooded in from four large windows, offering a breathtaking view of the surrounding landscape.

With the dining room finally finished—and my twisted ankle on the mend—we gathered together. Ursula was on hand to direct us, of course, as were Kevin the cameraman, Dave the sound and lighting guy, and Gopher the PA. In addition to this company of usual suspects, Corey Regan stood by with Sparky, our master electrician.

Before we began the day's shoot, I made sure to speak with Fiona, in case there was anything I needed to clear up about keeping her birth father from her for so long. "How are you feeling?" I said softly, taking a seat beside her on the steps of the grand staircase, off the front foyer.

She looked at me and sighed. "I don't know, to be honest. I always thought my father was a humble farmer. Then I'm told my biological dad died in a plane crash when I was two. Now, I learn he's still alive and living right here in Pleasant Woods."

Evidently, over coffee the day before, Evan had explained the entire circumstance regarding him being Fiona's actual father.

"I can't imagine what you're going through. But I'm here for you, whatever you need. Me and JP, both."

Fiona glanced up, tears glistening in her eyes. "Thanks, PJ. It's just . . . strange, I guess. Knowing I have this other family I never knew about. I've got a sister out there I haven't even met yet."

"Gracie is a great girl! Stephen told us she's a big Low-Fi fan," I reminded her, thinking back to the night we all went out to Drag Queen Queeraoke, when he made the announcement. "She'll be thrilled to learn you're her big sis."

We sat together, listening to the racket from the dining room, where the crew was setting up for the first sequence. I kept wanting to ask Fiona if she was upset with me for not telling her about Evan when she first came back from the mini tour. But my worry seemed selfish, compared to the turn her life had taken for the second time in seven months.

Fortunately, I didn't need to voice my fear as Fiona spoke up. "I'm not mad at you. I totally get why you guys didn't say anything at first. Evan told me he asked you to let him do it."

"Okay, good. I'm just sorry it took him a while to get around to telling you."

"Better late than never, I guess."

"That's what I always say!"

With the air cleared, we returned to the dining room and assumed our places at the mahogany table, ready for Kevin to roll his camera as Ursula called out: "Action!"

JP, the ever-charismatic cohost, led off the conversation. "We've been busy around here . . . What do you guys think of the dining room, now it's finally finished?"

"I love it! Especially this blue paint color," Fiona said.

"It's called Midnight Sapphire," I said for the benefit of our viewers at home. F and F were already aware of this fact, since they were the ones who chose it.

"It's a little dark," Finn complained, craning his neck as he took in the four walls from his seat at the table. "But I'll get used to it, probably."

Off-camera, I could see Ursula's ears prick up. He wasn't even on set for two minutes, and already Finn Lowenstein was being a total pain in her butt.

"This furniture is awesome! It fits right in with the house," said Fiona, running her hand along the tabletop. "Like it was right here when Woods Hall was first built."

Finn readjusted his yarmulke, trying to hold back. But alas, he couldn't resist making his opinion known. "It's a little old-fashioned for my taste. But again, I'll get used to it. Probably."

His fiancée folded her hands. "If you didn't like the paint color *or* the furniture when we picked them out, why didn't you say something?"

Hearing this back-and-forth bickering, Ursula's hands flew up in frustration. "Cut! Cut! Cut! We need to keep things positive, you guys. Unless you want all your Low-Fi followers hearing your lovers' spat, okay?"

JP nodded in agreement, trying to lighten things up. "Well, I think we can all agree the new chandelier is a showstopper."

Sparky, the electrician, grinned from across the dining room. The middle-aged man had a rugged appearance, with short-cropped salt-and-pepper hair, a thick beard, and gray eyes. His build was solid, his shoulders broad, and his arms muscular. His weathered skin was tanned from years of working outside. He wore a dark blue work shirt with the sleeves rolled up to reveal his sinewy forearms, and a pair of faded work pants with steel-toed boots.

"Thanks, JP. Corey helped me hook it up. Man, I gotta tell you, the old wiring in this place is a real piece of work," said Sparky, laughing to himself. "Had to rewire the whole dining room just to get that fixture up and running."

Fiona seemed more than thankful for the change of subject, and the chance to ignore Finn and his childish behavior. "Well, it looks awesome!"

"Had to be extra careful with them old wires. Some were frayed and barely holding together. I don't know how this place hasn't gone up in flames yet," Sparky reported, sounding surprised.

Finn gazed up at the unlit chandelier. "Wow, that's pretty scary. You guys sure it's safe now?"

"Absolutely. We updated all the wiring and added in some modern safety features," Corey assured the homeowners and everyone else present. "Plus, with the new light fixture, this room's gonna look brighter than ever."

"All we gotta do now is turn her on," said Sparky.

Before the master electrician could walk over and flip the switch, Finn stood up. "I'll do it!" He pushed back his chair and stepped out from behind the dining table.

"Wait a sec! Let's shoot this bit, in case we wanna use it," said Ursula, making the executive decision as executive producer. "Roll sound! Roll camera! Go, Finn!"

The musician burst into action, slinking his way across the dining room with great determination. As Finn flicked the light switch upward, something horrific happened . . .

A bright spark and a loud cracking sound shot out from the wall, sending a jolt of electricity coursing through the young man's body.

Finn cried out in pain, falling backward, and hitting his head on the hardwood floor with an audible *thud*.

"Cut!" Ursula yelled at the top of her lungs.

Everyone at the table jumped up in a frenzy, while Finn just lay there, dazed and disoriented. His hand appeared blackened and charred as he clutched it, groaning.

Fiona rushed to his side, her face full of worry, and helped him sit up. "Are you okay?" she asked, her voice trembling.

Ursula answered for him. "I think he'll be fine. We just need to get him to a doctor."

Gopher the PA stepped forward, brandishing the on-set medical kit. "I can take Finn to urgent care down in Fernridge."

"I'll go too," Fiona offered, gazing at her future husband with concern.

Sparky the electrician looked confused. "I don't understand what went wrong. I checked the wiring in that switch myself."

Corey piped up, a hint of mischief coloring his deep voice. "Emma Woods strikes again!"

JP gave me a knowing glance, and I shook my head slightly. After uncovering the hidden video projector inside the secret passageway, we both had our doubts whether a ghost ever existed. Still, someone was responsible for the most recent so-called accident to befall Woods Hall.

We were beginning to think we finally knew *who*.

Half an hour later, I texted Fiona, anxious for her to reply.

Hey! How's Finn doing?

He's OK, but he wants us to sell Woods Hall and be done with this haunted house biz.

No!

After hitting *send*, I made it a point to add a disclaimer. Despite Ursula dubbing my favorite astrologer a fraud, I still held out hope that Miss Zelda's upcoming visit to Woods Hall would yield a positive result.

The séance could be our chance to finally figure out who killed your mom.

But what if something bad happens and I get hurt?

Reading that last part, I stopped to think before writing back to Fiona. More than anything, I needed to ease her worries and make her realize we shouldn't give up.

I promise we will take EVERY precaution to ensure that everyone is safe!

We were so close to solving this mystery, I truly believed we could do it.

Chapter 39

Woods Hall bustled with activity on Halloween night.

The time had come to shoot the final episode of *Domestic Partners'* third, and most frighteningly intense, season. The air outside was crisp, and the waxing crescent moon appeared a sliver against the dark night sky.

With the crew of PNN's *Ethereal Encounters* on hand—dressed in all black and looking identical to our own executive producer, Ursula—they transformed the historic manor home into a spooky set. No expense was spared in their decking out the halls with cobwebs, skeletons, and other creepy decorations.

In the dimly lit dining room, the crew moved with precision, hard at work setting up for the season finale séance. A large black cloth covered the antique mahogany table in the center, the top adorned with an assortment of trinkets, crystals, and flickering candles . . . and a vintage Ouija board.

As I laid eyes on the game, memories of childhood flooded back. My sister, Pamela, used to beg me to play with the Ouija board at our grandparents' house. But the thought of who we might make contact with, if we did, always freaked me out. Now, as an adult, a twinge of terror overtook me, seeing the board set up on the dining table at Woods Hall, the fears of my youth still fresh in my mind. The eerie atmosphere of the impending séance only added to my unease. I kept telling myself it was just for fun. There was nothing to be scared of. But deep down, I still felt a sense of dread over what would happen once Miss Zelda did her thing.

The lead investigator from *Ethereal Encounters* called out to anyone within the sound of their voice. "Can I get everybody's attention, please? We're ready to begin."

They were a tall, imposing non-binary person named CJ, with a penetrating gaze that seemed to see right through the darkness, as if they could pierce through the veil of the unknown and uncover the truth. Their outfit that evening combined a mix of masculine and feminine clothing. A black button-up shirt with a subtle floral pattern, they paired with dark skinny jeans and black boots, with accessories including a silver chain necklace and a black leather cuff bracelet. "Remember, stay focused and don't let your guard down. We're here to uncover the truth about the spirit that haunts this house," CJ reminded us.

Hearing the sincerity in their voice, I waved to get Ursula's attention. "I thought you said the PNN producer told you the whole thing's rigged," I said, leaning in to whisper in her ear.

"I just said that to shut Finn up. These people are dead serious about contacting the ghost of Emma Woods, right here and right now."

"So, Miss Zelda *isn't* a fraud?"

"Not according to CJ over there. They say the old lady is totes legit."

I'd be lying if I didn't admit this new bit of info warmed my cold gay heart. I just knew my fav astrologer couldn't be a fake! On far too many occasions did my horoscope ring true. Take for instance the one I read earlier that morning, first thing after I woke up.

Daily Horoscope for Monday
SCORPIO (October 23–November 21)

You may find yourself a bit uneasy as you face the fear of the unknown on this All Hallows' Eve. As you navigate these uncer-

tain waters, a hidden truth will be revealed. Stay strong and coura-
geous, dear scorpion!

"Well, that's good to know," I told Ursula, feeling positive. Although learning of Miss Zelda's legitimacy made me even more
nervous about partaking in a séance than ever before.

Suddenly, a gust of wind howled through the dining room,
causing the candles to blow out. The crew all jumped at the sudden
darkness, as did both Ursie and I. Quickly, we composed ourselves.
All of us knew it was just a draft, but the hairs on the back of our
necks stood up on end, that's for sure!

Once the candles were relit, CJ checked and double-checked
each piece of equipment to ensure everything was in working
order. Me, JP, Finn, and Fiona took our seats around the dining
table—the four of us dressed in all black, like everybody else in the
room—leaving vacant the velvet-covered chair at the head as we
waited for our telepathic leader to join us.

Around the perimeter of the room, our *Domestic Partners* crew
congregated, not a one wanting to miss out on the evening's spec-
tacular spectacle. Kevin and Dave were all set to capture the scene
on tape. Gopher the PA stood by, ready with his trusty slate. Sparky
the electrician was also there, as was Yannick the plumber. Corey
the contractor brought along his actress girlfriend Ashley, who we
hadn't seen in person since the first night we all met at Top Dog,
two months ago.

CJ spoke into the mic attached to their headset. "Okey-dokey,
send in Miss Z!"

The electricity in the air was intense. All eyes turned toward
Miss Zelda as she hobbled into the dining room. The woman in her
seventies (*maybe* eighties, it was hard to tell) carried herself with an air
of confidence and grace, her eccentric appearance only adding to her
mystique. Her face was lined with wrinkles, but her violet eyes still

held a spark of youth and vitality. Her dress consisted of a flowing, dark jewel-toned caftan and a vibrant silk turban with gold accents, wound tightly around her head, concealing her hair. Her fingers were adorned with an array of chunky rings and bracelets that clinked together softly as she slowly moved across the hardwood floor.

CJ pulled out the seat at the head of the table, and they helped guide Miss Zelda down. Ursula called out "Action!" and the séance officially commenced.

"Welcome, my friends. I am Miss Zelda, your guide for this evening. Before we begin, I must ask you to turn off your cell phones and clear your minds of all distractions. We must create a sacred space for the spirits to communicate with us."

First off, I had no idea she spoke with an accent. Thinking about it, I'd never seen her on video, I only ever read her horoscope column online. But was it Polish or Czech or maybe Russian? She reminded me a bit of Madame Rose from *Clue VCR*—a game I was *not* afraid to play with my sister at our grandparents' house, back when we were kids—so for all I knew, it could've been Hungarian! Let's just call it *Slavic* and leave it at that.

Secondly, I absolutely loved her mention of silencing all mobile devices during her pre-show announcement. I wondered what she might do if someone's phone went off in the middle of her performance?

Miss Zelda closed her eyes in concentration. "Are we all ready? Let us start by taking hands." Creating a circle of energy among the group, we did as instructed, all except for Finn, who kept his freshly bandaged right hand resting on the tabletop. "We are here to celebrate the fiftieth birthday of Emma Woods . . . and mark the anniversary of her journey to the other side, twenty-five years ago on this very night. Emma, are you here with us?" the medium asked in a hushed voice, her fingers tightening around mine. "Emma Woods, if you're here, please identify yourself."

Before we could proceed any further, a technical snafu occurred. Apparently, the EVP (electronic voice phenomena) reading box used by the PNN people to record the voices of unearthly apparitions (or something like that) developed a software malfunction, causing us to cease with the séance.

"Let's take a ten and see what we can do to get it fixed," CJ, the lead *Ethereal Encounters* investigator, suggested.

"That's a cut!" Gopher shouted, alerting us all to the inconvenient delay in production.

Like Pavlov's dog hearing a bell, everyone in the dining room reached for their phones and powered them up. Finn rolled his dark eyes, obviously annoyed by the interruption. He rose from his chair and headed to the craft services table, set up on the newly installed island in the chef's kitchen. Before he disappeared, I happened to notice both Corey and Ashley walk off in the same direction. The young woman mumbled something to her boyfriend about being *bored to death*, a phrase I found rather appropriate under the given circumstances.

Just then, my phone buzzed with a message from my mother: **Help! Bella got into some Halloween candy. What do I do?**

"I just got a text from my mom. I need to give her a quick call," I told Ursula, rising from the table and reiterating the context to JP so he wouldn't worry.

"Hurry up, okay? We're taking a *hard* ten," Ursula informed me as I slipped away down the hall, barely paying her any attention.

Before I could dial my mother's number, I overheard Finn talking with Corey and Ashley in the kitchen. Huddling around the island, the trio didn't notice me lurking behind the propped-open swinging door. But they talked to each other in hushed tones, so it made me stand back, thinking something suspicious might be going on.

"Bro, you need to take it easy this time. You overdid it when you shocked me with that light switch," said Finn, his voice stern.

"Sorry, dude. I just wanted it to be convincing."

"We're trying to make this house look haunted, not actually scare anyone to death," Finn retorted.

They continued their chat, causing me to realize what, exactly, had been lurking in our midst this entire time . . .

Finn Lowenstein was in cahoots with Corey Regan and Ashley Starr (presumably her stage name) to create the *illusion* that Woods Hall was haunted. Which now begged the question: *Why?*

"What are we gonna do if that old lady fortune teller really summons the ghost of Emma Woods?" asked Corey, sounding frightened for the first time since we met him.

"Dude, chill. The sea witch told us already, Miss Zelda's a fake. The only ghost we're gonna see at the séance is standing right here. Now go get ready," said Finn, continuing to issue the orders.

Corey gazed at his girl with adoring eyes. "This is it, kiddo. Your big moment on national TV. You got the wedding dress all set to go, upstairs?"

"I left it laid out on the bed like you told me, boo. But the thing weighs a ton! I'm gonna need some help putting it back on," the would-be actress begged.

From the dining room, I could hear Ursula calling both Finn and me to return to set, ASAP. Frozen, I watched through the crack between the swinging door and the door frame as Corey and Ashley entered the butler's pantry. They pushed on a panel next to the tall, skinny cabinet . . . and it popped open, revealing the secret passageway leading upstairs to the third floor.

"On my way!" Finn called back to the TV show executive producer, after Ursie beckoned him a second time.

Left alone in the chef's kitchen, I took in the newly completed renovations and recently installed high-end appliances. JP was super jealous of the shiny, thirty-six-inch gas range with its red control knobs, four cast-iron burners, charbroiler atop, and convection oven below. Me, I admired all the counter space. Our kitchen at

home was so tiny! But at least it wasn't a galley, which was something I hated most about our apartment back in Williamsburg.

With the clock ticking, I needed to catch up with Corey and
Ashley, to stop them from doing whatever they were planning.
Turning around, something in the corner of the room caught my
attention, sparking an idea in my mind.

The dumbwaiter!

Chapter 40

The musty smell of old wood and dust filled my nostrils.

Before I could second-guess myself, I climbed inside the dumbwaiter and pulled the door shut. Making myself as small as possible, I held my breath as the tiny contraption started to ascend, my heart pounding. The small space was cramped, the ride jarring, and I almost lost my balance trying to squat in place and brace myself at the same time.

Halfway up, I started having a panic attack. A knot formed in my stomach, and my palms started sweating the second I realized there was no turning back. The walls of the dumbwaiter closing in, I tried calming myself, mentally and physically. But with my chest tightening and my throat feeling constricted, it made it pretty difficult to breathe.

The sense of impending doom grew stronger with each passing moment. I felt like I was losing control of my own body. My hands started to shake, and I broke out in a cold sweat. I felt dizzy and lightheaded, my vision becoming a blur. The noise around me sounded distorted, and I could hear my own pulse pounding in my ears.

The panic attack intensified as the dumbwaiter finally reached the third floor of Woods Hall. My mind raced with thoughts of danger and disaster, like I was truly on the brink of collapse. A sense of terrible dread overcame me, along with an overwhelming and all-consuming fear.

Thankfully, once the tiny elevator stopped moving, I immediately felt better.

Slowly, I lifted the dumbwaiter door and peered into the master suite. I could see Corey, standing near the canopy bed, helping Ashley into the wedding dress costume. For my sake, the couple seemed too distracted to hear the dumbwaiter ascending the narrow shaft. The cheap materials of the gown hung awkwardly on Ashley's thin frame. The dimly lit room made it difficult to see things clearly. But it wasn't too hard to tell the wedding dress was a poor imitation of both Princess Diana's and the replica worn by Emma Woods on the night she died, twenty-five years ago that very evening.

The synthetic blond wig appeared even cheaper, with an unnatural shine that made it almost plastic-looking. Never mind the terrible styling! The color was far too brassy, lacking the natural variation and depth of human hair. The coarse texture didn't come close to mimicking the softness. Her so-called diamond tiara was clearly rhinestones and plastic.

"Don't forget the music box . . . and cry real good and loud this time," Corey ordered Ashley as he adjusted her wedding veil. "We gotta make this ghost look as real as possible."

His girlfriend nodded, her bright green eyes wide with excitement and nervous energy. "I'll do my best," Ashley promised, her voice unsteady.

"And try not to move around too much, till I get the ghost effect aimed at you with the video projector."

Suddenly, my phone vibrated in my pocket. Quickly, I silenced the mobile device and checked the message from my mom: ***Did you get my text?***

Starting to panic again, I feared Corey and Ashley could hear the racket I was making, hidden away inside the dumbwaiter. So, as quietly as possible, I texted back: **Shooting the show. Can't talk. Call Pam for help, sorry.**

Too bad, at that point, I totally dropped my phone.

Corey stopped in his tracks, his ears pricking up, as if he noticed something coming from within the walls of the bedroom. "You hear that?" he asked, turning back to the woman wearing the tacky wedding dress, bad wig, and ridiculous crown.

Luckily, Ashley shook her head, taking the heat off me for a second while I retrieved my mobile from the floor of the mini-elevator.

Holding my breath, I remained completely silent, waiting to see if the couple would further investigate the current situation. After a moment, Corey shrugged off any concerns he had and continued helping Ashley prepare for her big moment. Sighing in relief, I watched as they finished up and disappeared into the secret passage-way, exiting the master suite.

The coast clear, I rode the dumbwaiter back down to the ground floor and hopped back out in the kitchen, hitting the tile mere moments before Ursula arrived.

She bellowed from just past the swinging door. "I said a *hard* ten, PJ. What's the holdup? Let's go!"

"Sorry," I apologized, thanking my lucky stars Ursie didn't catch me climbing out of a literal hole in the wall.

As we rejoined the group in the dining room, a sense of unease washed over me. I needed to let JP know what I just overheard in the kitchen and witnessed in the dumbwaiter. But there wasn't any time to pull him aside and fill him in before we resumed with the shoot. I couldn't shake the feeling something wasn't quite right, and Corey and Ashley's plan to fake the haunting of Woods Hall (with Finn's help) was just the tip of an otherwise larger iceberg.

Speaking of Ashley . . . the wannabe actress was nowhere to be seen.

"What happened to your girlfriend?" JP asked Corey as he returned without the younger woman in tow.

"She wasn't feeling too good, bro. I called her an Uber and sent her back to the apartment."

I shot a silent glance in Corey's direction, as if to say: *Sure, you did!*

From her usual spot looking over Kevin's right shoulder, Ursula gave the go-ahead to resume shooting. "Picture's up! Roll sound, roll camera!"

"Sound is speeding!" Dave declared, momentarily.

"Camera's rolling!" Kevin confidently announced.

Gopher held up the slate. "*Domestic Partners*, episode three-point-ten, scene three, take two."

"Action!"

Miss Zelda began guiding the heart-shaped wood planchette around the Ouija. JP and I, and Fiona and Finn, sat huddled around the table, our fingers resting lightly on the board.

"Are we really doing this?" Finn asked, his voice shaky. He was a better actor than I originally thought, based on his improvisations during our earlier tapings.

I still couldn't figure out why the Low-Fi band member was involved in the plot to make Woods Hall appear possessed. I suspected he might have *some* ulterior motive. Maybe Corey was coercing or blackmailing him? Whatever the reason, the betrayal bothered me. For the past eight weeks, we worked tirelessly renovating the old manor, so Finn and Fiona could finally move in and start a family. The fact that, all along, he pretended to be afraid of ghosts, and he willingly participated in his near fatal electrocution . . . Well, I had a feeling the daughter of Emma Woods and Evan Savage-Singer wasn't going to be very happy when she found out all the nefarious things her fiancé was up to!

"I've been communicating with spirits for decades," Miss Zelda assured all of us in the room, both on-camera and off. "Trust me, children . . . there is nothing to fear. Now, please. Pay your full attention."

The dining room fell silent. Everyone at the table focused on the Ouija board, waiting patiently for any movement or sign of communication from the other side. Miss Zelda placed her fingers lightly on the divination tool, posing questions aloud. "Is there someone here with us?" she asked, her voice hushed and reverent.

At first, the planchette seemed to move of its own accord, zipping around in random patterns. But then, gradually, it started spelling words, each letter being called out in turn by the astrologist . . .

E-M-M-A

A shiver ran down my spine as I realized we might actually be communicating with the spirit of the long-dead former beauty queen and automotive heiress.

"It's her," whispered Miss Zelda, her violet eyes darting around the room, as if searching for something. "I can feel her presence here with us. She's trying to communicate." Her hands shook slightly as she lifted them off the spiritualist device. She gazed up at the group gathered around the table, her expression serious. "We need to keep trying. We're getting close. Emma is here . . . and she wants to tell us something."

The old woman breathed deeply and closed her eyes. She took a moment to get in the right headspace, preparing herself to connect with the spirit world. Her face assumed a serene appearance as she spoke in a soft, calm voice. "Emma, dear. Can you hear us? We want to help you. Please, if you can, tell us what happened to you on Halloween night 1997."

With bony fingers, she lightly touched the planchette, allowing it to glide gently across the board. Her eyes remained closed, as if she was lost in deep concentration. Slowly, the device moved methodically, spelling out a series of letters . . .

R-O-Y-C-E

Opening her eyes, Miss Zelda let out a deep breath. "Does anyone here know of this person?"

For the benefit of the astrologer—as well as our *Domestic Partners* viewers at home—I explained the identity of Royce Anger, the young son of the Woods Hall housekeeper, Kathleen, the woman who married Emma Woods's husband Bill, shortly after her unfortunate demise.

"And do we know what has happened to this boy?" Miss Zelda inquired.

"He's not a boy anymore. He's in his mid-thirties . . . if he's still alive," said Fiona.

When Miss Zelda still appeared uncertain, Finn stepped in to clarify. "This Royce kid was almost Fi's stepbrother."

Fiona leaned forward, her elbows on the table, her piercing blue eyes fixed on Miss Zelda and the Ouija board. She clasped her hands together in front of her, as if in prayer. "Ask Emma if she knows where Royce is now," she said, her voice tight with emotion. "Maybe she can tell us?"

Her fingers vibrating on the planchette, Miss Zelda repeated the question. "Emma, please tell us what has happened to this Royce person. Where can he be found in this present moment?"

The dining room filled with tense anticipation as everyone watched the board resting on the tabletop. Then, the wooden heart started moving again, slowly at first, before picking up speed. From the looks of things, it appeared to be gliding across the Ouija board on its own. The movement was smooth and deliberate, as if controlled by an unseen force, spelling out its answer . . .

H-E-R-E

Stunned, we all stared at each other in shock. It made no sense. Was the Ouija trying to tell us that Royce Anger was among us? As we exchanged bewildered glances, struggling to comprehend the implications, the overhead lights flickered momentarily, casting eerie shadows across the room. A sudden thud echoed from somewhere in the manor, making us jump. The air became charged with an unsettling energy, as if the walls themselves were whispering secrets.

Miss Zelda's hands trembled as she slowly withdrew them from the planchette. "This is highly unusual," she murmured, her voice tinged with both fascination and unease. "We must proceed with caution and inquire further."

JP exchanged a glance with me, concern etched across his face. I could tell he was contemplating the implications of the Ouija board's cryptic message.

My mind raced, trying to process. How was it possible for Royce Anger to be here in Woods Hall? Was he hiding in some secret passageway, lurking within the mansion's shadows, evading our discovery? If so, why had he returned after all these years? And what was his connection to Emma Woods and the unsettling events surrounding her death?

A flurry of questions swirled in my thoughts, but no clear answers emerged.

"I think we need to find out more," Fiona began hesitantly, breaking the silence. "We can't ignore this."

Miss Zelda nodded, her experienced eyes focused on Fiona. "Agreed, my dear. We shall continue, but I urge everyone to remain vigilant and open to the possibility of unexpected revelations."

The planchette rested motionless on the Ouija board, waiting for our next question. Fiona took a deep breath, her determination shining through her eyes. "Emma, can you tell us if Royce is really here?"

The planchette moved again, spelling out its reply in a deliberate manner, one letter at a time . . .

Y-E-S

A collective gasp filled the air. This revelation sent chills down our spines.

Sensing the urgency and uncertainty all around, JP spoke up. "Miss Zelda, could you ask Emma where, exactly, in Woods Hall we can find Royce Anger?"

Miss Zelda nodded, her brows furrowed in concentration. "Of course." Gently, she placed her fingers back on the planchette. "Emma, dear. Please tell us where we can find this Royce person?"

The planchette began to move once more, first landing on the letter *C*, followed by *O*, then *R, E,* and *Y.*

Shock rippled through the dining room, leaving everyone momentarily stunned, our carpenter Corey included.

Fiona's voice trembled as she posed the question on all our minds. "Why is the spirit of my dead mother spelling out your name, Corey?"

Taken aback, his face contorted with confusion. "I don't . . . I don't know. Your guess is as good as mine."

Suddenly, the planchette whirred to life, spelling out a seven-word warning . . .

YOU CAN'T HIDE FROM YOUR PAST, ROYCE

A jolt of realization surged through me. I had a flash of memory, a connection, like solving an elusive puzzle. I remembered a key detail from one of my favorite novels, *Tales of the City* by Armistead Maupin. The name of the transgender landlady at 28 Barbary Lane, Anna Madrigal, is an anagram for *a man and a girl.*

And then it hit me.

My heart pounded as I blurted out: *"Corey Regan is Royce Anger!"*

The room fell silent, and so I fully explained my theory.

"What's an anagram?" asked Finn, his lack of understanding evident by his twisted expression.

Realizing not everyone might be familiar with the term, I further elaborated. "An anagram is when you rearrange the letters of a word or phrase to create a new one."

Processing this revelation, all eyes turned toward Corey, whose face contorted with guilt. "It's true," he said finally, his voice steady and full of conviction.

It was a lot to take in. A member of our *Domestic Partners* crew had such a dark and hidden history. The past was catching up with us in the most unexpected way, leaving us grappling with a sober reality.

The sense of impending doom hung over our heads like a shroud.

Halloween 1997

The little vampire watched his mother, the housekeeper, work.

Nine-year-old Royce stood in the shadows as Kathleen served guest after guest after guest. The party was a grand affair, with Pleasant Woods's finest turning out to wish Emma Woods well on her twenty-fifth birthday. Wearing a white wedding gown as the Princess of Wales, the former beauty queen received a lavish diamond necklace from her husband, Bill, as everyone looked on in their colorful Halloween costumes.

All except for his mother, who was made to wear her ugly servant's uniform, same as every other day of her miserable life.

As the night wore on, tensions grew between Bill and Emma. From a distance, Royce observed them arguing, a pair of plastic fangs clenched tightly in his mouth. His eyes gleamed with excitement as his wish was granted.

The fight ended with an upset Emma storming off. Curious, the small boy followed the lady of the house, sneaking into the dumbwaiter and riding it all the way up from the kitchen to her third-floor bedroom. Inside, Royce could hear Emma alone in the master suite, listening to the melancholy tinkling of her favorite music box, all the while crying. Outside in the hall, an unknown man begged Emma to open the door. She refused, telling the intruder to go away, before stepping onto the balcony.

After a moment, Royce recognized Bill's voice, calling out to his wife to allow him into the room. Again, Emma refused the order, shouting angrily at her husband. She'd never leave him free to run away with Kathleen Anger, no matter how much he and the other woman loved each other. In fact, she wanted the housekeeper fired, and her and her son removed from the house, *immediately*.

Hearing this, Royce sprung out of the dumbwaiter, his black cape fluttering behind him like the wings of a tiny bat. "This is for my mom!" He ripped the diamonds from around Emma's slender neck, then pushed the young woman . . . to her *death*.

The world seemed to slow down. The chill of the night air, the dim glow of the moon, and the haunting melody of the music box all bore witness to this harrowing act. In that heart-stopping moment, young Royce was a whirlwind of twisted emotions and exhilarating triumph. His tiny chest heaved with the adrenaline of the act he'd just committed. The diamond necklace clutched in his hands felt like a trophy, a symbol of his newfound power and vengeance. He accomplished what he'd set out to do: to rid himself—and his poor mother—of the wicked woman that was Emma Wheeler-Woods.

The rush of relief and joy surged through the boy like an intoxicating wave. It was the exhilaration of a predator capturing its prey, the thrill of a hunter tasting victory. For the first time, Royce felt a sense of control over the oppressive circumstances of his life, a liberation he'd been longing for. But amidst the ecstasy, a flicker of doubt danced at the edge of his consciousness. Did he mean for Mrs. Woods to die? He grappled with this question, his young mind struggling to process the enormity of what had just transpired.

In that crucial, heart-pounding moment on the balcony, it wasn't a carefully calculated decision. It was a surge of anger and a desire to assert dominance over the woman who held his mother in the chains of servitude, a chaotic mix of revenge and desperation. Royce wanted to punish Emma for the torment she'd caused his mother, but he hadn't anticipated the fatal consequences of his actions.

Regret clawed at him, but he suppressed it. He couldn't afford to dwell on remorse. He had to maintain his façade of fearlessness and defiance. The repercussions of his actions were too profound for a child to fully comprehend, yet the nine-year-old was acutely aware there was no turning back.

Bill Woods burst through the bedroom door. The boy rushed out, his heart racing. Emma's scream rang loud in his ears, haunting him as he hurried down the dark corridors of Woods Hall. It was the cry of a life extinguished, the echo of his innocence lost, and the beginning of a dark, troubled path that would shape his destiny. He didn't know where he was going, but he knew he needed to get out of there. He knew he had to find a way out . . . and fast.

Turning a corner, Royce saw a faint light coming from the end of the hall. He sprinted toward it. Without hesitation, he climbed out the window and onto the slate tile roof. The wind howled, and the cold, late October air bit at his pale skin. As he crept along, he spotted another smaller window, slightly ajar, and peeked inside at an empty room located in the attic. Crawling through, he closed the window behind him. He was safe, momentarily at least.

Catching his breath, the boy realized his tiny hand held something . . .

The diamond necklace belonging to Emma Woods!

Royce regarded the lavish piece of jewelry in awe, marveling at its beauty. He knew he shouldn't be happy, but he couldn't help himself. The stolen object was his revenge for every wrong committed by the terrible woman. The necklace rightfully belonged to his mother, and he would see that she received it.

As he sat in the attic, his mind wandered. He thought about his poor mom, still working as a lowly housekeeper. He couldn't bear the thought of her being mistreated any longer. Then, he remembered something Kathleen told him when he was just a little boy, about a secret passageway leading from the attic to the outside of Woods Hall. It was a means for the servants to escape if ever there was a fire. Royce knew he needed to find this tunnel, so that he could make his getaway.

Searching the attic, he moved boxes and old furniture aside, until he found what he was looking for: a small trapdoor hidden behind a stack of crates. He pulled it open and saw a ladder leading down into darkness. Without hesitation, Royce made the rickety descent. He followed the narrow passage, trying to keep his balance as he stumbled along in the dark.

After what felt like forever, he spotted a light. He quickened his pace, eager to see where it led. Getting closer, he realized it was an opening in the tunnel, and the illumination he saw came from the moon and stars, high above in the sky. Climbing out, Royce found himself in a small clearing in the woods behind the old manor home. He glanced over his shoulder, back at Woods Hall, looming in the distance. He knew he could never return there again.

Trotting through the forest, the young boy felt a freedom unlike any before. No longer a prisoner, he could start a new life for himself and his mother.

Emma Wheeler-Woods was finally *dead*.

Chapter 41

His expression turned dark.

With a quick, fluid motion Corey reached into one of the five pockets of his work pants and pulled out a handgun, eyes narrowed and jaw set. A cruel sneer twisted his lips as he squared his shoulders and stood firm his ground, holding the weapon with a steady, practiced grip.

A picture of ruthless determination, it was evident Corey Regan, aka Royce Anger, wasn't afraid to shoot if he had to.

"Enjoying your little game?" He grabbed Fiona by the arm and yanked her from the velvet-covered dining chair, holding the gun to her head, snarling. "Cuz you don't know the half of it. I killed Emma Woods . . . and I'll kill her daughter if I have to."

As Corey held Fiona hostage, everyone in the room froze, unsure how to react to the sudden turn of events. The tension in the room was palpable, with the crews from both *Domestic Partners* and *Ethereal Encounters* frantically trying to capture everything on camera. The rest of us struggled to come to terms with the cold, hard fact: We'd been working alongside a murderer this whole time. It was shocking to think someone we trusted kept hidden such a dark secret.

Fiona's blue eyes widened in fear as Corey pressed the gun to her temple. "Don't you dare move!" he growled, his voice thick with an anger befitting his given surname. "And turn those cameras off. Now!"

A moment of stunned silence lingered in the dining room. Everyone looked at each other, unsure of what to do. The folks from PNN exchanged worried glances, wondering if they should comply with Corey's demand or continue recording the events unfolding in front of them.

CJ, the lead investigator, raised their hand in a calming gesture. "Corey, please. We can work this out."

Corey shook his sandy head, his grip on Fiona tightening, his voice filled with fury as he retaliated. "I said turn 'em off! I don't want any of this getting out. I don't wanna be remembered as a killer. I got my film career to think of."

"That's a cut!" Ursula commanded both camera crews, who willingly complied.

Miss Zelda's face went pale as she sat rigidly in her chair, her gnarled hands clasped tightly together. "Dear Lord, what have we gotten ourselves into?" she whispered. Then, she spoke directly to Corey. "You must put down the gun, son, and surrender to the authorities. You cannot continue on this path of violence and deceit."

"No way I'm going to prison. I'd rather die than spend the rest of my life locked up." Corey tightened his grip on Fiona, his finger hovering over the trigger.

As tensions rose in the room, one thing became clear . . .

This séance would be remembered as one of the most haunting and dangerous experiences of our lives.

Suddenly, JP stood up, his arms raised in a show of surrender. "Corey, hey. Don't do this. Just put the gun down, and let's talk," he said, his voice calm and steady.

Corey's gaze flicked nervously from floor to ceiling as he contemplated his next move. "You think I'm stupid . . . You think I'm just gonna give up and let you turn me in to the cops?"

Tearfully, Fiona stared at him, whimpering. "Please, Royce. Let me go. I was almost your sister."

Corey smiled sinisterly. With one hand he grabbed Fiona's honey hair, pulling her head back to look at him. His other still held the gun. "And thanks to *your* mother, my own mom couldn't be with the man she loved."

"That didn't give you the right to murder Emma," said JP, his voice laced with disgust.

Corey let out a bitter laugh. "Her own husband didn't care. Bill Woods saw me run out of the bedroom that night, after I pushed his wife off the balcony. He told the cops to call off their investigation . . . to protect me. Said Emma fell to her death, even though he knew it wasn't true."

An eerie silence settled in Woods Hall. Corey's words were a revelation, a glimpse into the festering darkness that had driven him to such heinous actions. The fact that Bill Woods had stood idly by, allowing a young boy to get away with murdering his wife, spoke volumes about the couple's marriage.

"But why did you feel the need to kill an innocent woman?" JP pressed. He needed to understand the depths of Corey's madness, to grasp the guy's motivations for what he'd done as a child.

"Emma Woods wasn't innocent!" Corey spat out the words, his face contorted with a volatile mix of anger and hatred. It was a venomous release, the culmination of years of suppressed rage and bitterness. "Woods Hall was our home, first. Me and Mom lived here *way* before Emma ever did. But just cuz she married Bill, she swooped in and took everything from us."

The room felt like a pressure cooker, the atmosphere thick with the poison of Corey's words. He was unraveling, peeling back the layers of a tormented psyche, revealing the twisted reasoning that drove him to commit this unforgivable act.

"Emma was a snob, a heartless wench who treated us like we were beneath her," Corey continued, the bitterness seeping through his every syllable. "She flaunted her wealth, her status, her beauty, while me and my mother were relegated to the shadows. We were invisible, insignificant to her. She deserved to pay for what she did to us."

His eyes blazed with a manic intensity, and the room seemed to close in on itself, suffocating under the weight of Corey's wrath. It was a confession fueled by madness, a descent into the abyss of a damaged mind. The ghosts of the past, the ghosts of Woods Hall, seemed to watch in silent judgment.

"Mom loved this house," Corey ranted, his voice rising to a crescendo of fury. "But Emma stole it from us . . . *our home, our pride, everything!* Killing her was the only way to reclaim what was rightfully ours."

He was a storm of rage and resentment, a tempest that had been brewing for years, now unleashed in a torrent of confession. The revelation of Corey Regan's true identity as Royce Anger had peeled away the last remnants of his sanity, exposing the twisted core of his being.

The room held its breath, grappling with the chilling reality of what the man had just admitted. It was a moment that would forever stain the walls of Woods Hall, a moment that would echo through the annals of all our lives.

Corey took a deep breath, trying to steady his shaking hands. He let go of his strong hold on Fiona and began pacing back and forth. His eyes darted around the dining room as he relived the painful memories of his past, feeling the anger and resentment boiling inside him. Finally, he stopped in front of the window and stared out at the dark sky, his jaw clenched tightly, before continuing with his confession.

"You don't know what it's like watching somebody else get everything you deserve. My poor mom! Even after Emma was gone, she couldn't catch a break. Bill's stupid old man . . . No way was he gonna let his son tarnish the Woods family name by marrying the lowly housekeeper. Even though he already had a kid with her."

As he spoke, Corey's voice grew louder and more agitated. "Oh, yeah. I knew Bill Woods was my dad. Mom told me, way back when I was little. She promised me someday we'd all be together. I just had to wait and be good. But when old William Woods the third got in the way," he spat bitterly, "I killed him too."

The room fell silent again, the severity of Corey's words hanging heavily in the air. "That's what happens when you let a kid fix your coffee . . . and they put rat poison in it, accidentally-on-purpose. My own grandpa, can you believe it?" He laughed maniacally, glancing at his colleagues gathered around.

Like with every good mystery, it was time to come clean and reveal the truth regarding his motives. "When the news broke about Fiona inheriting Woods Hall, I knew it should've been mine. I just had no way to prove it, legally. Mom wasn't allowed to list Bill as the father on my birth certificate, so it was my word against everybody else's."

JP leaned forward, his forearms resting on the table, as he locked his eyes onto the handsome man holding the gun. "And you wanted this house for yourself, as the first-born son of Bill Woods and his rightful heir?"

Corey shifted his weight from one foot to the other, his eyes flickering nervously about the dining room at everyone in it. "Look, I know what you're all thinking . . . But I need money to finance my horror feature. You're an actor, JP, you know how it is. Movie making is mad expensive! So, I came up with a plan. 'Member that haunted house company? They contacted you guys," he said, addressing Fiona and Finn, "asking if you wanted to sell Woods Hall."

The firm Corey referred to was the potential buyer Campbell Sellers told us about, the one who saw one of his billboards and reached out to inquire about the status of the property. The very same one who contacted Fiona after she inherited the old manor, stating they wanted to buy the home and turn it into an actual haunted attraction.

"I remember," Fiona confirmed. "What about it?"

Corey's hands shook as he continued wielding his weapon. "Well, I happen to work for that company as a special effects artist. It was my idea to scare Fiona and Finn into selling. The owner promised me a fat commission if I could get him Woods Hall . . . which I totally could," he bragged.

After listening in silence, my mind swimming with a thousand different thoughts, I finally spoke up. "By making it look like the old house was haunted?"

Corey nodded, proud of his accomplishment. "You got it, PJ. Using the skills I picked up in film school."

Here, he began spelling out the exact way he went about doing what he did.

"It all started with meeting you guys at Top Dog on that first night. Me and Ashley kept an eye on Low-Fi's social media posts. That's how we knew right where to find you. Then, at the Woods Hall open house, there were so many people running around here . . . we just snuck onto the property early, with the setup crew, and installed a few fog machines out in the back garden."

Now that he mentioned it, I had a vague memory of seeing Corey and Ashley on that morning. But at that point, we'd only met them the one time, so I guess it didn't register. Plus, we meet so many different people at those open houses, it's hard to keep track of who's who.

"During all the chaos, I got inside and installed a flicker box. Used it to control the lights when the guys were giving PJ's sister a tour. The banging sounds you heard . . ." Corey looked at me across the table. "Just a mallet hit against some pipes."

JP raised an eyebrow. "Wait, so Ashley was the ghost we all saw during the Low-Fi concert? And she dropped one of the planters off the balcony and almost hit Fiona."

"Correctamundo," Corey concurred. "Yep. I set up a video projector and used special effects I created. Pretty low-tech stuff.

Good enough to make Ashley look like a ghost, from a distance, though."

"What about Chippy? That was Ashley up on the balcony too, then," said Ursula, still cowering behind Kevin and his camera.

"Now you're catching on. Earlier that night, Fiona posted a group pic of the crew at Chianti, on dinner break. So, we head on over to Woods Hall, sneak in the side door, and take the secret staircase in the kitchen up to the third floor."

"Which you knew about since you grew up in the house," I said, picturing a young Royce Anger running about the old manor home, wreaking havoc.

"Exactly!" Corey confirmed with a wink, before continuing his speech. "Up in Emma's old bedroom, Ash dresses up to look like her on the night she died. Chippy gets all spooked when he sees a ghost, falls right off the ladder, hits his head and breaks his arm. Leaves you guys looking for another carpenter. That's when I get the call. Thank you very much, Ursula!"

"Next time I won't hire anyone *not* affiliated with HDTV," she muttered, feeling duped by Corey's deceit.

"Once Chippy's out, I replace him on the renovation crew and get twenty-four-seven access to the property. That's how I made the lights go out, the night PJ was here all by himself working on the half bath. You thought Emma's eyes in her portrait were watching you?" Corey asked me. "That's cuz *I* was watching, the whole time. After I hauled the powder room door out to my truck, I snuck back inside and hid in the secret passageway. I could see every move you made from inside the walls. I had full reign over this whole house. I locked and unlocked doors . . . wrote messages in fake blood on mirrors . . . set up fog machines and made music boxes mysteriously play. I even rigged the light switch in here, last night when we shot the dining room reveal," he said, gesturing with his gun to the spot where Finn received his electric shock. "Sorry about that, Lowenstein."

Opposite where I sat, Finn's eyes widened in surprise when Corey mentioned his name. Furtively, he glanced around, fidgeting in his seat. I could see his hands shaking slightly as he gripped the armrests of his chair.

Since I already knew he was conspiring with Corey and Ashley, it didn't surprise me to see Finn quaking. As much as I didn't want to be the one to tell Fiona her fiancé betrayed her, I waited with bated breath for Royce Anger to do it.

Sure enough, he did.

Chapter 42

A smug grin spread across Corey's face.

His captive audience had no other choice but to remain silent, intently observing the man once known as Royce Anger. "Finn, dude, you really sold it. The way you jumped back and acted shocked when that switch sparked . . . it was perfect."

Fiona stared at her fiancé in disbelief. "Finn, what's he talking about?"

His face reddened as Finn shifted in his seat. "Uh, it's nothing. Don't listen to him, doll. The guy's a psycho!" he shouted at Corey, putting on a brave front to try and save face with Fiona.

"You guys were in on this together?" she asked, her volume rising as she made the connection.

Corey's eyes glinted with amusement. "Yeah, baby! Your boy was a big help. He gave my boss at the haunted house company a call, a couple months ago. Said he didn't want this place, asked if we'd take it off your hands. Got me a key early on, so I could get in here and set up all my special effects stuff. He even tipped me off to when you guys weren't gonna be around. Made it a heck of a lot easier to do my job."

Fiona's gaze flickered between the two men, her expression a mix of hurt and anger. "I can't believe this. You betrayed me, Finn.

You went behind my back and made me think my birth mother's ghost was haunting this place."

Finn's shoulders slumped as he let out a heavy sigh. "Look, Fi . . . I did it for us. We don't need this big old house. We belong back in Brooklyn . . . Think of the money we could make off the sale. Let's just take it and go home to New York."

Fiona shook her head, her voice trembling. "This is my home . . . My *family's* home. And I don't care about the money. I've got more than enough now, thanks to Emma and Bill Woods. But you . . . ." She clenched her fists to control her emotions as Corey prevented her from physically lashing out at Finn.

He hung his head, looking every inch the guilty party. "I'm sorry. That dude never told me he was really Royce Anger. I had no clue he killed your mom when you guys were kids."

Corey chuckled, enjoying the meltdown had by his young accomplice. "Oops, my bad. Guess I forgot to mention that part."

Fiona turned to Finn, her eyes flashing. "You knew how much Woods Hall means to me. I wanted it for *us*. I trusted you."

"I'm sorry, babe. I just thought . . ."

"You knew better than me?" Fiona snapped. "You thought you could make decisions for us without even asking?"

"I didn't mean it like that," said Finn, desperation creeping in as he stood up at the table.

Corey tightened his grip on Fiona, at the same time pointing the gun at her fiancé. "Easy, killer. Oh wait, I'm the only killer in this room . . . that we know of, at least."

Fiona turned her back on Finn. "I can't even look at you. We're done."

"Fi!" he screamed, like a wounded animal crying out.

Corey grinned with glee, thrilled with the part he played in breaking up the musical couple. "You heard the girl. Bro, she's just not that into you, no more."

Finn Lowenstein slunk down into his seat, utterly at a loss and totally defeated.

As far as I was concerned, the comeuppance served him right. I wondered what sort of punishment the guy might receive after the Pleasant Woods police force arrived on the scene.

Oh, yes. Once I learned of the plot concocted by Corey—but before I climbed out of the dumbwaiter—I fired off a text to Detective Paczki, alerting him to the goings-on at Woods Hall. A quick check of my Shinola watch made me think Nick and his cop buddies would come storming the old manor home momentarily. Until then, I knew we needed to stall.

So, I asked yet another question . . .

"What's in it for you if somebody turns Woods Hall into an actual haunted house?"

Corey's face twisted with disgust as he answered. "I could care less about Woods Hall! But I *do* care about this . . ." He reached into another pocket and, this time, pulled out a rather sparkly object.

Emma Woods's missing diamond necklace!

A collective gasp erupted in the dining room. The lavish piece of jewelry reflected off the lights set up by the TV crews, putting on a dazzling display and shining with a blinding brilliance. The intricate design of the necklace, combined with the glint of the diamonds, created an almost mesmerizing effect for all who admired it.

"After I killed Emma, I knocked a hole in my bedroom wall and hid it behind the plaster. But I never got a chance to get it out before they shipped me off to live with my grandparents, after Bill and my mom died." Corey's breath caught as he stared longingly at the necklace he held. The weight of it was both exhilarating and terrifying. "For years, I dreamed about getting back into this house and ripping this sucker outta the wall."

With his attention focused on the diamonds, Fiona saw this as her chance to make an escape. Her heart racing, she slowly retreated, eyes locked on the gun in Corey's other hand. She knew she had to act fast if she wanted to survive.

Corey continued with his story, scarcely noticing his prisoner inching further away from him as he rambled on. "Which is what I finally did. Sorry about the mess, JP. Looks like I'm *not* gonna get a chance to fix that hole in the plaster after all."

My partner rolled his eyes.

"Now I finally got this old thing, I can sell it and put the cash toward funding my horror feature."

As she backed away, Fiona's foot bumped into one of the instruments set up by Dave, our lighting and sound guy, knocking it over. The loud clatter caused everyone to jump, including the madman Corey. His eyes darted toward the sound, and for a split second, his attention was diverted from the diamond necklace. It was the opening Fiona needed.

With lightning speed, she bolted toward the doorway. Corey reacted quickly, whipping around and pointing the gun in her direction. At the table, Finn's eyes widened in horror. Without hesitation, he jumped up and rushed toward the woman he loved, positioning himself in front of her.

Corey whirled, his finger tightening on the trigger of the handgun. The sharp *crack* of a gunshot echoed through the room—causing the rest of us to shield our ears and duck for cover, JP and I included—as Finn took a bullet. A look of pain contorted his features, and he clutched at his left shoulder with his bandaged right hand.

From under the table, we could hear Fiona scream. Peeking out, I watched her freeze in terror as Finn collapsed. A deep red stain soaked through the fabric of his plaid flannel shirt.

Corey sneered, his eyes wild and crazed as he turned the gun on his almost-sister once again. "Mighty brave of you, dude, to defend your lady," he told Finn. "I'd've done the same thing for mine."

Speaking of Ashley . . .

I wondered where she was the entire time her boyfriend held the crews of two different TV shows hostage. And why were we allowing him to get away with it? There were far more of us than there was of him.

"We gotta do something!" I hissed at JP, beneath the dining table.

"I'm not getting myself killed," he spat back. "Where's your phone? Text Nick Paczki and tell him what's going on over here."

"I already did. He's on his way."

Without warning, the Woods Hall dining room plunged into darkness. A dense fog rolled in, accompanied by the tinkling tune of a music box and the sound of a woman weeping. The smoky haze swirled around the table, creeping into the corners, making it impossible to see more than a few feet in front of us.

JP and I both climbed out from our hiding place, in time to witness a ghostly apparition float through the wide doorway. She raised the arms of the flowy wedding gown she wore . . . and she went *"Wooo!"*

Corey started choking on the fumes given off by the fog. Before he could catch his breath, JP launched himself at the contractor, tackling him from behind and knocking the gun from Corey's hand. Me, I was never one to condone any sort of physical violence. But before I even realized what I was doing, I lunged for the weapon and picked it up before Corey could.

"Where are you, boo?" Ashley cried out, confused by all the commotion. She searched the foggy room, desperately trying to locate her boyfriend in the thick pea soup.

JP wrestled the big man to his feet, holding him tightly as I pointed the gun at him, my first time ever holding a firearm. TBH, it felt sort of cool to be doing something so butch.

While Fiona tended to Finn's wound, we detained Corey and Ashley as the fog began to dissipate, long enough until the PWPD arrived on the scene. Ursula and CJ attended to Miss Zelda, making sure the famous medium didn't sustain any injuries during the scuffle.

Detective Paczki pushed his way through the crowd of people gathered in the hallway outside the dining room, each person feeling lucky to be alive. Nick's team took the suspects into custody, including Finn Lowenstein of Low-Fi, who it was determined also needed medical attention. "Okay, what's going on here? Peter, I got your text."

JP and I recounted the events of the past hour, and how they played into the bigger picture of the (alleged) haunting of Woods Hall . . . and Emma Woods's death on Halloween night, twenty-five years before.

The hunky police officer listened intently, his brow furrowed as he took down the details on his phone's notes app. When we finished, Nick rubbed his bushy mustache with a thumb and forefinger, lost in contemplation. "We'll have to go over all the evidence and see if it'll hold up in court. But from what you fellas are telling me, this should be an open-and-shut case."

"Whatever we can do to help, just let us know," I said, handing over the gun to the detective.

Nick tucked the weapon into an evidence bag. "Thanks . . . and I gotta say, I'm impressed by the two of you. You certainly made my job a lot easier."

JP grinned, looking pleased with himself. "Just doing our part for Pleasant Woods . . . again."

As the detective followed the other officers out of the old manor home, Fiona emerged from the shadows, her face pale but determined. "I just spoke to Miss Zelda."

"What did she say?" I asked, almost forgetting the interrupted séance.

"Remember when the Oujia board spelled out Emma Woods's name? Miss Zelda insists it was for real. She told me my birth mother really spoke to her." Fiona choked back a sob. "And she said . . . she's proud of me."

"Of course, she is . . . I mean, look what you did here tonight," JP said.

Fiona laughed softly, then she sighed. "I'm so ready for Halloween to be over."

"So are we!" JP and I said, pretty much at the same time.

That night, Fiona Forrest got to experience the joy of sleeping in the guest bed at 1 Fairway Lane, with Mr. Fuzzy Face, aka Jackson Russell, cuddled up beside her.

Epilogue

The New Year's Eve party was in full swing.

Music, laughter, and the sound of clinking glasses filled the ballroom as Fiona Forrest's closest friends and neighbors surrounded her. The renovations at Woods Hall were finally finished, and the young woman was now living in her new home, proud of the hard work put into its transformation.

JP and I were there, of course, ready to celebrate the festive occasion, along with the wrapping of yet another season of *Domestic Partners*. It'd been forever since we'd gotten all dressed up and gone out anywhere. JP looked handsome in his black tux, and I cleaned up rather nicely in mine, if I said so myself.

"Well, we did it," I told him, finding it hard to believe.

JP nodded in agreement. "It was a lot of hard work, but this place looks amazing now."

"Feels good to show it off, huh?"

"Sure! But what're we gonna work on next?"

To paraphrase the late, great William Shakespeare: *That* was *the question*. Maybe I'd finally get around to writing that new novel?

As the evening progressed, guests mingled and explored the newly renovated spaces of Woods Hall. Fiona looked radiant in a sparkling silver gown. She greeted everyone with a smile, happy to see them enjoying themselves in her home. She even stopped by the step-and-repeat backdrop to pose for selfies, promptly posted to her personal social media account.

My favorite was the one of Fiona with her baby sister, Gracie, and her two dads, Evan and Stephen Savage-Singer, along with her adopted parents, Gregg and Gina Forrest. With her entire family together in one place, she couldn't have looked happier or smiled any brighter. And it was nice to finally meet the couple who'd taken Fiona in once she'd been orphaned as a child.

On the dance floor, JP and I spun circles, something we rarely got the chance to do. Swaying to the music, our eyes locked on each other. I stared lovingly at my domestic partner, both on-screen and off. "You look super sexers tonight."

JP blushed. "*You* look super sexers. Seriously, Pete. I wanna put you in my pocket and take you home with me." Then his voice softened, and he became serious. "I'm so grateful to have you by my side, now and for always."

I wrapped my arms tightly around his neck, staring up into his bright blue eyes, on the verge of tears at hearing his heartfelt words. "Thanks, hon. I feel the same way. It's been an incredible year . . . I can't wait to see what happens in the next one."

JP's big arms pulled me closer. I rested my head against his broad chest, and he spoke into my ear. "As long as we're together, I know it'll be amazing."

Shortly before midnight, Fiona stepped onto a small platform erected by Chippy, fully recovered and reinstated in his position as contractor. The ballroom fell silent as she began to speak. "Thank you all for being here tonight. It's been a long journey, but well worth it. And I've got an exciting announcement to make . . . I've decided to continue my musical career as a solo artist."

The room erupted in applause and cheers as Fiona's friends and neighbors congratulated her. "That's amazing!" I exclaimed, giving her a big hug. "It'd be a shame if you quit singing because of what happened."

After his arrest on Halloween night, Finn Lowenstein faced both criminal and civil consequences for helping to aid Royce Anger, aka Corey Regan, and Ashley Starr (not her real name either) in their quest to make Fiona think Woods Hall was haunted, thereby causing her to relinquish the property, as well as the injuries sustained by Chip Carpenter. Charges included assault, reckless endangerment, and conspiring to commit fraud. A lawsuit was even brought against Finn by Chippy, seeking damages to cover medical bills, lost wages, pain and suffering, and other expenses related to his falling off the ladder.

Suffice to say, Fiona called off her engagement.

The young woman sighed as she pulled away from my embrace. "I just can't believe Finn did what he did. I thought I knew him better." She shook her honey-colored head, clearly struggling to come to terms with the circumstances. "But I can't let him stop me from pursuing my dreams. I need to keep going, even if it's just for myself."

Breathing deeply, she forced a smile. "Anyway, enough about all that. Let's enjoy the party." She raised her glass, toasting to a fresh start and new beginnings.

As for Corey Regan, aka Royce Anger . . . He would soon be off serving a life sentence, without the possibility of parole, for confessing to the killing of both Emma Woods and her former father-in-law, William Woods III, when he was still a child. Due to there being no statute of limitations for murder in Michigan, the state was able to charge and prosecute him for the offenses as an adult, even though his crimes were only recently found out. Ashley was also charged for the part she played in faking the haunting but received a reduced sentence for agreeing to testify against her former boyfriend.

Stepping down from the stage, guests gathered around Fiona to offer their congratulations and express their excitement for her new venture. Chippy approached with a wooden music box in his hand. "Made this for you . . . It's a symbol of your new beginning."

Fiona opened the box, and the tinkling melody of "Auld Lang Syne" began to play. She couldn't help but tear up at the thoughtfulness of the gift. As the music filled her ears, Fiona closed her eyes and breathed deeply. Despite the joyous occasion, she couldn't shake off the weight of everything that happened. She felt a whirlwind of emotions, from discovering the truth about her birth mother's murder to finding out her potential stepbrother had a hand in the haunting of Woods Hall.

She wiped away a tear and gazed about the room, seeing so many friendly faces. She realized how lucky she was to have such a supportive community in her new home of Pleasant Woods. But she couldn't shake off the feeling of emptiness inside her. Finn's betrayal left a deep wound that would take a long while to heal.

Fiona stared down at the music box in her hands. It was a representation of hope, a reminder that despite the darkness she'd experienced, there was still light in the world. She took another deep breath and made a decision. She wasn't about to let the past hold her back any longer.

A middle-aged woman in a stunning emerald-colored dress that hugged her curves perfectly stopped by to say hello. For a split second, JP and I didn't recognize Margot from Home FurEver, dressed to the nines for New Year's Eve. Her usually wild curly hair was now sleek and styled, falling gently across her shoulders. The bold color of her lipstick matched her dress, and her eyes were accentuated with a subtle smoky shadow.

"Girl, look at you!" Fiona cried, greeting the dog rescue woman in her fifties.

"Thank you so much for the enormous donation," Margot said, her eyes lighting up with gratitude. "We were blown away by your generosity."

Fiona beamed brightly. "That diamond necklace didn't belong to me . . . I certainly don't need it. Selling it and donating the money to help all those homeless doggies was the least I could do."

Soon it was 11:59 p.m.

The room buzzed with excitement as everyone raised their glasses, ready to begin the countdown and ring in the New Year. Fiona stood next to me and JP.

"This is it," I told her.

"Another year older . . . and not much wiser," JP joked.

"Ready?" Fiona asked, checking the time on the ginormous flat-screen TV she insisted we hang on the wall over the fireplace.

"Ten, nine, eight . . ."

As the countdown neared its end, I closed my eyes and made a wish . . . for a year filled with love, happiness, and new beginnings. A year where JP and I could continue to grow our relationship and our business and make even more beautiful memories together. I also wished for the strength and resilience to face any challenges that came our way, knowing we could overcome them together.

"Three, two, one . . ."

With the clock finally striking midnight, the whole of Woods Hall erupted in exuberant cheers. Fiona kissed both my and my partner's cheek . . .

Then we kissed each other.

Haunted House How-to for DIY-ers

Haunted to Death was a ton of fun to write, especially the parts about the (allegedly) haunted mansion and coming up with all the ooky-spooky things that one would expect to find in such a place. Intentionally, I wanted the old manor home to resemble something more out of *Scooby-Doo*, as opposed to *The Haunting of Hill House* which, as of this writing, I still haven't seen since the trailer totally freaks me out!

Don't get me wrong, my partner, Craig, and I both enjoy a good scary movie, and we look forward every year to the Halloween season, although the pressure of finding the perfect costume has always intimidated us. In the past, we've opted for couples' outfits since we are, in fact, *that* couple. Highlights from our decades together include Akbar and Jeff, gay twin brothers from Matt Groening's comic strip *Life in Hell*; the rap-happy Tweedles from *Alice in Wonderland,* Dee and Dum; and *Are they or aren't they?* Bert and Ernie of *Sesame Street* fame.

While we do decorate the outside of our historic 1924 Craftsman Colonial, we've never gone about turning it into an actual haunted house. I think it might be fun to do this sometime—once the renovations have finally been completed. So, here are some tips I've put together and suggestions to follow, dear reader, should you, too, wish to create your own Woods Hall–inspired haunted manor.

Step 1: *Set the Stage*

- Location, Location, Location: Choose a spot that exudes an eerie atmosphere. Whether it's an old mansion, a dilapidated barn, or your own living room, the setting is key.
- Ambiance is Everything: Use candles and dim lighting, eerie music and spooky sound effects piped in from hidden speakers, and discreetly placed fog machines to set the mood. Create an otherworldly atmosphere that sends shivers down spines.

Step 2: *Haunting Decorations*

- Ghostly Apparitions: Hang white sheets, create floating ghost props, or use mannequins draped in eerie garments to give your haunted house a ghostly feel.
- Cobwebs Galore: Strategically place faux webs made from polyester fiberfill, pulled apart into thin strands and stretched across doorways and corners, to add an air of neglect and decay. Clear fishing line can also be utilized to create a crisscross pattern with additional lines to mimic spiderwebs. This can be particularly effective for outdoor decorations.

Step 3: *Ghoulish Props and Effects*

- Jump Scares: Set up hidden jump scares with animatronics or volunteers dressed as frightening characters to really spook your guests.
- Interactive Elements: Add sensory experiences like bowls filled with "eyeballs" (peeled grapes) or "entrails" (spaghetti) for a tactile thrill.
- Mirrors and Illusions: Use mirrors and optical illusions to create a disorienting effect as guests pass through the darkened corridors.

Step 4: *Thematic Rooms*

- Choose Themes: Create different rooms with unique themes.
  A spooky laboratory, a haunted bedroom, or a cursed library.
  Let your creativity run wild!
- Clues and Mysteries: Scatter hidden clues throughout the
  rooms to engage your guests in an intriguing storyline or your
  own cozy-style whodunit mystery.

Step 5: *Costumes and Characters*

- Haunted Hosts: Enlist friends or actors to dress as ghosts,
  witches, and other paranormal beings to interact with your
  guests. If you're feeling creative, write a script for them to
  follow to keep them from having to improv.
- Mysterious Costumes: Encourage your guests to come in
  costume to immerse themselves in the spooky experience.

Step 6: *Safety First*

- Safety Precautions: Ensure your haunted house is safe for all
  ages. Provide well-marked exits and use caution with any
  special effects that you incorporate.
- Age-Appropriate Frights: Tailor the level of scariness to your
  audience. Some guests may prefer a lighter experience.

Step 7: *Share Your Experience*

- Capture the Moments: Set up a photo booth to capture your
  guests' reactions and create lasting memories.
- Social Media: Encourage your guests to share their experiences on social media with a designated hashtag.

Step 8: *Keep the Mystery Alive*

- Create a Legend: Develop a backstory or legend for your haunted house to give it a sense of history and display it, scrawled in "blood" (red marker or paint), near the front entrance.
- Annual Tradition: Make your haunted house an annual tradition that keeps guests coming back for more each Halloween season.

Now, with this *Haunted House How-to* guide in your hands, you're ready to turn any space into a spine-tingling, cozy mystery experience. Start creating your own haunted house that will leave guests having a ghostly good time!

Disclaimer: Remember to prioritize safety when creating a haunted house, especially if it's open to the public. Ensure all visitors are aware of any potential scares or risks before entering.

Acknowledgments

If you're still reading, thanks! I realize you've invested a lot of time in getting this far, so I will keep the rest short and sweet, which is always easier said than done for me . . .

To my editor, John Scognamiglio—without whom there would be no *Domestic Partners in Crime* cozy mystery series—thanks so much!

Thank you to everyone at Kensington Publishing who had a hand in the publication of this book—with a long overdue shout-out to Carly Sommerstein, production editor extraordinaire, for dealing with my quirky writing style that isn't always (quote-unquote) grammatically correct, and all the crazy emails I've sent to complain about the copyedits that were made to improve my quirky writing.

Much appreciation to Timothy Sandusky, my very first beta reader, and to all the Bookstagrammers who participated in such a super creative *Haunted to Death* cover reveal this past Halloween.

Michigan-based readers, please support your local indie book-stores, including the ones who've supported me these past three years: Pages Bookshop and 27th Letter Books, both in Detroit, Sidetrack Bookshop in Royal Oak, Book Beat in Oak Park, Schuler's Books in Ann Arbor and Okemos, Bettie's Pages in

Lowell, and Two Dandelions in Brighton. Surely, there must be others . . . Please seek them out!

As always, I wouldn't be the writer I am without the support of my real-life Domestic Partner in Crime, Craig Bentley, and our two good doggie boys, Clyde and Jack, aka Clydie and Jackson. Daddy Frank loves you guys!